ORTEGA MAFIA – THE ENFORCER

A DARK MAFIA ROMANCE

STELLA ANDREWS

Copyrighted Material
Copyright © Stella Andrews 2023
Stella Andrews has asserted her rights under the Copyright, Designs and
Patents Act 1988 to be identified as the Author of this work.
This book is a work of fiction and except in the case of historical fact, any
resemblance to actual persons, living or dead, is purely coincidental.
All rights reserved. No part of this book may be reproduced or transmitted in
any form without written permission of the author, except by a reviewer who
may quote brief passages for review purposes only.

18+ This book is for Adults only. If you are easily shocked and not a fan of
sexual content then move away now.

18+

NEWSLETTER

Sign up to my newsletter and download a free eBook

stellaandrews.com

ORTEGA MAFIA

THE ENFORCER

Revenge, domination, control and power.
Love doesn't come into it when you are fighting a war and
sometimes the best weapons are the most unexpected.

Flora

I ran from two monsters into the arms of another.

Domenico Ortega.

Mafia Prince

His dark good looks, brimming with masculine intensity, make my heart beat a little faster. The way he stares at me through those demonic eyes causes me to shiver, and it's not out of fear. When he speaks, his voice is husky and laced with dangerous intent, and I crave every syllable. Then there's his magnificent body that could crush a woman's heart as well as a man's soul, and I would gladly sacrifice my own to his.

Then I discovered the people I ran from are on his wanted list and he locked me in his mansion as part of a twisted revenge.

Fraud, dishonesty and theft aren't the only things he wants from me.

He also wants my soul.

He's not the only one.

It turns out he's not the villain in my story after all.

There is something more sinister out there who hides behind sick rituals and blood drenched altars.

Will my dark Prince come for me or will my story end **unhappily ever after?**

Buckle up for a dark, twisted ride of family secrets, lies, and revenge.

Somewhere in the middle of mayhem, a love story grows that has a very hard beginning.

Fans of Dark Mafia Romance will love Ortega Mafia.

PROLOGUE

FLORA AGE TWELVE

THE DAY MY LIFE ENDED

I jerk awake and as soon as my eyes open, I'm aware something's wrong.

With a start, I sit up; the sheet falling from my shoulders, my eyes adjusting to the darkness informing me it's not morning at least.

I listen keenly but only register my own frantic breathing, making me wonder if I woke from a nightmare. I only wish I had because the nightmare is not of my dreams. It's standing by the window waiting for me.

The moonlight illuminates the shadow and for a second, I wonder if it's human at all. In hindsight, I was right because this person has never been human and probably never will be.

"Diana?" My voice is whispered, almost fearful and as she turns, even from the distance, the excitement in her eyes is the first thing I notice.

"Listen." she whispers in a voice laden with glee. It's as if something so magnificent is happening, like a kid discovering Santa is real.

I do as she says and strain to hear whatever is causing her joy and at that moment, I am rewarded with a bloodcurdling scream.

"What is it?" I'm so afraid and wish like hell I hadn't woken up and was still blissfully unaware, content in my dreams.

"Judgment day."

Her whispered response is laden with joyful ecstasy and her excited giggle is followed by another scream of the damned.

Before I can ask more questions that I really don't want the answers to, footsteps approach from the hallway outside.

Diana turns toward the door as it flies open, and my breath catches when I see the anger on my father's face.

"Follow me." His command leaves no room for discussion and grabbing my dressing gown, I fasten it quickly around me and slip on my shoes, wondering what can be so dreadful to pull us from our beds at night.

Diana rushes to catch up with him, leaving me running behind them, fearful of what happens next.

The darkened hallway offers no explanation and the sound of shouting and slamming doors adds drama to a situation that definitely doesn't need any.

My father ushers us down the back staircase, and as we spill out into the night, I'm grateful for the dressing gown I grabbed in haste.

Diana is still in the sheerest nightdress. The moonlight acting as a torch as it illuminates her naked body beneath the thin fabric. Her long blonde wavy hair flows to the small of her back and her bright blue eyes are lit with an excitement I will never understand. She's always been the same. She craves danger, is almost intoxicated with it and there is no doubt in my mind at all that danger has knocked on our door tonight and whatever time we had in this museum of horror has now expired.

My father opens the door of one of the usual black SUVs that we have become accustomed to and urges us inside with a haste that tells me not to question him.

Just before he closes the door on his two daughters waiting for an explanation, I note the weariness mingled with pain in his eyes as he demonstrates rare emotion.

"I'm sorry." He appears defeated, broken and nothing like the strong man we have grown up with and feared to an extent.

"Daddy…" I make to speak but he slams the door shut and thumps on the roof of the car, causing whoever is driving it to screech from the place we called home with an urgency that doesn't escape me.

I am so fearful and shiver in my seat, hoping my sister can offer me an explanation. Diana always knows everything. She must know what's happening now, but as I turn to ask the question, my words stick in my throat because the power flashing in her eyes unsettles me a little.

She turns to look at me and if anything, I don't recognize her as she says in a voice straight from Hades itself, "It's just you and me now, kiddo."

"What do you mean? Where's mom?"

I am so fearful for her answer because I know my sister and she thrives on drama, especially one of her own creation, and her low laugh confuses me as she hisses. "Dead."

"No!" My hand flies to my mouth as she shrugs, apparently unconcerned.

"It was inevitable."

"What was? I don't understand."

"That's typical of you, Flora. You have never understood and probably never will."

"Then tell me." My voice quivers because I realized from an

early age never to ask questions because in our world the answers aren't what you want to hear and this is no exception as she says almost with happiness, "She was murdered by Mrs. Matasso."

"No!" The tears break free, and I sob, "What are you saying?"

She shrugs. "Save your tears baby sister because our mother was caught screwing the great man himself and his wife took exception to that."

"I don't understand. What do you mean, screwing?"

Diana just laughs out loud and says in the voice that always made my blood run cold.

"Fucking, Flora. Our mom was Carlos Matasso's whore, and his wife wasn't happy about that. She took a knife to her heart and cut it out and ended up dead because of it."

I stare at her in complete shock, not really understanding what is happening and then she leans closer and sneers in my face. "Do you realize what this means."

"No." My voice trembles as she hisses, "A fucking war. Giselle's family will seek revenge, and our father will fight to save the man who was screwing his wife. If that's not fucked up, I don't know what is and guess what, little sis?"

She throws her head back and laughs out loud. "I can't fucking wait to watch them all burn."

There has always been something deeply disturbing about Diana Corlietti. I've always known that ever since I learned to crawl as a baby. I have watched her over the years develop into a great beauty, innocent and bewitching on the outside but rotten to the core inside. She has always scared me, but not half as much as she does now because it appears that the deepest pain in our life this far has released her tainted soul from its hiding place.

At this moment I am more afraid than I've ever been, and

it's not because of a future without our parents. It's because she is walking beside me into mine, and that scares me more than anything.

CHAPTER 1

FLORA

NINE YEARS LATER

Senator Billings makes my flesh creep. I wish I had never agreed to this, but he is such a huge benefactor to our gallery I had no choice. My boss Desdemona Gray gave me no choice, really. Accompany him to a swanky event and secure his patronage for another year.

"Champagne?" He reaches for the bottle in the ice bucket beside him and pours me a glass, leaning forward as he hands it to me without waiting for my answer.

There is no point in telling him I don't drink because he won't be interested in that. In fact, I'm certain the only thing he's interested in ends with me beneath him later on tonight. I'm not a fool. I understand how things works in Vegas. A rich, important man believes he has free access to any woman he wants for the right price. This time the price on my head is worth millions and will ensure the gallery continues to enjoy its position as the premier art gallery in town.

I can still remember the ice in Desdemona's voice as she issued the ultimatum.

"If you want a career in the art world, you must grow up and realize it comes at a price. If you're not up to the job, there are plenty more where you came from, which would be a waste of a promising young talent. Play by the rules and who knows, you may even get your own art exhibition out of it. One night with our business benefactor is a small price to pay for your future career. Don't blow it."

"To a satisfying evening."

The senator raises his glass to mine and licks his full wet lips as he openly drools at me from across the limo. There is no mistaking his intention regarding me tonight, and a slight shiver freezes my blood as he openly undresses me with his eyes.

I wish I hadn't worn such a revealing dress, but Desdemona insisted on it. She took me to the store and personally selected it and at first I was overawed by how beautiful it was.

Long, flowing gray silk that appeared to be cut from molten steel. It lapped around my ankles and clung to my curves, holding them so gently it made me sigh with pleasure. I have never owned a dress like this and the fact she insisted I wear nothing underneath so as not to disturb the flow of the fabric, makes me wonder if that was the real reason at all. I can tell my nipples are straining against the soft silk due to the fact I'm freezing. The bastard has the temperature so low I am shivering, not only from fear but from the cold as well. The champagne isn't helping and then the reason for it becomes clear as he says with a lecherous wink, "You appear cold, my dear. Why don't you slide in beside me and I'll warm you up?"

His meaning is clear and the message flashing in his eyes warns me not to refuse, but I pretend to ignore it and just smile sweetly.

"It's fine. Thank you. I'm very happy sipping this amazing

champagne while I learn more about your interest in art. I heard you are one of the most knowledgeable connoisseurs of the masters and I've been looking forward to hearing your thoughts about them."

I rest the champagne glass against my lips and hold my breath because I need this job and don't want to give him any reason to doubt my sincerity. However, flattery obviously works because he puffs up with his own self-importance and proceeds to bore the pants off me, that is, if I was wearing any, and speaks about his own discernment for the remainder of our journey.

I am grateful for my quick thinking as the car pulls to the front of an insanely large house, telling me I have escaped one mauling at least, and I gaze out in wonder.

Houses like this don't come cheap and certainly not in Vegas. In fact, it's a little incongruous even for Vegas, and it strikes me it would be more at home in the English countryside as the home of a lord. A sprawling mass of tradition piques my interest because I have always been intrigued by the past. I devoured the history books and learned everything I could about English history, not to mention Italian and Greek. It's my passion that is given a home when I unleash the artist inside me and paint what I see in my mind.

I can almost reach out and touch the history of this place even though I believe it is younger than I am. That's the trouble with Vegas. It's a land of smoke and mirrors, and this is just one example.

"Where are we?" My voice is laden with awe and the senator says with pride. "We are at the gala evening of one of the most powerful men in Vegas, Lucas Emiliano, aside."

"The Casino King?"

He nods and then laughs. "Mind you, unlike Lucas, this man doesn't follow the rules. It should make for an interesting evening."

I fall silent because at the mention of the Casino King I realize just how powerful the senator is if he considers that man an associate.

Lucas Emiliano rules Vegas and is usually just a name that is whispered in hushed conversations around town. I was told he married last year and by all accounts is very happy. His wife Ella Emiliano is a good customer of the gallery, but I am never permitted to meet her. Desdemona prefers to deal with her account, but I have seen her and always thought how friendly she seems. Word on the street is she's an amazing artist herself and obviously has an appreciation for it because she has bought an eye watering number of paintings from us, telling me that money is definitely no object to them.

"So, whose party is this?"

I'm curious because I have never heard of anyone as powerful as Lucas and the senator grins. "Domenico Ortega. He runs several Casinos in town…"

His voice trails off as I cease registering his words. I know that name and it only means one thing to me. Mafia.

My mind runs away from me as I suffer an anxiety attack that hasn't hit me as hard since I came to Vegas. Not since I ran from *them*.

It's like white noise all around me as I try to get my emotions under control. I thought I was done with that world. I *prayed* I was done with it, but tonight I will be breathing the same air as one of them. I may never have heard of the Ortega's themselves, but I know their kind. I *am* their kind and I've promised myself I will never glance back at a past I have tried to erase from my memory.

"Come my dear."

An arm snakes around my waist, diverting my attention back to more imminent danger, and as his hand grasps my ass, he winks suggestively. "You know the score. Don't let me down."

I am on information overload so don't react and he obviously takes that as an encouraging sign because he leans in and his stale breath hits my face as he whispers, "Perhaps we can indulge in a group session. There's always one at these events somewhere. I'll make some enquiries."

The horror must show on my face because he grins, "Don't worry, I'll look after you and guide you through the most amazing night of your life."

He squeezes my ass hard, which jolts me into action and, tearing myself away from him, I say in a high voice, "Can we go inside? I'm cold."

He nods, obviously taking my enthusiasm for getting inside as my desire to get started and he nods, a pompous smile gracing his lips as he guides me through the huge portico into a wood paneled hallway that has stepped straight from an episode of The Crown.

We are greeted by a freaking butler who almost bows to the senator and says politely, "Good evening, sir. Allow me to escort you to the ballroom."

Senator Billings reaches for my arm, and I grit my teeth as I follow by his side, vowing to type up my resume first thing tomorrow morning because, obviously after tonight, I am going to need a new job.

CHAPTER 2

DOM

As I glance out of the darkened window, I note the headlights of a procession of limos snaking up my drive and sigh inside.

I hate this.

I detest the people who flock to my home intent on a night of debauchery, fine living and a conversation at a future dining table about how well they know me.

I hate this shit.

The amber liquid in the glass catches the light and it deserves its title as the demon drink. It could almost be the flickering flames from hell dancing in the glass, and the burn is every bit as brutal as it slides down my throat.

I will need at least ten of these to get me through another excruciating evening in the company of people I don't give a shit about. In fact, I don't believe there is anybody alive that I *do* give a shit about—not anymore.

A gentle knock on the huge oak door makes me turn.

"Come in."

My voice sounds weary, defeated already and I pray I'm only required to make an appearance for one hour at the most before I retreat back here, possibly with a willing companion to suck my cock.

"Sir."

Pasquale, my right-hand man, enters with purpose, and I growl, "It's too early."

"There's something you should know."

My ears prick up because Pasquale would only interrupt me if it was important, and I jerk my thumb toward the chair set before the flickering flames in the grate.

I pour him a whiskey and top up my own glass and then regard him through narrowed eyes, waiting to hear something I'm not gonna like. "Your stepmother."

The hairs on the back of my neck stand to attention as soon as that name falls from his lips because I couldn't hate anyone more than I do that woman.

"What about her?" I almost spit the last word because any mention of Diana Corlietti rouses the beast inside me, and Pasquale wastes no time.

"She has a sister."

"I see."

This is news to me because so far we have discovered very little information about the woman who destroyed all our lives and it wasn't for lack of trying.

"A sister."

I swirl the liquid around my glass and wonder how best we can use this to our advantage.

I glance across at my closest confidante, and the unusual excitement in his eyes stirs my interest.

"She's here."

Just two words that cause the sleeping lion that rests inside my soul to lift its head and sharpen its claws.

"Is she now?"

I take a moment to absorb the information and Pasquale adds, "She's the guest of Senator Billings."

"A whore?"

I'm surprised when Pasquale shakes his head.

"She works for Desdemona Gray at the Barrington gallery. I'm guessing she's here to secure his business for another year."

"Then she *is* a whore."

Pasquale laughs and his eyes flash as he grins. "Not in the usual sense, but we all know what Desdemona expects from her staff. Especially the pretty ones."

When I think of the woman who has fallen to her knees before me many times, I must agree with him. Desdemona herself is the biggest whore around because she will do anything to keep her gallery in business. A blow job in exchange for securing another sale worth millions, among other things. I'd like to say she was worth it, but my experience of that woman makes my blood run cold. However, Pasquale has tossed a grenade into the room and I'm about to pull the pin because if this woman is Diana Corlietti's sister, she deserves everything coming to her.

"How do you know?"

I'm mildly curious, not doubting Pasquale for a second, but we have found no leads at all on my stepmother and I'm curious.

"I saw them arrive on the monitor."

"And that's your information?"

I raise my eyes and he nods. "At first I believed it was Diana herself. The resemblance is astonishing. I checked the guest list and noticed she was added this morning as a replacement for the senator's long-suffering wife. Her name is Flora Corlietti. I'd say that's proof enough."

"Why wasn't that name picked up before now?"

I feel the tension enter the room because everyone in my operation knows I must be informed the moment that name is mentioned, and Pasquale shifts in his seat.

"Eddie was responsible for checking the guest list. He's

waiting in the chamber."

Eddie is one of my soldiers and will be regretting his complacency because any guests in the chamber are usually bolted to the wall as they await punishment for their sins. I run a tight angry ship and haven't earned my name, The Enforcer, lightly because I deal with my own shit in the most aggressive way possible.

The rage burns inside me like an erupting volcano as I picture a satisfying outlet for my anger later on tonight. Eddie will learn the consequences of sleeping on the job because I don't pay my men well for nothing. I expect them to do their fucking job and not to let me down and the fact that name was scratched on my guest list should have waved a fucking red flag in his face.

Pasquale waits for my instruction, and I nod, setting the glass down on the table, something stirring inside me as I sense this gala may be more fun than I first thought.

"Leave Eddie to stress about what he's done. I'll deal with him in the morning." I growl, standing and straightening the cuffs on my black silk shirt.

Reaching for my black Armani custom made jacket, I shrug it on and catch a glimpse of my reflection in the ornate mirror above the fireplace. If anything, the anger reflects back at me because I wear it well. I am always angry and now I have a target for that anger. Flora Corlietti will regret walking into my home tonight because I am going to punish her for her sister's sins and then get my revenge on the woman herself.

As I reach for my revolver, I tuck it by my side and glance across at Pasquale, who stands waiting for instruction.

"Perhaps we should mingle with our guests. It would be rude not to, don't you agree?"

A slight smile ghosts his lips and his eyes flicker with an excitement I recognize. We are both hunters. It's why we work so well together and tonight I am going in for the kill.

CHAPTER 3

FLORA

I am positively breathless. Swamped by desire and it's not for the disgusting senator pawing at me. It's this place. The Ortega mansion. I have never seen anything like it. Drowning in antiques and breath-taking paintings. There is nothing here I don't like. I'm in awe of my surroundings and long to explore at my leisure. To take my time and savor every delicious morsel of history that this house provides.

I am enchanted and gaze around me, trying to remember every single object to salivate over later.

The senator is not so enamored and grabs my arm and merely his fingers on my bare skin makes me want to hurl.

The fact he is leaning a little too close for comfort and has an iron grip on my arm tells me I'm not going to escape him anytime soon.

I follow him around the most amazing ballroom and zone out a little as he makes small talk with men like him. I don't even register their salacious smiles or whispered conversations with the senator, which I'm pretty certain involve some kind of group session later on tonight. This is a world I want no part of but this house, I want all of it. Every single delicious piece of information I can discover about the story behind the various objects that surround me.

I am brought back to reality when the senator's hand runs down my back and he says smoothly, "This is Flora, my assistant for the evening."

I gaze up into the eyes of a man who makes me want to pass out with disgust. He is openly staring at me with a hunger I recognize and he nods to the glamorous woman beside him who looks much like me. Disgusted.

Like me, she is young, impeccably dressed, with nothing left to the imagination, and I want to hurl when the man says openly, "So we are agreed. A foursome in one of the rooms provided. Shall we say one hour?"

"Excuse me." I stare in disbelief and make to protest but Senator Billings nods and pulls me into his arms on the dance floor with a rough, "Do as I say, or you'll be walking the streets tomorrow."

I open my mouth to tell him exactly what I think of him, when he shocks me by fastening his disgusting lips to mine, making me choke back the bile. I push him hard against the chest because this is so not happening, and he tightens his grip and hisses, "You fucking whore. You will do as I say or…"

"Or what, Senator?"

I'm shocked when the senator pulls back and stares past me and turns an interesting shade of gray. His eyes hold more fear in them than I have ever witnessed before, and the sweat starts to bead on his forehead. He licks his lips and stutters, "Domenico, I—"

"Mr. Ortega to you." Another deep voice interrupts, and I swear my blood freezes when I sense the menace behind me. I don't even want to look because it's as if the devil sits on my shoulder and my entire body is fighting against death as it struggles to survive whatever this is.

I have no choice though, as Senator Billings spins me

around to face what can only be described as a beast. A man is glaring at us as if he wants to kill us on sight and my heart starts thumping as I stare at menace in human form. Dark hair frames the most magnificent features. Turbulent eyes glitter with danger and the dark stubble gracing a strong jaw reminds me this is all man. His body is barely contained by the designer suit he wears so stylishly, and I swallow hard when I register an arm that could crush us to dust with one thump. As his arm lifts, the jacket parts and I shiver when I see the gun positioned by his side and my legs tremble as I try to remain conscious while I stare at a man who will forever star in my nightmares.

"Of course, I'm sorry, Mr. Ortega."

The man who spoke is equally terrifying and is glaring at the senator as if he wants to rip him apart for pleasure. There is no denying the nature of these men and I must be having a post traumatic episode because I can't move an inch. If I could, I'm certain I'd be running right now and for once, I'm grateful that the senator is holding me up.

"I asked you a question." A simple phrase that is loaded with possibilities and I wouldn't want to be the senator right now. Hell, I don't even want to be *me* right now because it hasn't escaped my attention that this man appears to want to rip me apart as well.

"It was nothing; a joke." The senator stutters.

"I don't see her laughing." Domenico Ortega is obviously not going to let him off and it would be amusing to watch the disgusting senator suffer if I wasn't freaking terrified right now.

The senator turns to me and drapes his arm around my shoulder with a familiarity that makes my flesh creep.

"Tell him, Flora. We were only messing around."

"Take your filthy hands off her."

The sentence comes out as a low growl, and I stare in shock as the senator springs away from my side as if I'm toxic.

Domenico flicks the senator a disdainful expression and says in a dark tone that offers no argument, "Leave."

I almost faint with relief to get the hell out of here, but as I make to move, a huge arm reaches out and pulls me roughly to his side. "Not you."

"But…" I foolishly open my mouth, causing him to turn and, for the first time, stare straight into my eyes and what I see there tells me I should be extremely afraid right now. Terrified even because this man is not saving me, he's declaring war on me.

As the senator is ushered away by the other man, I sense the attention of the room upon us. It's as if the whole town is witnessing my humiliation because I have no doubt in my mind this man is angry and I doubt it's because of the company I keep. For some reason, his anger is directed at me and with one jerk of his hand, the music starts playing once more and he tugs me effortlessly against his rock-hard chest. Before I can react, those immense arms lock tight around me and before I know what is happening, he proceeds to move me around the dance floor, apparently in no hurry to let me go.

I'm in shock and rendered speechless by fear. What is happening? Why did he intervene and why is he so angry with me? Maybe he knows I'm only a lowly assistant and doesn't think I'm good enough for one of his parties. I can't even contemplate why this has happened and if I survive the night, I'm booking a one-way ticket to London, taking me as far away from this man as is humanly possible.

His scent is overpowering, and it's not just his aftershave. There is something so incredibly attractive about the man holding me tenderly, which surprises me because he appears anything but tender.

I can feel his heart beating against my cheek and for some reason, it makes me feel safe. Inside his arms, I am protected. However, what happens when those arms fall away from me? I doubt he will let me walk away. Something is telling me that already and I quickly run through an escape plan in my mind because God knows I'm going to need one.

The music changes and if anything, his arms tighten even further and as we move around the room, I'm glad nobody can see me engulfed in this wall of muscle because my cheeks must be flaming right now. What is this? Does he think I'm a whore and expects me to swap punters for the night? It wouldn't surprise me, but what shocks me the most is I'm not disgusted by that.

What would it be like to be with a man like Domenico Ortega? My own body is betraying me as it wakes up to that possibility, and I must physically restrain myself from bending toward him like a flower facing the sun. The trouble with balls of fire is they burn and I'm in no doubt at all that he would burn badly.

We must dance for several songs, and I'm shocked when his fingers trail against the back of my neck in a surprisingly tender move. In fact, this man, despite his size, is incredibly gentle as he holds me like a precious flower, almost fearful that I'll be damaged.

The heat from his body is welcome, and it strikes me that I'm no longer cold. If anything, I'm burning up because this is seductive. Just being the focus of his attention is overwhelming but being in his arms is like a drug.

When I don't think he will ever let me go, he stops abruptly and without saying a word, fastens his bear like grip around my wrist and almost drags me from the room like a cave man claiming his mate. I nearly fall as I stumble to keep up with him and, as the door closes, it effectively silences the noise from the gala.

Now the silence is oppressive, threatening and suffocating. Extreme danger is beckoning and I'm certain I won't leave this place with my dignity intact, if I'm allowed to leave at all, that is.

Finally, I muster some courage from somewhere deep inside and say in a rather high voice, "Um, thanks, but I can take it from here."

I may as well have saved my breath because he completely ignores me, causing me to say a little louder. "Please stop. I want to go home."

Suddenly, I am flung hard against the wall and as I catch my breath, he grips my neck in one hand and forces me to stare into his obsidian eyes that are brimming with anger.

"What did you say?" He hisses as he leans closer, his breath dancing across my face, causing me to squeak, "Please, I want to go home. I'm sorry if…"

His huge hand presses against my mouth, effectively silencing me, and as I stare into his turbulent eyes, I wonder what the hell I've done to make him so angry.

Then for some reason, he stares at me and if anything, I would say he was fighting his own battle and then his hold lightens and what I see should scare me more because the extreme anger has been replaced by raging desire.

"Who are you?" He whispers and I gulp, "Flora. I work at the Barrington Gallery. I'm so sorry if…"

"No." he stops me mid-sentence and whispers, "I know you."

Now it's as if I'm in an asylum and I am seriously wondering about this man's mental health as he relaxes his grip and stares at me with a yearning I'm not certain how to deal with.

"I…"

He shakes his head and places his finger on my lips and stares at me with an expression that steals the breath from my lungs. If anything, the sight of me is torturing him and I wonder about that. Does he think I'm someone else? It can be the only explanation. Because I don't believe he is seeing me right now.

I'm shocked when his finger traces a light path down my cheek and the emotion in his eyes makes me freeze because who wouldn't be intoxicated by this attention from a man as magnificent as he is?

Then, from out of nowhere, the anger returns, and I watch the violence erupt in his eyes as he hisses, "You smell like revenge."

He dips his head closer and inhales deeply, shocking me by dragging his tongue the length of my face before hissing, "You even taste of revenge."

"I'm sorry, I…"

My foolish words leave unchecked, and before I know what is happening, he silences me with his lips. However, this is no gentle kiss. This is brutal. A promise and a declaration of war. This kiss damns your soul to hell because it's rough, painful and damaging. I can taste my own blood as it fills my mouth, and the pain is only chased away by the fear in my heart. This is not a kiss of desire, its retribution.

CHAPTER 4

DOM

It's like watching pain stand before me in human form and there are no meds to help me. I wasn't prepared for the extent of the emotion that gripped hold of my heart the minute I saw her. Unlike Diana, though, this incarnation has none of her hard edges and that is what I'm struggling to deal with. I want to tear her clothes off and fuck her senseless before pushing the barrel of my gun into her mouth and blowing her to hell. I'm unsure how to deal with the feelings she has created and as soon as she opened that pretty little mouth, there would only be one possible outcome.

I craved a taste; had a desperate need for it. It's as if I was back home with the woman herself as I tried to sate a thirst that has never left me. Diana Corlietti was the first and last woman I have ever loved, and I have vowed to end her life in the most brutal way. The fact she has a substitute in her place right now is interesting, but it will never be enough all the time the woman herself still breathes oxygen in the same world as me.

The woman crushed against the wall ceases to exist. She has

manifested into the darkest revenge, and I am blinded to her rights and even her existence. I will strip everything from her before using her to crush her sister, and I will enjoy every fucking minute of it.

I won't do what's right. I never have, and I offer her no regard as I punish her mouth so cruelly for daring to speak at all. This woman will experience the full extent of my anger, and nothing can save her now.

When I pull back, I wipe her blood from my mouth and grabbing hold of her wrist hard; I pull her along with me with a purpose I haven't felt for quite some time now. I have no emotion inside me but revenge, and if she believes compassion exists alongside it, she is laughably mistaken.

The party may as well be over because I will not be revisiting it tonight. My men will ensure the guests have a good time before parting with their hard-earned money in an auction that will bring millions to my chosen charities. They are my smokescreen of respectability, allowing me to exist in a town that takes no prisoners because Vegas was crafted from insanity, which is why I fit in so well.

We reach the chamber and if this woman believes she's getting out of here anytime soon, she will be disappointed because she is about to learn the repercussions of her foolish visit to my home, and I am blinded by anything other than rage right now.

I open the door and pull her roughly into the room and her gasp of shock tells me she's seen exactly what happens to anyone who betrays me, because chained to the wall is the man who let me down so badly this evening.

With no word to either of them, I fling her hard against the stone-cold wall and cuff her without care, noting her shivering body in the flimsy dress that does nothing to disguise her soft curves and the stirring in my pants reminds me how much I always desired her sister. This woman *is* Diana in my mind right now and as I step back, I cast my eye over the length of her and sneer.

"Tell me your name."

The panic in her eyes amuses me as she stutters, "Flora, um, Corlietti."

I glance at my soldier chained beside her and sneer.

"This woman is the reason you're here, Eddie."

He nods, resigned to his mistake, and the startled surprise on Flora's face gives me a moment's pleasure.

"Why?" Her soft breathless question is like balm on a sting, reminding me of the power a woman holds over a man. Soft, seductive and painfully addictive. I always craved that in her sister, and it appears Flora is no exception, because I have an overwhelming urge to release her from captivity and take her to my bed instead.

To crush this desire, I must give my anger free rain and in a sudden move, I power my fist into Eddie's chest, causing Flora to scream in startled surprise.

"Stop! Oh my God. What are you doing?"

Eddie's grunt of pain is his only reaction because he knows he won't escape his punishment and will suffer it like the fool he is.

I answer her in a dark, even tone. "Eddie knows I have a vendetta against your sister. The sight of your name on the guest list should have been reported at once."

"My sister—Diana?"

At the sound of her name, I smash my fist against Eddie's jaw, the sound of bone breaking making a satisfying sound in the room.

"Please stop." Flora's confused sob is a pleasure and I growl, "Why the fuck should I?"

"It's not his fault you're pissed at my sister."

In a moment's bravery, her furious voice bounces off the walls of the chamber, which impresses me a little. Like her sister, she has fire inside that sweet soft package and that interests me way more than the addictive fragility of the outside.

I turn my attention to her and love how she cowers under my murderous glare, and yet she tilts her face bravely toward me and says tightly, "Let him go. Let us *both* go because we are not the person you want."

I lean closer and can almost touch her fear as I growl, "Now where's the fun in that?"

Then I spin on my heel and leave her chained to the chamber wall, probably wondering what the fuck she's done to deserve this.

As I slam the door and turn the key, I notice Pasquale leaning against the wall, watching me.

"Having fun?" His amused grin makes me smile and as he falls into step beside me, I say with some satisfaction. "It's a start."

We take the short walk to the control room and as we push inside, my soldier Vinnie glances up with an unreadable expression. I know he will hate the fact there's an innocent woman involved, and I growl, "That woman shares the same blood as a devil. She's not as innocent as she looks."

He lowers his eyes and glances back to the monitor and I say with a growl, "Turn up the volume."

We take a seat in front of the monitor and watch with interest how our latest guests deal with their predicament.

Flora's voice is first as she whispers, "I'm sorry."

Eddie says nothing as I expected because he knows this beating is inevitable. His life will be spared, but it will be a painful lesson in loyalty.

Flora carries on. "That man is a fucking bastard. How dare he chain us up like dogs? He's a fucking disgrace."

Pasquale laughs softly beside me, and I grin, loving the

anger on her pretty little face.

For a few moments there's silence and I can tell she is fuming, and I can't help my attention fall on her shivering body, noting the way her nipples have hardened against the cold and the gray silk does little to disguise what's underneath. My cock is begging for release because it has always craved her sister and it appears this woman will be a welcome replacement.

Then Flora says in an urgent whisper, "Listen. I have a plan."

Pasquale snorts beside me and I almost expect him to pull some popcorn from his jacket and sit back and watch because he is enjoying this show more than any on the tv.

"OK, this is the plan. We need to act fast because we may not have long."

Eddie just shakes his head and groans, knowing whatever she has planned is futile, but she obviously doesn't heed his warning because she says with some excitement, "OK, when he comes back, I'll plead with him. Tell him anything he wants to get him to untie me. As soon as he does, I'll take my chance and grab the gun he has inside his jacket. I'll use it against him as a warning and chain him up in my place before setting you free. Then we will lock him in, and you can help me escape. Tell anyone we meet that you were told to throw me out and then we can both run to the cops."

Pasquale bursts out laughing and even Vinnie joins in and I cast an amused glance at the foolish woman who doesn't realize just who she's dealing with.

If anything, I'm impressed by the fight in her. Most women would be screaming and crying by now, begging to be set free, but not Flora Corlietti. She is trying to figure a way out of this, and I must give her some credit for that.

"Oh man, this is priceless. I could watch this show all night."

Pasquale is having a great time as he leans closer, waiting for the next part of the show.

"Maybe we should test her theory. Give her a chance to make good on her promise." I say with a low laugh. The two men in the room laugh along with me and for the first time in ages, I feel a little of the pain seep away and leave a lightness inside that hasn't been there for some time.

CHAPTER 5

FLORA

I am still in shock. This is a nightmare I never expected to be involved in and I might have known it was because of her. Diana. The demon on my shoulder who just won't go away. Even though I haven't seen her for years, she is still affecting my life and whatever she has done to this incredibly scary man is obviously going to be paid for by my blood.

However, I'm not a Corlietti for nothing and mafia blood flows in my veins too, so I push away my fear as I have been trained to do and formulate a plan that may actually work.

The soldier chained beside me gives nothing away, and that doesn't surprise me either. He is shit scared and I understand why. Domenico Ortega is a bully. A powerful bully at that, and I realized it as soon as I first set eyes on him. I've met his kind before and so I harden my heart and sharpen my anger to stand up to this bully and show him what happens when he picks on a woman who isn't scared of him. OK, that's a lie because that man freaking terrifies me, but I need to believe in myself, and I must remain strong to escape.

Luckily, I don't have long to dwell on that because loud

footsteps outside alert me to someone heading our way and I prepare myself for the fight of my life.

My breath catches as the door opens and I swallow hard as the man himself enters the room.

It's as if the air changes when he enters. The oxygen dragged from it and replaced with menace, seeping through my body, choking me and suppressing life as he turns that malevolent gaze on me and strips my resolve in an instant, with a cold, hungry look of disgusted desire.

It's obvious I affect him, probably because of Diana and I don't even want to know what she did to cause him to hate her so much, but I can kind of guess.

He moves closer and for some reason, it causes my heart to flutter, a physical reaction that is definitely not needed at this point in my life. I need to hate him, detest him even and wish him dead, but for some reason my body has other ideas. That alone surprises me because that emotion was long since buried after the trauma I experienced not too long ago. It catches me unaware and as he stops in front of me, I stare at a man who is both beautiful and ugly. An oxymoron with the emphasis on moron because I can only think of him in that way. I can't allow my body to betray me too, even though betraying Flora appears to be the general rule of life, and so I lower my eyes and say with resignation, "Let me go."

"Is that all you've got?"

He barks out a laugh, causing my anger to bristle, and I stare up into dark stormy eyes and say through gritted teeth,

"Listen. Your problem is with my sister, not me. To be honest, I don't blame you either. That bitch probably has it coming and if anything, I'd help you if I wanted to, but quite honestly you aren't exactly the friendly sort, so why should I help you when you're obviously as big a bully as she is?"

I glare at him with defiance and hold my breath as he leans

closer, his lips dancing dangerously close to mine, and he whispers, "In the absence of your sister, you'll do."

His aftershave is seriously amazing, which is a strange thought to have right now. The scratch of the scuff on his jaw grazes against my cheek as he moves closer, and I close my eyes, anticipating the end of life as I know it because I'm not a fool. I get he is only playing with me and whatever he has planned will involve my total humiliation.

I jump when his hands land either side of me against the wall, imprisoning me in a wall of muscle and yet the heat from his body causes the shiver in me to fold toward it like a life-saving drug.

"Please let me go." My voice sounds weak and pathetic, and yet it's all I have. We both know I don't deserve to be here, and yet here I am. At this powerful man's mercy and I need to think of something and fast to bring him down on my side.

"I'll help you." I blurt out weakly and his low laugh tells me what a fool I am.

"You will help—me?" His low laugh is almost sensuous and coupled with the seriously sexy scent and the warmth from his body, my mind is scrambled along with my principles.

"Yes." My voice is weak and breathless, telling him exactly how he is affecting me, but I couldn't care less about that. This is one of those moments in life that happen so rarely I am powerless against it because right now, chained against this chamber wall, Domenico Ortega owns the whole of me and he knows it.

I stiffen when his hand flies to my wrist and caresses it softly. At least it feels like that, before I realize he is unfastening the lock. As it falls away, his hand slides around my waist and he holds me close against him as he does the same with the other wrist. As my arms fall free, his own wrap around me in a soft embrace, the warmth from his hard body providing welcome shelter from the cold.

A hard object brushes against my chest and I realize it's the gun he has tethered to his side and now my escape plan is urgent as he reminds me how much danger I'm in right now.

It would be so easy to reach inside and grab his gun. To press it against his heart and demand he set us both free. This is the moment I've been waiting for and as my mind scrambles for the bravery my heart needs, I jump when his finger tilts my face to his and I stare into two dark glittering promises of my downfall.

"Now is your chance, my little spitfire."

His lips graze against mine and my body strains toward his as a seductive moment of danger and desire collides, making escape the furthest thing from my mind right now. Then, as his breath mingles with mine, I lean a little closer, causing him to laugh softly.

"What's the matter, baby? Has your bravery deserted you?"

"I'm sorry."

I'm not even sure where I am in this moment because his seductive voice is causing every thought to leave my head.

"Now is your chance to defeat me."

His fingers brush against my face and I lean into it. Loving the tenderness of a man who, at first sight, appeared severely lacking in that. Maybe it's because I've had so little kindness in my life. I crave this more than anything and would even sacrifice my freedom for a tiny bit more of it.

His other hand slides down the silk dress and rests against my ass, causing me to weaken further as his musky scent stirs the pheromones in the air. His hand closes around mine and presses it against his chest, the smooth metal of the gun at odds with the warmth from his body. As my fingers close around it, a small moan escapes me as he whispers, "Now is your chance, baby girl. This is your moment to slay the beast and set your fellow captive free. What are you waiting for?"

His lips trail against mine in a sultry dance as he teases me and if I could have anything in life right now, it's to experience one kiss with him. I almost believe I'll get my wish when he leans closer and then I hear the click of the barrel of the gun against my temple as he hisses, "Time's up."

I freeze as the realization hits me because he's right. I wasted the one chance I had for one more moment with him and as he grips my wrists behind my back with one hand, he pushes the barrel of the gun in deeper.

"As escapes go, baby girl, yours was laughable. Did you really think you could overpower me and turn my own weapon on me?"

"You heard." I stare at him in shock, and he laughs like a demon. "There is nothing I don't know about except one thing."

"What?"

Despite my imminent death, I am still intrigued by him, and he leans in closer and whispers, "If you fuck as good as your sister did."

Like a bucket of icy water, his words cleanse any desire I had toward him at the mention of that bitch and I hiss, "I am nothing like her and I never will be."

"I'll be the judge of that."

His hard cock pushes against my leg and for some reason, that weakens me further. "Then you'd be disappointed."

My voice almost breaks because that is an area that weakens me more than anything and possibly it's the defeat in my voice that saves me because he lowers the gun and steps back a little, the interest showing on his face as he whispers, "A damaged angel. I kind of have a weakness for those."

"What do you mean?" I've already forgotten the poor soldier hanging beside me. I disregard the fact we're in a dungeon of sorts and I'm freaking freezing and I totally turn a blind eye to my predicament right now that could end with my brains decorating the dank, depressing walls. All I crave is more of his time and when he pushes me back against the rough stone, I almost expect him to cuff me against it but this time he presses in harder and whispers, "Perhaps I should fuck you against this wall and let my soldier watch. Perhaps I should strip you naked and let him have a turn. Would you like that, baby girl?"

"No!" Suddenly, my mind resets to default and the full horror of my situation hits me and his words unleash the demons inside that I have struggled to keep locked away.

"Please no." The tears blind me as my past reaches out and punches me square in the heart. A panic attack builds and my heart beats frantically against my chest as if trying to make a run for it. The sweat chases away the chill and causes me to panic and as my eyes widen and the tears spill, I know he has the measure of me. He has found my Achilles heel, and he is stomping on it hard.

CHAPTER 6

DOM

Now, this is an interesting development. Just the promise of humiliation has broken this woman more than any angry word or threat of violence. It's as if I have stirred an unwelcome memory, something that happened in her past that's scared her shitless. Her entire body is trembling with fear as she faces something so dark, she is more afraid of it than anything and, curious about that, I whisper, "What can you see, baby?"

Her eyes are glassy and it's as if I'm not even here, and she whispers in a voice laden with fear. "I see *them*."

"Who?"

She stares directly at me and the pain in her voice is hard to ignore as she hisses, "Diana and *him*."

At the mention of that woman, I feel like smashing my fist against the wall. However, evidently Diana also made an enemy of her sister and in this moment, everything changes for Flora Corlietti. I recognize that expression of devastation. In fact, I own it because I see it every time I look in the mirror when I'm alone at night. It's obvious we share something so devastating it may well be to my advantage, and so I change the direction I was heading in and do something alien to me. I relax my hold and pull her close against my body, and this time I protect. This woman needs it and for some reason, as she slumps against my body and my arms naturally lock around her, I like how it feels.

It doesn't take me long to make my decision and with a cursory glance at my soldier, I growl, "I'll deal with you later."

His eyes fall to the ground, and I hope he's learned his lesson well because I have no intention of doing anything other than roughing him up a bit and then setting him free to head back to his duties. The most important thing on my mind right now, is Flora and I sweep her off her feet into my arms, loving her yelp of surprise and the way her arms instinctively cling to me.

"What's happening?" She sounds fearful and perhaps she should be because I am not letting her go anytime soon. If anything, her behavior has earned her my close protection, and that involves me by her side twenty-four seven.

"You're coming with me." I growl, giving her no indication of what fate has in store for her, and as we leave the chamber, I have a very different future in mind for her.

* * *

SHE IS SO fragile in my arms. Like a feather, in fact, and just as soft. Despite her similarity to her sister, this woman appears to be nothing like her inside. It's confusing my feelings toward her and while I deal with them, I need her with me because letting this beauty go is not an option at all.

"What's happening?" She whispers against my chest, and I growl, "You are going to help me bring your sister down."

She falls silent, and I wonder what's running through her mind right now. She must be terrified, but rather than struggle, she's lying compliant in my arms and to my surprise my hold tightens a little.

I'm not sure why I'm so protective of her. It started when the senator laid his dirty hands on her. I *hated* it. I hated seeing another man's hands on this woman and I put it down to the fact I cared so much for her sister. I told myself at that moment she was Diana, and I was blinded with lustful rage.

The past two years has been torturous and not just because I would have given anything to spend one last night with the only woman I have ever loved. However, that ship sailed when she chose my father instead. She fell pregnant with his child and turned her back on me and I will never forgive her for that.

It wasn't just me, either. She was also screwing my brothers and when we discovered her duplicity, we left, never to return. But that's all changed now because the king is dead. The self-styled mafia king and, as one of his heirs, it's time to return and claim my throne.

We reach my private rooms that are accessed through a door off the main stairwell. It's the only place in this mansion where I can drop my guard because nobody ever comes here but me. Outside of these rooms, I am the brutal boss of all I survey and run the Ortega mafia business with an iron fist, reporting directly to my father. Now he has gone, the only person sitting on his throne is his widow and if I have anything to do with it, she won't be there long.

* * *

I SET Flora down on her feet and she peers around her nervously. "Where am I?"

"My private quarters." I growl, ripping off my tie and unfastening my shirt, an act that causes her eyes to fall to the floor and an embarrassed blush to stain her cheeks.

"What's the matter, princess? Are you scared of a man's skin now?"

She shakes her head. "I'm scared of you."

"You should be."

I reach for the whiskey and pour a generous amount into a glass before chucking it down in one go and refilling it to the top.

Then I drop onto the couch and say roughly, "Come here."

She lifts her eyes and I relish the uncertainty on her face and growl, "Now!"

"Why?"

I almost roll my eyes because she is seriously questioning my command and I sigh heavily. "Because nothing has changed. You are still my prisoner and I want to make your life a misery."

"No, you don't." Her voice shakes, telling me she's foolishly brave and even she knows that, and I lean back and regard her through malevolent eyes.

"And why is that, baby girl? I'm dying to hear your reply."

As I lift the glass to my lips, my eyes flash as she says nervously, "You want to make Diana's life a misery and I'm the closest thing to making that happen."

"Correct."

I shrug. "You say I want to make her life a misery. I disagree." I arch my brow. "I *will* make her life a misery before I end it and it won't be easy on her."

"You want to kill Diana?"

She shifts a little closer, which interests me more than anything. She appears to delight in this news, which tells me Diana has even made an enemy of family. I'm not sure why that shocks me, because that woman has no heart anyway and so I nod.

"I don't *want* to kill her. I will kill her, though."

"I don't understand."

She reaches my side, and her expression is loaded with curiosity and I jerk my thumb to the floor.

"Kneel."

"Excuse me." She looks horrified and I say in a menacing voice, "I said, kneel. You are still my prisoner until I say otherwise."

I almost think she's going to refuse, and I get off on the fact her eyes fill with tears and her lip trembles, but she obviously realizes she has no choice and with as much dignity as she can muster, she sinks to the floor before me.

I tilt her face to mine and say roughly, "All the time that woman breathes, she is my enemy. You are the closest thing I have as an outlet for my rage, and I won't apologize for my actions. You have the same blood running in your veins and you look so alike you are a welcome distraction. So, here's the plan."

Her eyes fill with unshed tears and yet the expression in them is hard to ignore because despite her situation, Flora Corlietti is fascinated by it, by me even, and this may be more enjoyable than I thought it would be.

I lower my voice to a heated whisper. "Until she's dead, you're her substitute. That woman has a huge debt to repay, and you have just taken that on. The quicker you help me, the shorter your stay will be. Until that happens, you take her place and I mean that in every way possible."

The flicker of fear in her eyes turns me on because I get off on a person's fear of me and I always have. Diana was the first woman who faced that fear and made it hers, and it will be interesting to see if her sister shares the same skill.

"I still don't understand."

Flora is nervous, just the gentle quiver to her lips as she speaks tells me that and, if anything, I admire her bravery. However, I am too far gone to offer her mercy, so I lean back and growl, "You will satisfy me in every way, starting with sucking my cock."

"No!" her strong response almost amuses me, and I raise my brow and say with interest. "No?"

"You heard me, asshole. I'm not a whore."

"Did I say you were?"

"You obviously think I am."

Reaching out, I grab her hair and pull her face to my crotch and hiss, "You're no fucking whore, but you are now. My whore and you will do whatever the fuck I tell you to."

If I was expecting a fight, I'm a little disappointed when she slumps back and says in a voice, shaking with fear. "Please, I'll help you, but I can't do that."

"Why not?" I am dismissive of her request, and she raises her eyes and the pain in them gives me a moment's interest as she whispers, "Because I'm celibate."

This time I laugh out loud, as if she's cracked the biggest fucking joke. "Celibate. You're fucking kidding me. What are you, a nun or something?"

She shakes her head sadly. "I'm not, but I tried to be."

That comment takes me surprise. "What do you mean, tried to be?"

"I went to the convent and expressed my desire to take the oath. They turned me down."

"Because...?"

"Because I wasn't good enough."

A lone tear escapes and I watch it roll down her cheek with a fascination that's growing by the second for this fragile creature.

"Not good enough. What does that even mean?"

She shrugs. "They told me to think about it. Take a year out and live in the real world. If I still wanted it after one year, I could return, and they would accept my request."

"Interesting."

In all my life, I've never met a woman like Flora and briefly wonder if she's playing me. Diana would. It's definitely something she would cook up, so I shrug off her request and say fiercely, "Request denied. Now suck my cock or end up chained against the chamber wall while my soldier fucks you for my pleasure."

The hatred in her eyes gives me an instant hard-on and as I settle back, I love the resignation on her face as she reaches for my belt.

CHAPTER 7

FLORA

How have I ended up here? On my knees in front of a man who scares the shit out of me. Even when I pleaded with him, he shrugged it off and I couldn't hate him more than I do right now. My thoughts bizarrely turn to Senator Billings and what I would be doing if Domenico hadn't laughably saved me from him and I suppose out of the two this is the least abhorrent, but I wasn't kidding when I told him I was celibate. I am. I swore off men the minute I escaped from Diana and Mario and now here I am. Once again on my knees in front of a man who thinks he has the right to make me his slave.

My fingers shake as I take a deep breath and steel myself for something I've done a thousand times before. This is not new to me, no matter how much I wish it was. However, this time the man involved is a seriously sexy one, despite his rough exterior and arrogant demands. I should hate him. Detest every part of him, but somehow, I can't. If anything, I'm mildly curious about what he would be like. Would he be as tender as I think he could be? Despite his harsh words and angry stares, I sense a gentle giant hiding behind a suit of bitter armor. Did

Diana do that to him? Is she responsible for the pain he tries so hard to mask that peers out from behind his eyes when he's not looking?

I wouldn't bet against it being Diana. I know how she operates and even family wasn't a word that afforded any leniency. If anything, it made her angrier and crueler and Domenico Ortega may hate and despise my sister, but it will never be as much as me.

So, I push aside my panic attack and concentrate on getting out of this as soon as possible and if I do as he says, it may be faster than I hope for because I know men like him get off on control and if I resist, it will only make him more interested.

My fingers shake as I reach for his belt and the fact he leans back and watches me through a narrowed gaze causes my cheeks to burn. It takes me longer than normal because I am battling my own inner demons and yet as his pants fall open, I take a deep breath, preparing myself for what happens next.

My heart thumps as I steel myself to do something I'm more curious about than afraid and I swallow hard when his cock springs free, even angrier than the man himself appears to be. My eyes water, not just from the tears but at the size of the weapon he conceals in his pants and as his hand settles on my head, I face the inevitable and prepare myself to give him pleasure against my will.

The angry tip advances toward my mouth and as I open to allow it inside, I'm shocked when he pushes me away. I fall back and he says with a bored tone. "Change of plan. You took too long. I'm not interested anymore."

I peer up at him in startled surprise.

"I'm sorry."

"No need to apologize. You'll improve."

"I didn't mean for that." I'm incensed and his low laugh unsettles me a little. "What's the matter baby? Have I disappointed you? Were you looking forward to sucking on my cock?"

"You're disgusting."

I turn my face away because I can't bear to look at him a second longer and am surprised when a rough hand grips my face and forces me to stare into two malevolent, dark, flashing eyes.

"For your information, I lost interest because I don't force myself on anyone, even the sister of the biggest whore ever born."

"Then why?"

"Because I was interested in seeing what you would do." For a second his expression softens, and he appears almost human and for some reason, that fascinates me way more than it should. Then the emotion in them changes and he openly stares with a puzzled expression before gripping my face a little tighter, causing the tears to well up in mine and he whispers huskily, "You may look like your sister but there is something completely different about you. What is it? What did she do to you?"

It's as if he's picking at the lock of my deepest secret, shut away never to see the light of day and I freeze because how can I ever admit what my own sister did to me?

"I can't…"

I yelp as he increases the pressure, and it's almost as if my eyes are bulging from their sockets as he hisses, "Tell me."

Part of me wishes I could. To offload the burden I have carried with me that became so heavy I buckled underneath it. However, there's the part of me that is so ashamed I can't even say the words out loud. So, I freeze and just stare back at him with a hopelessness that he must be feeding off right now because I understand men like him. They get off on another person's weakness. They crave it to boost their own inflated egos and his appears to be bigger than most.

For some reason, he releases me and as I fall back, I half expect to feel the weight of his boot crushing against my ribs and I immediately curl into the fetal position to try to protect myself as best as I can. Instead, I'm surprised when strong arms reach down and pluck me from the floor and hold me so tenderly it brings tears to my eyes for an entirely different reason. As he gently rocks me inside a wall of muscle, I find myself relaxing into his warm chest, inhaling the musky scent of a man who is increasingly desirable the more unexpected his actions are.

I'm not even certain how long he rocks me in those huge arms, but it gives me a strength I thought had deserted me. Then, as his lips brush against my cheek, I have an overwhelming urge to experience his skin on mine because these clothes are a serious deterrent to what I really want.

His phone rings and his low husky voice makes me smile and I snuggle in closer as he growls, "What is it?"

I hear the urgent voice on the other end but can't understand the words. Italian perhaps, Spanish possibly. Domenico answers back with an angry tirade and his tightening hold tells me he's angry with what he hears.

Then he cuts the call and an angry rush of what I'm certain are expletives, pour from his mouth but he doesn't lessen his grip at all.

If anything, he tightens it further and then he sighs heavily and, to my surprise, buries his face in my hair and inhales sharply, his hand holding the back of my head as he crushes me to his chest. This is more intimate than what he demanded of me earlier, and I wonder about the monster holding me so possessively. It's as if I'm a comfort to him, and he doesn't want to let go of that and then he sighs and growls, "Duty calls, baby girl. Just when we were getting along so well." His low rumble of laughter surprises me and then as he pulls back, I should be afraid of the demonic gaze he directs at me, before grinning,

"But you are still my prisoner, and you know what I do to them?"

"No." I'm almost afraid to ask, picturing a return to the dark dungeon and being chained to the wall for the rest of the night.

"I restrain them until I am ready to indulge in my pleasure."

The man is a monster if he gets pleasure from imprisoning his victims and I squeal when his huge hand squeezes my wrist. Locking it in an iron hold as he pushes me from his lap.

"Where are we going?" I am pulled roughly after him as he stands and heads toward a door set at the end of the room and he says roughly, "To my bedroom."

My heart leaps because I wasn't expecting that. If anything, I thought he would take me back to the dungeon but instead he flings open the door and I gasp when I see a room dressed in black with charcoal and silver walls. The bed that stands in the middle of it is simply huge and the covers dressing it are luxurious in their dark decadent shades. A black fur throw lies at an angle draped across the bed and the plethora of cushions make me long to dive headfirst into the purest luxury. Hidden lighting illuminates the various paintings hanging in gilded frames, and my mouth waters. I'm almost certain they are original, as I spy two from my favorite artist, Picasso.

"Are they...?" My voice sounds hungry as I openly drool at the magnificence looking down on me and Domenico shrugs and says with a hint of pride, "Original? Yes, baby girl. I don't tolerate imitations which brings me to you."

He spins me around and, holding my face in both hands, stares deep into my eyes and if anything, the hunger in his has intensified, causing me to be strangely attracted to him. It's as if the only thing he wants in life is me, and it's a heady experience.

The hunger in his eyes makes my heart flutter and the way he licks his lips with a tortured groan should have me fearing for my respectability. Instead, I am transfixed in a moment that could damage souls forever because God help me I want him to want me as much as he obviously does my sister. I'm not a fool. I know it's her face he sees when he regards me through those tortured eyes, and it hurts—a lot.

To him I am Diana, not the damaged second. Not the one who is half the woman she is and probably always will be. I am nothing, not like her. Diana is the type of woman who would make the history books. A woman able to explode empires with a smile and a gentle kiss. To bring down warriors and kings and have them all fighting over her and the lustful glance he is throwing my way isn't for me at all. I know that in my heart, which does a good job of breaking it because who wouldn't want to be desired as much as he obviously does her.

CHAPTER 8

DOM

When I look at Flora, I only see Diana. When I look *inside* Flora, I see the woman I always hoped her sister would be. I am conflicted, more than I thought possible. On the one hand, I want to fuck Diana out of my soul. Rape, hurt and tear her apart before feeding her to my men to finish off. I want the cruelest end to that woman, and I want it to be by my hand. However, when I'm with Flora, I have different desires. To protect, to cherish and to, for want of a better word — love. Flora is everything I hoped Diana was and yet I can't break through the barrier her sister has built around my heart.

There is so much I want from Flora, but like me, she is damaged by association. Diana was the most beautiful woman I had ever set eyes on with what I thought was the purest heart and when you've lived my life, any hint of purity is like the hardest drug to an addict. I craved it. The sensuous, soft nature of a woman who loved, rather than destroyed. Her softly spoken words and feather like kisses, disguising a hot, sultry, sexy siren when she stepped from her innocence and unleashed the power on me.

I had never caught feelings until I met Diana, which is why it destroyed me when I learned she had been playing us for fools. Three of us. The sons of the bastard who created us and subsequently spent the rest of his life destroying us.

Now I have a chance to experience what I felt again. This time with the purer soul of her sister. Could Flora be the answer to my prayers? Can she save my own tortured soul and make me feel again?

More than anything, I want to see what it would be like. To spend time with her and push her to her limits. Make her fall in love with me, locked away here in my tower with no other distractions. No other temptations to steal her attention away from me. My princess locked inside my chamber until she gives me her heart—forever.

I'm not sure when things changed for Flora and for me, but one glance into those soulful eyes haunted with dark images from her past, declared war on my heart. Now I need to nurture the flower. To make her unfold and expose her delicious center to me, but not now. As I said, business has become an unwelcome guest at my party and so Flora and my fascination for her must wait its turn.

"Stay here."

"Where are you going?"

She is afraid and I suppose she should be because nowhere is safe for this woman all the time I breathe. So, I push away my fascination for her and pull her roughly onto the bed, forcing her on her back with one strong arm and reaching in my drawer for the cuffs I keep there with the other.

"What the...?"

As I snap her dainty wrists into the metal cuffs, her yelp of surprise brings a rare smile to my face.

"Would you prefer to wait with Eddie until I can deal with you? It can be arranged."

"Why?" The tears spill down her cheeks as she breaks

before my eyes, and I shrug. "I told you. Business comes first. You'll be safe in here, but I don't want you poking around while you wait. Make yourself comfortable. I won't be long."

Grabbing the metal cuff, I secure it around the bed post and stand back, loving how good she looks at my mercy.

"What if I need to…" she says nervously, and I laugh out loud.

"Hold it. If I see anything on this bed other than you, I will punish you for it."

"But what if I need to go now?" She says defiantly, an angry stain forming on her flushed cheek, and I sigh and walk toward the corner of the room. I grab the trash can, then head her way and place it on the floor, before grabbing her in one arm and tearing her dress off as if it's wrapping paper. Her mortified shriek makes me laugh as she sits naked before me and as I force her to squat on the bucket, I sat drily, "Go ahead."

"You fucking animal." Her angry hiss excites me, and I growl, "It's now or never, baby girl. Remember, one stain on my sheet causes a bruise on your ass."

The sound of liquid filling the bucket makes me raise my eyes, and she pointedly looks away as she faces the humiliation of peeing in a bucket while I stand watching.

As soon as she finishes, I grab a handful of tissues and rub them gently against her pussy and her horrified hiss makes me lean closer and whisper, "This is mine. I'll be visiting it later and this time I won't lose interest."

If anything, the sight of her lower lip trembling gives me an instant hard on and with a flick of my wrist, I spin her back onto the bed with a giant slap on her ass accompanying it. Then I grab the bucket and head to the door, slamming it on my way out before depositing the bucket outside for one of the servants to deal with.

Now my mind turns to business and all thoughts of Flora

ORTEGA MAFIA – THE ENFORCER

evaporate into thin air because anybody who disturbs my down time will suffer the most severe consequences.

* * *

THE MEN WAITING for me are extremely unwelcome, and I sense something has changed at lightning speed.

I stare at the detective, who appears as if he would rather be anywhere else right now, and I note how his eyes flick around the room and the perspiration beads on his brow.

I'm surrounded by my men who glare at the accompanying detectives almost like the moment before a battle cry and I lean back and say with disinterest.

"What's this about?"

Detective Woznowski shifts nervously on his seat and says with a slight break to his voice, "Senator Billings."

"What about him?" Just his name causes my temper to flare because I can't shake the image from my mind of his hands on my woman.

"He's dead."

That gets my attention and I lean forward.

"Since when?"

"One hour ago."

"What happened?"

I am genuinely confused and the detective shifts nervously.

"I was hoping you could answer that question."

"Me?"

I shrug. "The last time I saw him, he was being escorted from my party after unwelcome advances toward one of my guests."

I nod to Pasquale. "My associate escorted him out personally."

Pasquale nods. "His limo was called and the last we saw of

him, he was heading toward the gates. It's all on CCTV if you want to look for yourself."

The detective nods and says, grim-faced. "His limo was found at the end of the street, his driver's throat cut and the senator minus his heart."

The air is tense as I process this information because what the actual fuck is happening right now?

There is silence as we wait for the detective to speak and, with a sigh, he glances around the room.

"A dog walker called it in, and the scene has been sealed. We have stopped anybody leaving and will require your cooperation."

"How?"

"Fingerprints, witness statements from your guests. This is now a crime scene, and it won't be long before the press get to hear of this and it becomes a circus."

I stare at him thoughtfully, a thousand possibilities running through my mind because this is shaping up to be a fucking headache for me.

The detective exhales sharply. "I will start with you, Mr. Ortega. If you can dismiss your men, I will take your statement while my detectives take your, um, associates' statements. I'm sure you understand these must be done in complete privacy and then we will start with your guests."

"Of course." I glance up at Pasquale, who appears as mystified as I am, and I know they are giving us no opportunity to align our stories. As the room starts to empty the detective says casually, "Are there any other guests we need to locate? It appears that some were found in your private rooms and have been asked to join the rest in the ballroom. We have a warrant to search this house, but it would help us greatly if you could direct us to the right place."

I sense the anger building inside me as my world is ripped apart before my eyes, but I know cooperation is needed right now. Senator Billings isn't your average Joe, and his death will be all over the press in a matter of minutes. I am an easy fall guy and an attractive one. The authorities have longed to pin something on me and my family and this could be the gift they've been searching for.

"My girlfriend."

I lean back with a sigh. "You interrupted us, so I should head back and inform her."

"Just tell us where she is, and my men will fetch her."

"No fucking way." I glare at him, and he has the sense to back down immediately and says with a sigh, "Then I will walk with you."

My temper is starting to worry me now because I am so close to unleashing it on him, but I grind my teeth instead and stand, heading straight from the room without a backward glance, hearing him rush hastily to his feet and scurry behind me.

As I pass through the hallway, I note the painting on the wall that disguises the hidden door to my chamber. At least that's one thing less to worry about because even if they did discover it, which is extremely unlikely, it merely reveals a wine cellar disguising the entrance to my house of horrors. The fact the chamber is soundproofed makes me wish I had chained Flora to that wall instead. She would have remained undiscovered, and I wouldn't have to deal with the problem that is facing me now.

As we reach my private quarters, I point to the couch and growl, "Wait there. There is no fucking way you are seeing my girlfriend until she is respectable."

He makes to object, and I growl, "Non-negotiable."

He has the sense to shut his mouth and then open it as he says quickly, "One minute, Mr. Ortega, and keep the door open."

My blinding rage threatens to send me to jail as my gun lies heavy against my side, aching to be unleashed on the detective but I fight it down and head into my room, raising my finger to my lips when Flora makes to yell at me.

I waste no time in reaching for her cuffed wrists and releasing her, say in a low angry whisper, "We have visitors, darling. It appears that your date never made it home and they want answers. Remember, you are my girlfriend, and I will protect you. If you tell him anything but how much you fucking love me, I will punish you. Got it?"

Her eyes are wide as I pick up her discarded dress and pull it over her head, only to find I did a pretty good job of ruining it as it hangs ripped to shreds on her shivering body.

With an irritable sigh, I pull her with me into the closet and drop one of my sweatshirts over her head, noting how it falls to her knees, effectively disguising every one of her curves from the enemy.

Then, as I grip her hand, I whisper, "Play along, sweetheart, and you'll live another day. Protect me and I protect you. You know how it works."

I'm uneasy because this could end badly for me and yet I breathe a sigh of relief when she nods. "OK."

The tightening of her hand in mine tells me that Flora Corlietti knows exactly how this all works, and I'm not sure if I'm happy about that or not.

CHAPTER 9

FLORA

Things are moving so fast I can't keep up. One minute I'm naked and chained to the bed of the most frightening man I have ever met and the next I'm pretending to be his girlfriend.

The fact it regards the creepy senator is the only reason I'll play along, because of how serious this is. If Senator Billings never made it home, it's probably because Domenico did something to prevent him and whatever it was, I hope it hurt like hell.

If anything, I'm glad of his protection as I walk beside him out of the room and notice a man sitting on the couch watching us approach.

He smiles kindly, but I see the hunger in his eyes and it's not for me. He senses an opportunity to bring Domenico Ortega down and I suppose it's my history that makes me angry about that. I have lived with the mafia for most of my life and have been schooled in the rules concerning that. We protect our own against them all. The feds, the cops and the system. We close ranks and deal with our shit in our own way and even though this could be my way out of a scary situation; I understand it would only bide me some time because if you upset the mafia, retribution will be quick, painful and resulting in a long-drawn-out death.

"Excuse me, Miss…" The detective stands and holds out his hand and then drops it as quickly at the low growl from the beast by my side.

"Corlietti, sir. Flora Corlietti."

The fact his eyes are raised tells me he knows only too well where that name came from and the resignation in his expression tells me he already knows he will get nothing from me.

He nods toward the couch and Domenico sits down, pulling me beside him, anchoring me by his side as we face the detective together.

"Senator Billings." The detective stares me straight in the eye and I can't disguise the contempt in my own as I say wearily, "What about him?"

"He's dead. Murdered."

I glance up in astonishment and gasp, "But he just left."

The detective nods. "An hour ago. I need to hear about your involvement with him."

My mind is racing because what the hell do I tell him? The truth? I have nothing to hide, but then again, why would I be someone else's date to my boyfriend's party? Domenico's hold on me tightens, telling me I need to play this cool, and I say wearily, "I was asked to accompany him here tonight."

"Who asked?" The detective pulls out his notepad and starts to write.

"By my employer, Desdemona Gray."

"Of the Barrington gallery?" The detective glances up, his pen poised above the page.

"Yes. She asked me to accompany him to secure his business. She was hoping I could persuade him to invest in more work and acting as his escort for the night would be in a business capacity only."

"To your boyfriend's party. Do you think I'm a fool, Miss. Corlietti?"

"I don't know, sir. Are you?"

I play it cool because there is something a little creepy about the detective and Domenico's low laugh almost makes me smile.

I say firmly. "I told you it was in a business capacity. It has no bearing on my relationship with, um, Dom, and he was fully aware it was business. They both did, or at least I thought the senator understood."

"Why, what happened?" The detective leans forward, his eyes lighting with interest and I say with disgust. "The senator obviously had other plans for me, involving a few of his friends and when he attempted to assault me in full view of my boyfriend and his guests, he was thrown out for his trouble."

The detective's gaze falls on Domenico, who nods. "What did he expect? I'm sure any man would have stepped in and asked him to leave. You see, detective..." He leans forward and stares into the detective's eyes with a piercing gaze that could kill a man's soul on impact. "Nobody touches my girlfriend but me, and he overstepped the mark. But before you ask or insinuate that we had anything to do with his death, there are enough fucking cameras in my home that will prove we never left the building."

Domenico leans back and pulls me with him and the detective nods, scribbling in his book before snapping it shut.

"We will need access to the recordings." He says bluntly and then stands. "I trust you have no objection to our presence while we carry out our investigations."

"None at all." Domenico stands, pulling me with him so we face the detective as one unit.

"We will help in any way we can. If you need me, ask any one of my men and they will inform me."

The detective nods. "Thank you. That will be all—for now."

He stares at us both for a good few seconds before a look of resignation enters his eyes.

"I'll leave you to your evening. But Mr. Ortega, Miss. Corlietti..."

He glances around the room with a small smile on his lips before turning to face us and saying firmly, "Don't go far. We may need to ask you more questions."

We say nothing and watch as he leaves the room and only when the door slams behind him, do I relax the breath I was holding and then the fear returns almost as quickly when Domenico heads to the door and turns the lock, leaving me in no doubt I have been locked inside with a man I should fear more than fear itself.

"Good girl."

I peer through my wet lashes as he stands in the doorway with an unreadable expression on his face. For some reason, his praise creates a glow of appreciation inside me, telling me I'm fucked before I've even begun.

He advances slowly toward me and my mouth dries, my tongue flicking against my lips as I attempt to deal with the situation unfolding and as he stops before me, he reaches out and fists my hair, dragging my face to his. As our lips collide, the kiss he delivers is definitely not from a fairy tale. This isn't love's true kiss, this is a declaration of war, on me and as I frantically attempt to survive the attack, I hate that I'm loving every second of it.

My lips feel bruised as he pulls back and then drags the sweatshirt over my head, leaving me naked before him and as his hungry eyes run the length of my body, I hate the way it responds by shivering with desire at the thought of what he could do to me.

"Your cooperation changes nothing. You are still my prisoner and will pay your sister's debt."

"Please..." I stand shame faced before a monster, knowing

there is nothing I can do to change his mind but foolishly try, anyway.

"Please what, Flora?" He appears amused as he stands with his arms folded, watching me as if I'm a floorshow put on purely for his pleasure.

I raise my eyes to his and stare straight into two pools of obsidian beauty that sparkle with something I can't quite fathom. "Please don't do this. I'm not responsible for my sister. I never was."

"I know."

He shrugs. "The trouble is you look so alike it's as if she is here suffering for her sins. I have no loyalty to you, so why should I care if you want this or not?"

"Because somewhere deep inside you realize this is wrong, perhaps?"

I stare at him defiantly and he merely laughs out loud, as if I've cracked the funniest joke.

"Any feelings I had were beaten out of me before I could talk."

He steps closer and, leaning toward my face, snarls, "Then your sister made sure to destroy any hope I ever had of changing that. I don't give a fuck about your rights, your wishes or if it's wrong. I have no conscience and no heart, and you will soon learn that. If you hate every minute of it, blame your sister because she is the one who has put you in this position when she unleashed a wrecking ball on what I had left of a heart."

I know only too well what that feels like, so I sigh heavily and say with resignation. "Then do your worst and get it out of your system. This wouldn't be the first time I've suffered because of who my sister is, and I don't expect it will be the last. Unless you do me a massive favor and kill me in the process."

As the words spill from my lips, I prepare myself to fight

another battle caused by my sister and I'm surprised when he raises his hand and lightly touches my lips with his index finger. His thumb rubs across my lower lip and his voice is uncharacteristically gentle as he whispers, "What did she do to break you, baby girl?"

I wasn't expecting kindness—not from him and for a second I lower my guard and the tears well in my eyes and my lip trembles as I fight the demons that are circling.

"It doesn't matter."

"I disagree."

His voice is soft like silk and as luxurious as velvet. Husky, with an edge of desire that I appear to crave because I lean against his hand, loving the contact. It's nice being asked something about me, Flora, not Diana, for a change and as my chest heaves and my lip trembles, I am more vulnerable than I've ever been before.

CHAPTER 10

DOM

This is unexpected. Something shifted inside me when Flora pleaded her case and then accepted her fate. There is something lost in her that only a person who knows how that feels can recognize. She appears so vulnerable, so fragile and for some reason it's calling to the protector in me that I never realized was there.

It's not as urgent to tear her apart anymore, just to unlock the secrets she's guarding so bravely. Maybe I can use Flora in a different way than I first thought, and as the seed takes root, I pull her shivering body against me and wrap my arms protectively around her.

The trouble is, when I close my eyes, it's her sister that stands behind them and all the emotions that go along with that are there sharpening their claws ready for retribution. I thought her sister must be a lot like her, not only due to her appearance, but because she was the senator's whore for the night. Diana would have thrived on that role and been plotting to exploit the situation to her full advantage, but something is telling me that Flora is merely here to please her boss and keep her job. Nothing else.

So, I must contemplate this new situation and will need time to get my head straight. With a sigh, I gently guide Flora toward my bedroom and then, to her surprise, sweep her off her feet and tuck her inside the silk sheets, resisting the urge to take full advantage of the naked beauty in my bed. However, my inner bastard hasn't given up on me yet, so I cuff one wrist to the bedpost and try not to react to the hurt brimming in her beautiful blue eyes and growl, "Sleep. You will need all your strength tomorrow."

"Why?" The panic in her eyes turns me on because I've always thrived on a person's fear. It gives me the biggest high and the pretty woman in my bed waiting to discover my intentions toward her is causing my body to demand release. I want her and I haven't figured out yet if it's Flora I want, or Diana.

Without offering her any kind of explanation, I spin on my heel and walk away, more for my own sanity than her wellbeing.

As I retreat to the couch outside, I pour my usual whiskey and try to get my head straight. Moving across to the window, I swirl the amber liquid in the crystal glass, just as I did a few hours earlier, and contemplate my current situation. The fact Senator Billings was found murdered outside my home tells me it was intentional. Somebody wants to bring heat on me, and I need to figure out who. Reaching for my phone, I dial Pasquale's number.

"Boss."

His deep voice reassures me because of all my men, Pasquale is the one I rely on and trust the most.

"We need to talk. Meet me in my apartment."

I cut the call before he can answer and continue to stand by the window, watching the activity outside. Cops, the sheriff and possibly the feds are swarming around my home and grounds and there is nothing I can do about that. They will need to run their investigation and I'm convinced that a word in the right ear will make it all go away, but whoever caused this will not be so lucky.

A gentle tap on the door causes me to bark, "Come in."

As Pasquale enters the room, I turn and regard him with a hooded expression.

"What can you tell me?"

He will have run his own operation and he sighs, dropping onto the couch at the jerk of my thumb.

"We watched the footage and saw the senator's car leave. Our lookout had eyes on it until it turned the corner, which is apparently where it was ambushed, and they were taken out."

"Any indication of who ordered the hit?"

"None." Pasquale sighs heavily. "I've called in a few favors and asked our neighbors security to check their cameras. I've also called in a few of our men off the street to dig deep and get information by any means necessary. If someone does know and they're not far away, they had better be hiding well because we're sweeping this town for information and should have some intelligence by morning."

"It's a start, but I want to discover every fucking detail of the senator's life. His friends, colleagues and family. I want to know how he likes his eggs for breakfast, and I want it all yesterday. Whoever took him out either had a grudge against Senator Billings, or me and I want to rule out the first one before I deal with the next. If I am a target, they had better start running because I am pissed and spoiling to break a few souls over this."

Pasquale nods and as his phone rings, I nod, giving him permission to accept the call. After a few seconds, he says brusquely, "I'm on my way."

He glances up and excitement has sparked in his eyes, which immediately captures my attention and my glass hovers against my lips as he says pleasantly, "Perhaps we should start our interrogations a little closer to home."

"Meaning?"

"Eddie."

I raise my eyes as he shakes his head in disgust. "It turns out Eddie didn't just neglect to inform you Flora Corlietti was on the guest list."

"I'm listening."

"It appears that he was responsible for setting it all up in the first place."

"How do you know?"

"Desdemona Gray was a contact in his phone and when we checked it out, there were a few interesting texts that signed his death warrant."

He rolls his eyes. "Dumb fucking amateur. It turns out Eddie was fucking Desdemona along with half of Vegas and 'suggested' she send her young assistant on a date to hell with the slimy senator."

"Why would he suggest that, I wonder?"

My mind is racing because all my men are aware the Corlietti name is like waving a fucking red flag in my face and Pasquale says grimly, "I'm guessing you will need to ask the man himself that information."

The surge of adrenalin that races through my veins delights me more than any orgasm. I've always been a twisted bastard and my love for my job even scares me sometimes. Pain, violence and torture are the tools of my trade, and I wield them well. Eddie is about to discover that first hand, so I set my glass down and a sense of peace descends over me as I prepare to do something I'm insanely good at.

They don't call me the enforcer for nothing and most men in my position would delegate this job to a man lower down the ranks, but I lead by example, something Eddie is about to experience, and I can't wait to get started.

* * *

Two hours later and my body is streaked with Eddie's blood. I'm naked from the waist up because blood on my designer suits is unacceptable.

Pasquale is leaning against the stone walls, and I can sense his interest even now and it amuses me to think of the house crawling with cops, all happily unaware of the crimes happening around them.

Eddie's groans will only be heard by us because this chamber is soundproofed and hidden from even the keenest eye. Nobody knows it's here and even if they stumbled across it, it would alert us in plenty of time, enabling the security measures to snap into place, ensuring our privacy.

No, Eddie is fucked, and he knows it and as his life hangs in the balance, he knows there is only one way out—death. But not before he guarantees the lives of his family, of which he has two sisters, currently attending college, who are unaware their lives are now in his hands.

"Please boss, spare my family."

His pathetic cry washes over me like a passing breeze.

"Then tell me who is responsible. Who is trying to set me up and who murdered the filthy senator?"

To his credit, Eddie has held out longer than most and at first denied all knowledge and implied his phone was stolen and the evidence planted. Once I broke both his legs and severed his hand, he started to think differently and told me a fabricated story involving a man from his card game that he owed money to. If he wiped out his debt, in return, he wanted Eddie to arrange for the senator to be escorted by Flora Corlietti and he even set up Eddie with Desdemona as a cover story.

The trouble is, my instinct is telling me it's all lies, so as I reach for his other wrist, he yells, "Please, no more."

He is barely conscious, and I nod to Pasquale who chucks a bucket of icy water over him and as his breath labors and he is resigned to the fact that only his soul will ever leave this room, he finally tells me what I need to know.

"Mario Bachini."

"What about him?"

My anger increases as he speaks the name of Diana's stepbrother.

"He offered me money and a position higher than I would ever get with the Ortegas. I only had to make sure Flora Corlietti made it inside this building. I'm sorry, boss. I should have come clean."

My anger simmers like a bubbling volcano and even Pasquale appears nervous as that name bounces around my mind like machine gun fire. Mario fucking Bachini. How I hate the very mention of him. Diana's stepbrother and my father's consigliere. A man my father chose over his own sons to help run the Ortega Mafia and the fact he sent Flora here tells me he's intent on taking over as the new Ortega don.

With a roar, I drive my fist through Eddie's skull, effectively silencing him forever, and as I brace myself against the bloodied damp walls of hell, I feel retribution surge through my entire soul. Flora Corlietti must have been sent here to bring me down and whether she is part of it or not, I have played right into their fucking hands by declaring to the entire police force that she is my girlfriend. The senator's death was to frame me for murder, and knowing how those tainted minds operate, I'm certain of only one thing. This war has only just begun.

CHAPTER 11

FLORA

If I could sleep, I would. In fact, it's unusual for me to sleep for more than a couple of hours before the nightmares wake me. There has only ever been one monster who dominated them until now.

Domenico Ortega has invaded my subconscious even while I sleep, and I jerk awake after a vivid image of him advancing on me as I am chained to his dungeon wall. He scares me. There is something positively evil about that man and I'm not surprised he was drawn to my sister. Two halves of the same mold, perhaps. Possibly, although I always afforded Mario that honor before.

I shiver when I think of the despicable creature who came into our lives not long after ours was destroyed, along with my parents.

Two orphans with nowhere to go after our grandmother suffered a heart attack a year after we arrived on her doorstep on that fateful night.

The tears slide down my face as I remember the one woman who showed me more kindness than anyone else. She was the person I ran to for comfort and the only friend I ever had.

Grace Corlietti was a formidable woman who led a hard life herself. She tried to prepare me for the future, but nothing could do a good enough job of that because what happened next is the stuff of twisted nightmares and it's doubtful I will ever recover.

Once again, I cast my mind back to my meeting with the mother superior of the convent of the Blessed Virgin Mary. I landed on their door one night, thumping my fist against the ancient wood and crying for shelter from the evil I lived with. It was the only place I could think of to go and as they ushered me inside with kind smiles and gentle touches, I immediately knew I had found a place I wanted to call home.

The tears slide down my cheeks as I remember how loving they were. Sister Agatha, who became a surrogate mother to me, was the kindest person I have ever met. I was broken, and they repaired the damage. At least I thought they had, but I am so close to revisiting that nightmare and this time I may not survive.

The usual darkness circles and consumes me. I live in darkness. I always have and yet nothing compares to the darkness that exists in the Ortega mansion. It surrounds me. The demons that lurk in the shadows whisper that my life is here now. Is this my final resting place before the comparative bliss of the afterlife? Part of me hopes it is and then there's that will to live inside me that has always burned so brightly.

I'm not even sure of the time when he returns. The door crashes open, causing me to gaze up in startled surprise. I choke back the sob it causes when I peer at a warrior streaked in blood standing by the side of the bed, gazing down on me with fury flashing in his eyes.

"Mario Bachini."

He says the two words I detest most in the world and I swallow the bile that the name always brings.

"What about him?"

My voice shakes as I answer him and he growls, "I need to know everything you've got on him."

"Now?" I shift into a sitting position, hating the fact I'm chained to his bed, naked and shivering with fright.

His eyes flash and the scowl on his face, cause my fear to deepen and my eyes fixate on the blood that decorates his insanely ripped body like the deadliest war paint.

The moon casts his body in shadows and his dark close cropped hair gleams as it catches the moon's rays. His turbulent eyes glisten as he openly stares at my body and as they run the length of me, my face flames as my nipples peak and my desire runs its betrayal between my legs.

"I asked you a question." He snarls, advancing slowly, making me cower in fear and I lick my drying lips and whisper, "He's the devil who walks on earth."

The bed dips as he sits beside me and I flinch as he reaches out, causing him to say firmly, "I'm not going to hurt you—yet, anyway. I'm going to release the cuff, and I expect you to tell me everything you know about that man and his involvement with your family."

As he releases my wrist, I'm surprised when he gently presses his lips to the graze the cuff created. It's a sweet gesture at the scariest moment of my life and it disarms me a little. In fact, this whole situation is confusing because we are both nearly naked. Only his pants preserve his own modesty and I'm guessing even they will soon be gone and I'm not sure how I feel about that.

I'm not a fool. I understand how these things end. He will use me, then dispose of me, either dead or broken. I have accepted my fate, but I'm curious about the man who will make it happen.

For some reason, he keeps my hand clasped in his giant one and I expect it's preventing my escape, so I sigh and look to the floor as I prepare to tell him what he wants to know.

"He's not really our stepbrother in the usual sense."

His hand tightens in mine, and I shake my head in disgust. "When our grandmother died, we were orphans. Mario's family took us in and adopted us."

"The Bachini's?"

Domenico appears surprised at that. I expect it's because that family has a history of crime under their belt and ordinarily shouldn't be gifted an animal, let alone two vulnerable girls.

"I believe he had something on the adoption officer and his wife wanted a daughter. She got two instead, and we arrived late one night with nothing but the clothes we were dressed in."

I shiver at the memory and am surprised when a huge arm reaches across my shoulders and pulls me against a warm body that smells like death and salvation in a lethal cocktail.

"Mario was their son and even from that first meeting, I could tell he was trouble. He has a rotten soul and no compassion, and was the perfect accomplice for my sister."

My voice breaks as I sob. "Now I had two tormenters instead of one. There was no help from Mrs. Bachini either. She was much the same and adored Diana and hated me on sight. I became the object of all their derision and life was pretty bad from then on."

"How long?" Dom says tightly, and I shrug. "Three years. As soon as I was sixteen, everything changed."

If Domenico's arm wasn't holding me up, I would be trying to escape because revisiting this nightmare isn't something I'm keen on doing right now.

"What changed?" His low hiss tells me I'm not getting away with this and my voice is so soft I'm not even sure he can hear it.

"They put me up for auction."

"Who did?"

"Mario and Diana."

"What kind of auction?"

"One to sell my virginity to the highest bidder."

Domenico tenses beside me and I say in a dead voice. "I raised a bid of ten thousand dollars from a man old enough to be my grandfather. I was taken to his house and raped repeatedly. In the morning, Mario and Diana came to collect me and as I broke down on the back seat of the car, they laughed and told me to get used to it."

"The fucking bastards." Dom's growl tells me he is disgusted, which gives me a little hope at least and I nod sorrowfully.

"They weren't kidding, either. Every weekend when his parents were out, Mario invited men to visit. I was expected to entertain them along with Diana, and Mario pocketed the money they paid him for sex with us. It was degrading, humiliating and wicked and I had no way out. I couldn't even plead with my sister because she loved every minute of it. They both did."

I turn to look at the man dragging my sordid secret out and note the pulse throbbing in his temple and the grim set to his jaw.

"Diana was fascinated by Mario. She idolized him. He was everything she loved, and he took full advantage of that. They had one hell of a fucked-up relationship and they tried to drag me into it several times."

"How?" his voice is like a bullet firing from a gun and I jump at the menace in it.

"Threesomes mainly. Not with my sister, but with friends of his."

I can't check the tears that fall on my naked thighs. "You

must be disgusted and think I'm a freak and I wouldn't blame you."

I am so ashamed of my past and what I did to survive it and then I'm shocked when a low growl makes it way out from deep inside my captor and he rasps, "Your sister is a fucking bitch, and she will pay for what she did to you. I promise you that at least."

Then he drags my face to his and the flashing revenge in his eyes almost makes me fear for my sister—almost.

"I will kill them both and you will be free of them forever. Help me bring them down and you earn your freedom with enough money to be set for life."

"How?" I'm shocked because how on earth can I bring those people down? And Domenico stares deep into my eyes and hisses, "By becoming Diana."

CHAPTER 12

DOM

The rage that burns so hot inside me drove me to find the one woman who can give me the answers I seek. Mario's name set off a chain reaction that I am still struggling to deal with. When I learned Diana had brought her brother to live with her after I left, I never thought much of it. Then the stories began to filter back to me of a bastard soul who deserved his place by my father's side.

It appears that Diana always intended on driving us out and installing her twisted lover in our place and my father was so besotted with her he couldn't say no. I'm not a fool and I'm guessing this was probably her plan all along and when Flora sobbed out her story, fear gripped my heart and squeezed it tightly. I left my own fucking sister with those monsters, and I can't shake the dreadful realization I played a part in her death.

Eliza ran away soon after we left and now I know why. It was because of Diana and Mario, and hearing Flora's tale makes me wonder if history repeated itself. I was blinded by rage and regret that I never saved my sister because she perished along with my father when their super-yacht exploded in Dubai.

Eliza was innocent. She had run and my father was arranging her retrieval. It's why they were there, an exchange if you like, and yet they never made it off the boat. Two family members dead because of two rotten souls and if I was closer to my brothers, I would ask for their help.

But I'm not and it's all because of one woman. Diana Corlietti.

When I left Pasquale to dispose of Eddie's body and clean up the chamber, I had only one thing on my mind. To punish Flora for her sister's sins and send her back to her in pieces. Eddie's story painted a picture with Flora in the starring role and I thought she was the enemy sent to bring me down.

Then I heard her story, and any fool could see she wasn't faking the pain and in that moment, I knew what I had to do. Flora is as much a victim as the rest of us and as she spoke, a plan began to formulate in my mind. To defeat the enemy, you need to always be one step ahead of them and we are running to catch up. However, Flora will be the one to bring her sister and stepbrother down if it's the last thing I ever do.

Flora is waiting for a response and as I turn, I see the fear in her eyes, and it unnerves me a little. She is so like her sister it's confusing my emotions and as she stares through those beautiful pain-filled eyes, I want to chase that fear away.

I loved Diana, but it's amazing how quickly love can turn to hate and yet as I cup Flora's face in my hand, the emotion surges through me like a dam bursting.

It's as if all those emotions are now shifting onto her and I don't even register that I'm streaked with another man's blood. A man that I killed in cold blood and never gave it a second thought. Now I'm experiencing a different emotion and after hearing her story and watching the fear mix with resignation in her eyes, I do something alien to me and whisper, "You're safe with me, Flora. I won't hurt you."

I'm not even sure she believes me because her eyes flicker

with disbelief and she probably expects me to be like everybody else. I don't blame her for that and so I reach for the fur throw on the end of the bed and wrap it around her shivering shoulders.

"I'll take care of you, baby girl. You're safe with me."

"Am I?" Her lower lip trembles and I suppose she's right not to trust me, and I nod with a determination that's alien to me.

"I don't want to be like Mario or her. I am better than that and can tell you've been used along with the rest of us."

"Us?" She appears confused and the ache in my heart is growing by the second when I think of my sister who was the only innocent one caught up in all of this.

"I had a sister." My low growl comes from nowhere and it surprises me more than her. She says nothing, but the air is tense between us, and I should leave it there, but something is compelling me to unburden this grief onto her.

"Eliza. She was the same age as you."

"You say was. What happened?"

Flora's sweet gentle voice washes over me like balm and I sigh heavily. "She lived with us and when Diana moved in, I was happy she had someone her own age to hang out with."

"I'm sorry." Flora hangs her head because she knows what's coming and I growl, "Diana turned us all against her. Made out Eliza was causing her trouble and plotting to get rid of her. I'm ashamed to say, along with my brothers, we thought more of Diana than Eliza and made her life a misery because of what Diana told us."

A small hand creeps into mine and she whispers, "She's good at that. Don't blame yourself or your brothers for something my sister did."

Just this gentle act of kindness melts a little piece of my frozen heart and, as a piece falls revealing a jagged edge, it sharpens the pain. I take a deep breath and whisper huskily, "Eliza ran away after soon we left. My father was angry and searched the globe for her, but she remained hidden for well over a year until he heard she was under the protection of the Karim family in Dubai. A meeting was arranged in exchange for information my father had on the mafia king and when he went to collect, they were blown to fucking hell."

Flora's shocked gasp reminds me she's here because I'm so deep in my own thoughts I forgot that for a second.

I turn and gaze into her astonishing eyes that are brimming with compassion, and my breath hitches. She is so beautiful, so fragile, an innocent caught in the middle of a turbulent storm with nowhere to shelter. In this moment, I hate myself and so I lower my voice and whisper gently, "Together we will make them pay for what they have done to us, and every innocent person caught up in their despicable world. Will you help me, Flora—please?"

I hold my breath because this is alien to me. I don't say please. I don't request. I take and demand, but I am caught up in the purest moment of my life and it's as if an angel sits before me and I am pleading for forgiveness. I'm mesmerized as she slowly smiles, transforming her features like the sun chasing away a shadow and revealing the beauty within. This time my breath hitches as I gaze at the power of a woman and my heart beats a little faster as I fall under Flora's spell.

"Yes." Her shy whisper wafts toward me, hitting me hard in the heart, and I have an overpowering urge to chain her by my side forever.

However, I don't want to take this time. Not after hearing her tragic story and I must earn my right to be by her side, so I raise my hand and cup her face, marveling in the fact she leans into it and sighs with contentment and I whisper, "I'll ask you again. Who are you?"

She glances up in surprise, but I mean every word because there is something telling me Flora Corlietti is the most important person in my life right now and was sent here for a reason.

Is she part of this? Is she the best actress I've ever met, and will she ultimately bring me down? I don't have the answers to that, but I know one thing. I want this woman and I want to keep her safe. To protect her from this fucked up life we lead and wrestle her demons away from her.

"I'm nobody and I never have been." Her soft response to my question angers me and I grip her face tighter and growl, "You are everything and don't forget that. You are strong and brave, and I won't hear otherwise."

"It doesn't feel that way right now." Her low laugh reminds me of her situation and so I nod and say huskily, "Then let me rectify the situation."

As my hand closes around hers, I tug her up with me and without another word, I set about making Flora feel at home because one thing's certain, this is now her home and I'll fight anyone to the death who tries to take her away from me.

CHAPTER 13

FLORA

I'm not sure what's happening here, but something has changed. When Domenico stood by the bed stripped to the waist with another man's blood streaked across his chest, I thought my time was up.

However, after our conversation, my feelings changed toward him because even I know how my sister can drive a saint to crime. Whatever has happened is down to her, and he is probably right to doubt my involvement in this.

As I walk beside him, I have many questions, but one is burning brighter than the rest and I say fearfully, "Diana knows I'm here."

More than anything that scares the shit out of me because it wasn't only Domenico's sister who ran from that monster. I did, too.

He turns and looks surprised that I spoke, and I say falteringly, "I am hiding, much like your sister was. When the nuns sent me away, they gave me enough money for a bus ticket and a place to rent. I came to Vegas hoping the bright lights would shield me from view and when I took the job at the art gallery, I thought it would be the last place they would find me.

"What makes you think that?" He obviously considers me a fool, judging by his expression, and I say tightly, "Diana hates art. She hates anything to do with beauty and she always has. Her preference is gothic imagery and horror films. If I know my sister, she'd have thought I'd headed off to San Francisco because I always spoke of it as a child. For some reason, I always looked on it as Utopia, probably because our mother was born there and loved telling us tales of how amazing it was."

I say nervously, "I came here because this is the last place Diana would expect me to go. The trouble is, she knows I'm here, which means she's watching me."

I shiver as it hits me hard and I am so worried she will appear and drag me back to her disgusting life.

"It doesn't matter."

Dom's voice is gruff and dismissive, and I bite back.

"It matters to me—a lot, actually."

He stops suddenly and I wonder if I've angered him again, but I'm surprised when he says fiercely, "Nobody will harm you. They will have to come through me first and I don't rate their chances much."

"Why are you helping me?"

I'm so confused and then my heart flutters when he stops and stares into my eyes with an expression of yearning that catches me off-guard. "Because something is telling me it was always meant to be you, Flora."

"I don't understand."

He pulls my face gently to his and as his lips hover close to mine, he whispers, "I fell in love with perfection, at least I thought I had, but I didn't realize perfection comes from inside. You are perfect inside and out, which in my book equals everything I ever wanted in life."

My heart bangs like a base drum as he hovers against my lips, and I'm surprised when I lean a little closer with an overwhelming urge to know what love tastes like. I have been kissed before, but not with love. Desire, dominance, and possession but never love.

He breaks away and snarls, "Come. You need to clean up."

I'm not sure why I'm disappointed that he's interrupted what could have been an interesting experience, but I'm guessing I should be grateful for it.

As I follow him silently, it strikes me how fascinated I am by this man. He scares me more than anyone I've ever met, even my own sister and I'm wondering if it's because from the moment I sensed him behind me at the party, he had the ability to steal my breath away.

Even when he chained me up like an animal, it just piqued my interest further, and I doubt it's because he's the most magnificent man I've ever met.

His dark, swarthy good looks, brimming with masculine intensity, causes my heart to beat a little faster. The way he looks at me through those demonic eyes causes me to shiver, and it's not out of fear. When he speaks, his voice is husky and laced with dangerous intent, and I crave every syllable. Then there's that magnificent body that could crush a woman's heart as well as a man's soul and I would gladly sacrifice my own to his.

Yes, Domenico Ortega is the most intense man I have ever met, and it's like the hardest drug. Lethal, desirable, and the cause of the most massive high, followed by an incredible need for more.

He pushes open the door to a room I wasn't expecting. Unlike his own bedroom, this one is in direct contrast. Dressed completely in white silk, it shimmers in the moonlight that spills through the open window, causing the breeze to calm my already heated skin. The silk drapes billow and the white shagpile carpet bunches beneath my toes. The soft warm lighting calms and the inviting bed covered in silk sheets and a white fur throw makes my eyes heavy with the need to sleep.

Domenico says gruffly, "This will be your room. You will find everything you need and if there is anything missing, I'll get it for you."

I stare around in stunned surprise and whisper, "It's beautiful."

I've almost forgotten I'm naked, dressed only in his fur throw as I stand before him, my hair cascading down my back and my eyes wide with wonder.

I wander around the room, gazing with admiration at the exquisite décor and stylish touches that make this room a work of art. Then my eye is drawn to the most beautiful chaotic painting that takes pride of place on the far wall.

As I stand before it, I gaze in wonder at a masterpiece and whisper reverently, "Is that …?"

"A Matisse." He stands beside me and it's as if a shadow is cast over my soul as my heart beats faster. I have a strange yearning to hold his warm skin against mine, and I'm not even sure why I lean a little closer to the warmth emanating from his body. I have an incredible need for his arms to fold around me, which shocks me a little.

Is Domenico Ortega my knight in shining armor? Like fuck he is, and I must push away these fanciful thoughts and shut them down forever.

"It's stunning." I praise his choice in art, and he laughs huskily. "It's an investment, nothing more."

"So, you don't appreciate art for the beauty before you?"

I'm a little disappointed about that and he laughs softly.

"I appreciate many things, Flora. The curve of a woman's ass, the way her tits bounce against my chest as I fuck her hard and the beautiful sight of my cock filling her smart mouth."

I turn away in disgust because he has just proven to me that he is no different from the rest and when he snatches my wrist and pulls me back to face him, I'm surprised when he drags his index finger down my face and stares into my eyes with a heated desire that makes my breath hitch.

"I appreciate you, Flora Corlietti. Your beauty, your femininity, and your pure soul. You don't belong here; you don't belong with me, but I'm a collector of beautiful things and I've never met anyone that fits that description more than you."

"Collect me?"

I'm confused, and he nods, a wicked smile appearing on his face that tells me he has a plan for me that I may not be comfortable with.

"I won't let you go until you fall in love with me."

His words take me by surprise and my mouth drops as I peer through my lashes at a man who shouldn't talk like that.

"But you said…"

I falter, my mind racing to keep up because he promised I could start again if I helped him. I'm astonished when he pulls me flush against his body with a firm hand in the small of my back and as the fur throw hits the ground, my naked skin hits his.

I am overwhelmed by desire. His gruff tone increases it when he whispers, "I have until your sister dies to make you fall in love with me. When her timer runs out, so does ours. You will be given a choice. Leave and start again somewhere safe, away from this life—away from me. Or marry me and walk by my side into a turbulent future. A dark future filled with pain, anger, and horror. A mafia future that will be breath-taking in its intensity as you discover I love just as hard."

The way his eyes flash is compelling and feeling bold, I say breathlessly, "Then I'll look forward to experiencing your powers of persuasion."

A wicked smile lights up his face and his eyes flash with a danger I strangely crave. This moment is intoxicating, dangerous and destructive because he has unleashed a side of me I choose to ignore most of the time. I walked away from darkness, hell I ran away. Then why is it so enticing to race straight back into it and jump headfirst into the flames of hell, holding this man's hand as I go?

CHAPTER 14

DOM

I wasn't kidding when I told Flora I wanted her as my wife. Why the fuck wouldn't I? She is everything I dreamed of as a child since learning the power of attraction. Soft, sweet and vulnerable with a hidden steel inside. Kind, funny and gorgeous, with a body for sin.

I want to devour Flora Corlietti and break her over and over again just for my pleasure. I want to pick her up at will and play with her until she passes out from exhaustion and I want to do it for the rest of whatever life I have left.

Now I must use her to bring her sister down and the weasel that scurries by her side. Mario Bachini will suffer for daring to try to bring my family down, but most of all he will suffer for what he did to Flora.

My plan hit me as soon as I saw her trusting, beautiful eyes staring at me with desire. For a second, I thought it was Diana herself and it took me back to the time she controlled my heart. She looked at me like that—a lot and when we were together, it was inevitable we would end up in my bed.

She was my father's girlfriend and my lover. She told me

she was scared of him. That he made her do things she was uncomfortable with.

She played the innocent victim well and my need to protect her was strong. So many times, she told me she only felt safe with me. That if things were different, we would be together.

Her soft whispers of love settled inside my heart, causing my mind to bend against my own family loyalty. I would have done anything for Diana Corlietti, even murder my own father to set us both free but when I discovered my brother fucking her against her closet wall, that love turned to the most bitter hatred and any dreams I had evolved into twisted nightmares of how painful I could make her ending.

Betrayal is the cruelest form of torture, and I have lived with it far too long. First, my mother was murdered before my eyes and then my heart was brutally torn from me by the woman I loved and my bastard brother. Now I have regained control of a situation I never wanted in the first place and when Flora unknowingly walked into my home, my plan hit me just as hard as my feelings toward her.

It would be so easy to bend my lips to hers and taste perfection. To run my hands across her soft skin and lose myself in lustful desire. To thrust my cock in so hard she would scream my name and to drive her to the point of ecstasy before I spill my own seed deep inside, leaving her in no doubt at all about who owns her now. Because I do own her, she just doesn't know it yet and so, reluctantly I pull away and say gruffly, "It's been a long day and you need to sleep. I'll make sure our unwelcome visitors have left and we will talk in the morning."

Before she can say a word, I spin on my heels and head from the room, locking her inside so my captured beauty can't get away. As I pocket the key, I laugh to myself, imagining the pleasure imprisoning this woman will bring to my life. Yes, as plans go, this one is astonishing in its brilliance, but as for my other plans concerning Flora, tomorrow can't come soon enough for me.

* * *

Without even stopping to shower the blood from my body, I pace the corridors of my mansion like a warrior ready to do battle, streaked in the blood of his latest victim.

Luckily for me, Pasquale has cleared my home of all the unwelcome visitors and as I stop by the guard house, I relish the widening of my men's eyes as they see The Enforcer has been hard at work again—this time making one of their own suffer. I wear his blood like a promise. Step out of line and your life ends at my hand. They glance up as if fearful of catching my eye and I growl, "Where's Pasquale?"

Vinnie, one of my braver soldiers, speaks up. "He's in the den." Nodding, I spin on my heel and head off to Pasquale's own office that sits beside mine.

My consigliere enjoys a greater freedom than most of my men because, with no exception, he is my most loyal. The man I trust with my life and as I head through his door without the courtesy of a knock, he glances up and the grin on his face settles my heart.

"At least your evening ended well."

He nods toward my chest, and I grin, sinking down on the chair opposite him and reaching for a cigarette.

"Not as well as I hoped, but satisfying none the less."

I take a long drag and then regard him through hooded eyes.

"What can you tell me?"

"The detectives came up with nothing." He shrugs and reaches for his own cigarette, lighting the tip and taking a long, satisfying drag.

"His men searched but came up empty handed and none of

your guests had anything to add other than you were here with Miss Corlietti the entire time."

"Good." I puff out smoke rings and nod toward the crystal decanter of whiskey, causing him to reach for two glasses and set about pouring us a celebratory drink.

"The senator." I growl as my fingers clasp around the cool crystal.

"As the detective said, his heart was liberated, and his driver's throat cut."

"Anything from neighboring CCTV?"

"Take a look."

Pasquale spins his screen to face me, and I watch as the camera catches the senator's limo as it turns the corner.

I observe with keen interest as the image shows a black unidentified SUV screeching to a stop in front of it and then four black hooded figures spill from the car. An ambush of the deadliest kind that is shielded from the camera courtesy of the SUV.

It takes mere minutes before the figures head back to the car and I growl, "Zoom in."

Pasquale does as I ask, and I see a slim figure shrouded in black with a balaclava covering their identity, holding the senator's heart like a trophy.

"Why the heart, I wonder?" I speak almost to myself and Pasquale shrugs. "A trophy perhaps, or a gift for his widow. Perhaps a reminder to someone who pissed them off, and the senator is a warning. Who knows, it could be many things."

"Can you ID them?"

I peer a little closer but can make nothing out and Pasquale shakes his head. "The car is nothing special, with no license plates. The figures could be anyone, and the motive is undetermined."

"I don't like it."

I'm uneasy as I sense something is coming to bite me hard and Pasquale nods grimly. "I feel the same."

"Any more camera shots?"

He shakes his head. "Just a few, but they only show the retreating vehicle before it hits the highway. I had word from my man in the police control room and he told me the car was abandoned just outside Boulder and torched. There was nothing left of it when the fire crews got there."

"What about any cameras?"

"There aren't any." Pasquale sighs. "I'm guessing they knew that already, and our only chance is to wait for someone to spill the info we need as the soldiers sweep the city."

"Which they are doing now." I fix him with a hard look, and he nods. "Of course. By morning, we should have something at least."

I stretch out and take another long drag of the cigarette, loving how it calms my rough edges, and I say bitterly.

"I'm guessing this is only the beginning. Hit the streets hard. I don't like this at all and until we know who was responsible, none of us are safe."

Pasquale nods. "Consider it done."

I chuck back the contents of the glass and relish the burn before standing and heading for the door.

"Inform me the moment you have news. I'm heading to the shower and then to crash for a couple of hours."

Pasquale nods and turns back to his computer screen as I leave his den, confident he will do a good job of finding the information I need.

As I head to my room, I'm weary and not just from the late hour. I'm weary of this fucked up life that seems out to bite me whenever it can. Something deep inside is telling me who is responsible because even without proof, I know this has Mario and Diana written all over it. It is drenched in their evil and I know the stakes are high.

They want my father's business, which means they must take out his three sons first. I'm guessing I'm not the only one who will be targeted and so before I shower, I do something that sets my teeth on edge.

I call the only family I have left.

They both answer the group call immediately and for some reason my heart beats fast as I prepare to speak to my two brothers for the first time since I left that night.

Matteo speaks first.

"Domenico. It's been a long time."

Leonardo adds, *"You must want something."*

I grind my teeth and growl, "I have Diana's sister."

There's silence as I guessed there would be because if I'm certain of one thing, it's that my brothers hate Diana and Mario almost as much as I do.

Leonardo says grimly, *"What's your plan?"*

"To use her to bring down her sister."

"How exactly?" Matteo sounds interested, which doesn't surprise me because he's always been the master manipulator and I growl, "I'm using her to claim her inheritance."

There's a short silence as my words register because our father's last will and testament is due to be read next week, and I have been dreading every minute of it. I'm guessing he left everything to his merry widow, but the business is unknown. As his sons, we are the most likely successors and will be required to step up and take the business back from the current caretakers.

"How?" Matteo will be thinking through all the possibilities already and I snarl, "A visit to the bank should be a start. It needs to be soon because I'm certain Diana and Mario are trying to make certain we are in no position to claim our inheritance."

"What happened?"

Leonardo speaks up harshly and, as our older brother, he is

the one who is set to inherit the title of Don Ortega and is therefore the biggest target.

I fill them in and the silence that ends my story tells me they are thinking hard.

Leonardo growls, *"Then I guess we can also expect a visit. Thanks for the warning."*

For some reason, that simple statement melts my heart a little because even though we hate one another and always have, we are still family, and they are all I have left of blood. Mafia blood and it will need to count for something incredible if we are to unite and defeat the enemy within.

Leonardo sighs heavily. *"I'll see what I can find out. Thanks for the heads up. I'll step up security and break a few heads open to find what we need."*

Matteo adds, *"Same. We must work together for once in our miserable lives for the family."*

"For the family."

Leonardo adds and I say gruffly, "For the family."

The silence tells me they have cut the call and I sigh heavily.

For the family.

The family motto that is a fucking joke. We haven't been a family ever since we were babies.

Why the fuck do they think we'll be one now?

CHAPTER 15

FLORA

If I wasn't in hell, I'd think I was in heaven. It certainly feels that way as I languish in a hot bubble bath in the most insane tub I have ever seen. It is placed before a floor length window and the candles that flicker around me cast the room in a sultry light.

When I heard the door lock behind Domenico, it made me feel strangely safe. Fucked up perhaps, but I can't help my emotions. I wasted no time in exploring and as soon as I saw the huge bathroom, it was where I wanted to be most. I quickly began running a bath with hot sweet-smelling water, courtesy of the oils and foam I added. Then I lit every candle I could and sank into pure bliss, gazing out at the starry night wondering how the fuck mine ended up with me here.

I should be home right now, tucked up in the narrow bed in my condo not far from the gallery. I wonder if Desdemona will call me tomorrow, wanting all the details of my night of shame.

My heart hardens toward her because she fed me to the wolves willingly. She intended for the senator to fuck me in exchange for his patronage, and it makes me sick how close I came to that happening. In fact, it's been on the cards the entire night and I'm astonished to have got away with it.

When Domenico Ortega dragged me to his dungeon, I really thought my life would end in there.

Somehow, I survived and yet being chained to Domenico's bed brought with it a different kind of emotion because there, in that sinful room, my mind imagined a whole different story playing out. If anything, I was more curious than afraid and as I relax for the very first time tonight. I think about the man himself.

He wants me. He told me that and I have no doubt at all he meant it. I must help him to kill my sister. Can I do that? Will I do that? I'm not certain of anything anymore except how much I fear Diana and Mario. I hate them and I want them gone, but death—do I want that on my conscience?

If I help him, I will be free—or will I? For some reason, when he told me he wanted me to stay, it surrounded me in a warm glow. Why did I like hearing that? Why am I such a fucking basket case because who willingly chooses this life?

I close my eyes and he's still there. Watching me with an intensity that has my fingers caressing my body, almost as if he has that honor. I groan as a sudden burst of longing explodes inside me as I picture his wicked mouth coaxing my orgasm from deep between my legs.

Just imagining what he can do tells me my mind is fucked already because more than I want my freedom, it seems I want him more.

By the time I slip between the cool silk sheets, I already realize tomorrow will be challenging in so many ways. As my eyes close and sleep claims me in blissful ignorance, part of me hopes that when I wake, this will have all been a dream and the other part of me is disappointed about that.

* * *

"Get up."

My eyes flicker open at the gruff voice that tells me what happened yesterday was definitely no nightmare. It's a living hell and as I snap open my eyes, I close them just as quickly because crouching beside the bed is the man who starred in them. Rough, angry, sexy as fuck, and glaring at me as if I've done something to offend him personally.

I open them again when his husky voice grips my soul and shakes it awake.

"You will eat with me. I'm not letting you out of my sight."

He pulls the sheets from the bed, and I nod, slipping my legs to the side and hating how hard my heart is thumping, reminding me I'm still in extreme danger and I should play along because this man obviously doesn't expect anyone to disobey him.

"What time is it?" My voice sounds weak and fearful, laden with sleep and ignorance.

"Seven. We have a busy day ahead."

As I glance at him from under my sleep encrusted lashes, I'm doubtful he even slept at all last night. His hair is tousled and his jawline darker than yesterday as the shadow on it intensifies. His eyes are red and hold a weariness in them that I'm certain resides there in perpetuity. I'm guessing his life is no bed of roses either, courtesy of the job he does and for some reason, I pity him for that.

Mafia is a way of life that you either choose unwillingly or are born into it and his is the latter. Taught from an early age what it means to survive this world and I know a lot about that.

I swallow hard when I register he's shirtless but thankfully no longer streaked in another man's blood and the scent heading toward my heart like a wrecking ball is all man and devastating for my libido. I hate that I want him so badly. That I see past this situation and crave just one taste, making a mockery of my vow of celibacy. Just one sniff and one blinding look at this man has rendered that vow meaningless.

He stands and reaches for my hand, and I catch my breath at the dark glittering eyes that devour me with just one look and as I stumble to his side, I'm glad of the strength he possesses as he prevents me from making an idiot of myself before the day has even begun.

I follow him to the bathroom and shiver when he turns to me and with one surprising move, tears the t-shirt from my body as if it's paper.

I squeal and try to cover my modesty as he flicks on the shower and laughs softly, "Get used to it, baby girl. All the time you are with me, I will do with you whatever the fuck I like. Nothing has changed since yesterday except the way I will use you to rid the world of your bitch of a sister."

I don't even have time to process his words before he pulls down his sweatpants and my attention is grabbed by the sheer size of the cock pointing angrily in my direction and as I swallow hard at the sight of it, his amusement makes me hate myself already and I doubt it will be the last time today.

"Do you want some of this? Do you want to know what it's like with me inside you?"

"No!" I bark out and close my eyes so he can't witness my lying first hand.

"Liar." A low hiss by my ear causes me to screw my eyes shut even tighter and then his warm hand lies flat against my abdomen as he caresses it with a surprisingly light touch. His husky voice is close to my ear as he whispers, "I've thought of you all night. What you would taste like, how loud you can scream in ecstasy. What it would be like to own such a beauty. I couldn't sleep from a burning need to experience something pure. Do you understand what that's like, baby?"

His voice has changed and softly caresses my soul, calming it and bringing it firmly under his spell and I nod, my eyes closed against reality as I let his words soothe away the burn that being with him brings.

His lips rest against mine and my mind explodes like a lit firework. Images of skin on skin. Hot emotion pours through my body, burning like a river of the damned as my body betrays me in a spectacular fashion.

CHAPTER 16

DOM

I am torturing myself. It started when I left her last night. I couldn't shake the image of her naked and waiting for me. In my mind, she is Diana and I have such a burning need for that woman. An ache that prevents me from carrying on without feeling it at every turn and every movement. A desire that will not fade and an urgent need to have one more moment with her.

I try to remind myself that this woman is not Diana. An imitation, a carbon copy, and an impersonator, if I have my way.

However, Flora is fast becoming the woman Diana should have been. Soft, vulnerable, and innocent with steel running through her veins as she faces a hard life and moves through it with a bravery that should have been destroyed by now.

I am conflicted and when I see Flora staring at me through eyes brimming with tears, with an urgent need she can't disguise, giving me permission to do what the fuck I want, I almost can't hold back. I could have been there already. Tested my infatuation with a woman who certainly looks like the one

I fell in love with but with none of the hard edges. At least that's how it appears.

Her breath is soft and warm against my lips, her naked body shivering more with need than fear. I recognize the signs. I can tell when a woman wants me. Usually a whore or a woman plucked from obscurity to satisfy an urge that never passes. Now is my chance to test my emotions, tentatively, with care, hoping I'm not completely broken beyond repair because of one seductress who destroyed everything I ever wanted.

I reach out and touch the soft skin that flushes prettily as she stares into my eyes. I stare deeper and search for any hint of her true nature. Is she as pure as she makes out? Was she damaged as much as I was? Her breathing is rapid, and her pupils dilate as I run my thumb across those wet lips and hiss as an overpowering need catches me off guard. It's undeniable I want this woman, but is it the one standing before me, or the one hundreds of miles away plotting my downfall?

The desire is overwhelming me, dragging me down and into a place I lived once. A place I vowed never to go to again when I left what remained of my heart there. I can't inflict that same torture on my soul, knowing that once again it will be taken from me.

Flora is *not* Diana, I must keep reminding myself of that and to prove that more to myself than her, I push her, so she stumbles against the tiles, and I hiss, "Clean yourself up, we have dragons to slay."

I turn away so she can't witness the yearning in my eyes. The need to experience one final taste of something I resigned myself to losing what seems like a lifetime ago.

The sound of the water gushing from the showerhead may as well be my soul crying a river of damnation because I am under no illusions that woman crushed my soul to dust under her dainty heel.

I stare at the floor until the shower is silenced and I am in tune to every move she makes, even though it appears I'm disinterested. What a fucking joke that is. I am more than interested, desperately so, and it's only my hatred of Diana that is preventing me from exploring this desire for her sister.

A soft cough alerts me to her presence, and I raise my eyes and watch as she hovers nervously by my side.

"Um, I've finished."

"Obviously." I snarl sarcastically and, grabbing her wrist, I pull her down to the floor so she is kneeling before me, with a look of startled surprise and a fear I can almost touch.

"Drop the towel."

I know I'm being cruel and for some sadistic reason, I get pleasure from her fear. In my mind, this woman is Diana and I love seeing her kneel before me.

I reach out and grab her chin and force her to look up at me and snarl, "Just so we're clear, you are my prisoner. Speak only when asked and offer no opinion. Do as I say and don't think I care about you. You are nothing, a means to an end and a way to destroy your sister. When that happens to my satisfaction, you will be set free, exactly like I told you. Until then, you will be my shadow. Where I go, you do too. I am your puppet master, and I pull the strings. Whatever I say is law, and you get no privileges unless I say so. Any questions?"

To her credit, she merely shakes her head and casts her eyes to the floor in a submissive act that gets me instantly hard. What can I say? I'm a dominant man and not only because of my name. I crave control, which is why I fell so hard for Diana. She played me at my own game and turned it back on me, and I wonder if this is what Flora is doing now. I can't be sure, so I sigh heavily and snap, "On your feet. There's a closet in your room with enough clothes to choose something that fits. Dress respectfully and I'll be waiting. We need to eat and discuss the next step."

She nods and stands silently, which angers me a little.

Where is the fight in this woman? She must be playing a game because nobody in her situation would willingly accept what I'm asking. She should be pleading with me, begging me to let her go, but she's allowing me to treat her like the trash her sister is, and I wonder about that.

Once again, I lock her in her room and head to my own to shower and dress in my customary black suit. We have business to occupy us and it's important we pull it off.

My phone rings when I step from the shower and my brother Matteo says darkly, *"It appears to be my turn now."*

"What do you mean?"

From the edge to his voice, I'm guessing it's unwelcome, and he snarls, *"Last night I received a call from a rival family. Don De Luca."*

"What did he want?"

Don De Luca runs an operation in Garden City, and they respect each other's boundaries. Something is telling me that is about to change.

"His shipment of cocaine was seized by the authorities, and I was placed firmly in the frame."

"By whom?"

"One of my soldiers was delivered back to me this morning with his tongue cut out and his throat slashed."

"An informant?"

I can picture the scene because it's standard practice for dealing with anyone who squeals.

"It appears he told them I gave him the green light to inform the authorities, and Don De Luca has declared war."

"You think it's a set up?"

"Of course. The heat is now on me to prove my innocence and defend my family against attack. My casino was torched in the early hours and my staff only just got out in time. I'm guessing somebody wants us out of the picture and they are wasting no time."

"Does Leo know?"

"Of course. I told him just before I called you. He will be next, and it doesn't take a college diploma to work out who is responsible."

"Diana." I hiss through gritted teeth and his rough, "The fucking bitch herself," tells me my brother hates her almost as much as I do. That doesn't surprise me because, like me and Leo, Matteo also fell for her manipulative charms.

"What do you need?"

I offer him my assistance because the Ortegas may hate one another, but we are still family and that has always come first, and he barks, *"Nothing. We are all fighting our own battle in this bloody war. I just thought you should know. If you discover anything from your hostage that could help, call me because I'm guessing we'll need all the help we can get to slay this monster."*

"I'll see what I can drag out of her."

"She must have some information we can use against them. It needs to be quick information, though."

"Of course. Leave it with me."

Matteo sighs heavily. *"I could fucking do without this right now."*

"Same."

It's obvious we are being kept busy for a reason and my thoughts turn to the reading of my father's will next week and wonder if there is something written that is the catalyst for this.

"Matteo." I say gruffly.

"We need to get eyes on that will before next week. I have a hunch the answer is scratched in blood on there."

"It won't be easy. Our father used Ernest Bagway for a reason."

A low laugh escapes me when I think of the cunning man who heads up the most trustworthy law firm in town.

"There must be a way. If there is, I'm guessing you will find it."

"I'll do my best."

There's a short silence and then he whispers, *"Take care, brother."*

He cuts the call before I can answer and, for a second, I hold the phone with a strange emotion inside me. Brother. I wonder when that description ceased to mean anything in our lives, if it ever did in the first place, that is.

I pocket the phone and once again my thoughts turn to Flora, waiting for me to make my move. If it wasn't so urgent, I would enjoy every minute of this and drag out the pleasure. However, it's obvious time is a luxury none of us can afford and so, with grim determination, I head off to business.

CHAPTER 17

FLORA

What the fuck has happened to me? I'm an idiot. Obviously, something is seriously wrong with me because why am I not putting up a fight? It must be him. Domenico Ortega. Somehow, I feel safe and protected all the time I'm with him, which is a fucking joke because I am definitely not safe from that man. He appears to want to tear me apart for his own pleasure, and I only have one person to blame for that. My sister.

I wish he looked at me and didn't see her. The way he touches me sometimes tells me he is capable of great tenderness and love. He tries to disguise it, but it's there, standing center stage, yearning to be seen. He is damaged, probably beyond repair, and I understand a lot about how that feels.

The door flies open, making me jump and I swallow hard when I see the man himself, glowering at me from the doorway. I briefly wonder if I chose the right outfit. Respectful, he said. I chose a Chanel shift dress and ivory heels. A smart matching jacket makes me feel a million dollars and I expect the clothes I discovered in the closet weren't far off that sum due to the designers I found there. Dior, Givenchy, Versace and

Chanel were dripping from the rails. Valentino and Dolce and Gabbana were their accomplices, and I stared around me in awe at the magnificent sight.

Mafia money is dirty money, and I must remind myself of that and so I push away my awe and trample on my envy because I will not allow myself to respect this man.

He prowls toward me like a black panther, dressed head to toe in black Armani, looking like every dark dream I have ever had. I'd prefer to think I've only had a few, but it appears darkness follows me around because at night they creep into my subconscious and unleash a yearning inside me for a life I ran from in terror. I expect it's because I grew up around the mafia. It's all I know; hell, my own father was one. Cut down in his prime, fighting a war that included him falling on his metaphorical sword to protect the life of a grade A bastard.

Domenico stands before me and his dark glittering eyes hold a promise that whatever this is, will end when he says so and I stare at him defiantly and wait for him to speak like the good little girl I appear to be.

He says nothing.

Instead, he stares into my eyes with a yearning that tears at my heart, ripping it apart and exposing it to emotion toward him. I want to reach out and soothe away the trouble that surrounds him. He is conflicted; a fool could see that, and I'm surprised when he reaches out and strokes my face lightly, with a reverence that slays the monster inside me and turns it into a pussycat.

I lean against his hand and am mesmerized at how his eyes glitter with emotion, and I dare not speak and destroy this intimate moment. He is somewhere else. The instant realization that when he looks at me, he sees another is a crushing blow, which makes me wonder if he has stripped me of my sanity.

"You look beautiful."

His whispered words surprise me and a brief smile lights

my face, which causes a strange expression on his. I surprise myself when I return the favor, and reaching up, cup his cheek and whisper, "Let me help you."

The intensity increases and his hand snaps against mine and yet, rather than pulling my hand away, he deepens the hold. Skin on skin, minds connected, we both recognize a kindred spirit when we see one.

"How?"

His response catches me off-guard, and I lean a little closer. "I want to help you bring my sister and Mario down, and I think I can help with that."

"I'll ask you again—how?"

He doesn't even blink and as we stare deep into each other's eyes, I whisper, "I know their weakness. Hit them there and they will fall."

He nods and I'm surprised when he shifts closer and runs his hand around the back of my head and clutches my hair in his fist. His grip tightens and it makes my eyes water as the sadness inside him manifests into a cruelty I am used to. Then he pulls my face close to his and before I can react, his lips fasten on mine and still holding my head in place, he kisses me so passionately I forget to breathe.

It lasts a lifetime—at least it seems that way and as our tongues collide, they dance in a battle of wills. He tries to dominate me, but how can you when the person on the receiving end craves every bit of it?

It's as if he opens the floodgates because I can't think of anything but him right now. He has stepped inside me and blocks out the light, and as his hand moves lower and lifts my dress around my waist, I don't even recoil. If anything, I lean closer and as his fingers inch inside my panties and thrust deep inside, I moan like a whore as he invades my most intimate place.

I push down on those fingers and kiss him with a hunger

that even shocks me. The sweat runs down my back as he unzips his pants and pushes me hard against the wall. I am resigned to what will happen and rather than fear it, I crave it and as his cock hovers at my sodden entrance, he growls, "You're mine."

My legs part as he steps between them and as he thrusts inside, I cry out at the sensation it creates. This is fucking at its most brutal. There are no whispered words of love and permission granted. He is taking from me what he wants, whether I agree or not. The fact my slick betrayal is writing him a written invitation tells me there is no hope left for me. As my back hits the wall on repeat, I gasp as he powers inside me and experience nothing but heated desire.

I love it.

Every thrust, every groan and every thump of my heart because I have never felt so desired—so alive. It's wicked, forbidden and unexpected and if anybody told me I would be fucked against a wall by a man like him, I would have booked the first ticket out of town. But then I would have missed the most passionate experience of my life.

I scream as he bites my neck and grabs my breast, growling at the material covering it. Then I squeal when he rips that dress from my body as if it's from a bargain store and rolls my nipple against his thumb.

He is overbearing, dominant and so delicious. I could gorge on him all night and when he comes so hard the pictures shake on the wall behind me and I feel his hot cum spurting inside me, telling me that now I'm really fucked. I'm almost afraid to form the words, but as his hot breath fans my neck, I whisper, "I'm not on birth control."

To my surprise, he laughs against my neck and says huskily, "I guess that comes with being celibate."

The fact he's just fucked me renders that statement ridiculous and, to my surprise, I giggle as if he's the funniest guy in the world.

He pulls back and stares at me for a second, which silences my laughter and my breath hitches when he strokes my face with a heart wrenching tenderness and whispers, "Whatever happens, you are mine and I will take care of you. You're not on your own anymore."

"What do you mean?" I'm confused and my voice obviously demonstrates that because his wicked grin takes me by surprise as he growls, "Do you really think I can let you go now?"

"Why not?"

Now I'm really confused and his eyes glitter as he whispers against my ravaged mouth, "Because one taste was enough and now I'm addicted."

I have no words and he carries on. "You told me you would help me."

I nod and a sudden softness enters his eyes as he caresses my face in a surprisingly gentle move. "Nobody has ever said that to me and meant it."

"I don't understand." I really don't, and he laughs softly. "Usually, they tell me what they think I need to hear to get away from me. When you looked into my eyes, you pledged your help out of compassion. I read it in your expression."

For some reason I feel bold. Maybe it's because his cum is running down my leg, creating a connection I never really expected, and I smile shyly and reach out and touch his lips with a curiosity that makes his eyes glaze over.

"I see myself in you, Domenico. I experience your pain because that same pain lives inside me. We have a common enemy born out of betrayal and that makes us the most powerful people in this war. We have a job to do and must unite to win, so tell me how I can help you and I will give it my best shot because I can tell you are just as much a prisoner as I am."

He says nothing and just steps back and nods with approval and then says gruffly, "You have five minutes to change. No shower, though. I want to know you have my cum between your legs, marking you as mine."

His words make me smile and as I turn away, he says roughly, "Flora."

I turn and the darkness in his eyes should scare the hell out of me because this look tells me I've just gifted my soul to the devil, and that is confirmed when he growls, "Make yourself at home. You're mine now."

I turn away without another word and head back inside the closet, feeling strangely warm and fuzzy inside.

You're mine now.

I have never been important to anyone before and his ownership and dominance is the sweetest gift he could ever give me, because that means I'm not on my own anymore. I have Domenico Ortega and whatever that involves is fine by me.

CHAPTER 18

DOM

It's strange how plans alter with one expression and a few whispered words. As soon as I saw Flora waiting for me, looking so beautiful it all changed for her. The fact she is so sweet is like kryptonite to me because that is what I craved about her sister.

However, one taste of Diana revealed she had a bitter center, which is why I felt the need to sample her sister. Just to confirm she is made of the same stuff, so I could carry on torturing her in the name of revenge.

I am now conflicted because rather than a sour center, Flora's was sweet, giving me a craving for more.

The way she looked at me tore my heart out because nobody has ever looked at me like that. There is something hurting her, and I recognized the signs. Whatever was in her past will have consequences for whoever did this to her and as I witness the same expression in the mirror, I'm guessing I already have my answer to that.

When a man as damaged as I am holds something so pure in his hands, it's physically impossible to let it go and I meant what I said. Flora does belong to me now and all the time I have this protective yearning for her. She is going nowhere.

She is still my prisoner, of course she is because even if she is willing, nothing changes. My need is stronger than my compassion for her and yet something in her eyes is telling me she wants this too.

She makes it back within five minutes and I feel satisfied with how things are shaping up. Flora will become my ideal woman. Do everything I tell her and bend to my will. If she has any fire in her, I'm interested to stroke the flames because when she walked into my home, she may as well have left her soul at the door.

"Come, we must eat."

I hold out my hand and as her slender hand settles in mine, a powerful emotion grips me.

This protective streak I have toward her is surprising and I must remind myself it's there because of my deep yearning for her sister. However, as we walk silently toward the dining room, it's not Diana who occupies my mind. Somehow Flora has pushed her to the back of it, because all I see when I gaze at her now is my future beckoning.

As always, breakfast is waiting, and I pull Flora into the seat beside me and lift the coffee pot.

"Coffee, baby girl?"

She nods gratefully, "Please."

The steam and aroma from the pot is a satisfying one and as I reach for my mug, I have never needed the caffeine more.

A slight movement from the doorway makes me glance up and I note Pasquale looking weary as he heads into the room, closely followed by my butler, Monroe.

"You look like shit." I growl as he pulls out the seat opposite Flora and sinks into it wearily. I can tell she's surprised at his appearance, although she shouldn't be because breakfast has always been yet another business meeting for a man who has dedicated his entire life to it. For two years it has always been just Pasquale and me. If I have an overnight guest, they are usually escorted from the premises by Monroe with a fistful of dollars and a satisfied smile on their face. They never eat with me. Why would they? But I have never had a prisoner before and I kind of like it.

"It's all over the news. Senator Billings, murdered in an ambush. The press has moved in and no prizes for guessing what the word on the streets is."

"Tell me." I nod to Monroe, who sets down a plate of eggs and bacon before me and the same to Flora, whose expression tells me she's starving.

I lift my fork and nod to her to do the same and as she silently eats beside me, Pasquale carries on as if she isn't even in the room.

"Our soldiers on the streets speak of rumors about the senator. He's well known for his sexual proclivities, which aren't to most people's tastes."

Flora shivers beside me and I expect she's congratulating herself on being spared from discovering what they were first hand, and Pasquale says angrily, "Apparently, the good senator was playing off several families, one against the other. He had his fat finger dipped in so many pies he was overcome with greed. It could be anyone who decided enough was enough and took matters into their own hand, but the fact he was leaving your party after being publicly shamed means there is only one name in the frame in most people's minds."

"I'm guessing that would be me." I snort and wipe my mouth with the napkin and reach for more coffee, refilling Flora's mug as she waits like a statue beside me.

Pasquale is intrigued by the situation. I see it in his eyes, and I turn to Flora and say roughly, "Tell us what you can about Senator Billings."

She glances up nervously and can't disguise the hatred in

her expression as she whispers, "He's a regular at the gallery. Desdemona sees to his account personally, and I was surprised when she asked if I would accompany him here yesterday."

"That doesn't surprise me." Pasquale sighs. "That bitch has fucked most of Vegas just to keep her business going, and it's not the first time she's involved one of her staff. Perhaps the senator wanted someone who doesn't come with an STD and requested her latest protégée to test her loyalty to him?"

I shake my head. "Or the request came from someone else."

Flora looks as sick as a dog and nods, settling back against her seat and looking so worried it makes my blood boil for some reason.

"Do you think Diana knows I'm here?" Her voice is laden with fear which angers me, and I snap, "It's possible. I'm guessing she is counting on my infatuation with her to stir the pot and keep my attention off something more important."

Pasquale nods. "I had my contact at the airport run a passenger check on any flights into Vegas in the last month. There was no evidence of Diana Corlietti or Mario Bachini on any of them, even the private manifests."

"They could have driven here." I snap back and he shrugs. "Of course. If someone wants to remain anonymous, it's easy enough to do. I have the soldiers scanning the streets for any word on that, beginning with the car that we saw on the cameras."

"And the police investigation?"

I glance at Pasquale with a sharp expression, and he shakes his head. "It should be easy enough to deflect the heat from our door, but if you are their intended target, I'm guessing they have a few more surprises up their sleeves."

"Which is why our guest is so important."

I turn to Flora, who appears shit scared all of a sudden and as Pasquale stares at her with interest, I say gruffly, "You told me you would help. What is their weakness?"

I'm straight to the point because I will not waste time in ridding the Ortega family of the cuckoo residing at the head of it and Flora says bitterly, "Mario is their weakness."

Pasquale glances across at me and I say with interest, "How?"

Flora sighs, obviously hating the mere mention of his name, and she says in disgust, "Diana loves him."

Such a simple statement that wields a knife to my heart, plunging in deep and slicing it open.

"You think that woman has the capacity to love?" I say roughly and the tone of my voice obviously saddens my prisoner because her face falls a little and I watch a little part of her soul drop away.

"I know she does. But only him. A man who is her equal and shares her love of pain, humiliation, and greed. Somebody who doesn't care what it takes to win and will do whatever they must to achieve that."

Remembering her own sordid tale of what they did to her, I wonder if she is influenced by that, and Pasquale says gently, "Tell us."

Flora shivers in her seat and I experience an urgent need to hold her close, to protect her from the memory currently circling her like a vulture about to feed off her remains, but I can't show any weakness where it concerns this woman. If anything, I will be harder on her than most and I growl, "Everything. Tell us everything you can about them and leave nothing out."

As Flora raises her eyes to mine and stares at me for the first time since we sat down, I register the raw pain in her eyes as she faces her past and prepares to let it into the room.

CHAPTER 19

FLORA

Domenico Ortega demands the impossible. I have fought to contain the demons that circle my soul, and he wants to unleash them for his own ends. His consigliere is staring at me with a hunger for the information I guard inside a locked cage in my heart, but to defeat a monster you need to unleash an even bigger one and it will be a relief to set it free to haunt someone else's thoughts.

So, with a deep breath, I give them what they want.

"As soon as we became part of Mario's family, I noticed Diana infatuation with him. She would follow him around like a puppy dog and was obviously fascinated with that man." I say with distaste.

"He realized it too and used it to his advantage and manipulated her feelings. Something she excelled at herself, but it appears he used her own superpower on her. They became inseparable, and it wasn't long before they overstepped the boundaries, and she began sleeping with him."

I can sense the tension in the room as I say with distaste, "When his parents were out, I heard them. They made no secret of it, and I expect they wanted me to because they had no shame. Mario made my skin crawl the way he used my sister and then watched for my reaction. I was younger than them and never really understood the sounds that came wafting down the hallway into my room, but I guessed it to be wrong. Diana was besotted with him and walked around with starry admiration for a man who certainly didn't deserve any. He appeared pleased with her attention, but didn't share her feelings."

"How do you know?"

Domenico interrupts and I snap, "Because one woman will never be enough for that man. He would bring other women into the house and make Diana join them. What went on outside my closed doors still remains a mystery, but I can guess. Diana changed almost immediately and wore her love for Mario like a giant fucking green flag on her sleeve. He could do no wrong and took great pleasure in testing her infatuation for him and when I reached sixteen, he involved me in their sordid world."

I look down, so ashamed of what they made me do and the silence in the room offers me no compassion and so, with a deep breath, I tell them the news they require.

"It became almost impossible to live in that house. His parents hated me, and if I told them what their son and Diana were doing, they wouldn't believe me. You see, they were always so careful around the Bachinis. They played the model children and always pointed out things I had apparently done when it was them all along. Two against one became unbearable, and I had nobody to turn to. My grandmother was dead, sent to join my parents, and the only person I had left was Diana."

When I think of the information I guard inside my mind, a small smile escapes and I laugh softly, "However, it appears that even monsters are affected by demons they can't control, and I overheard a conversation that revealed Mario's during a family party. There were many guests, but when one particular family walked into the room, I noted Mario's expression change in a heartbeat."

I glance up and smile at the two foreboding men.

"There was a family standing there I hadn't seen before but evidently they were important to the Bachinis. Sam, Mario's father, raced over there like a rocket and Claire, his wife, wasn't far behind. But it was Mario's reaction that intrigued me when he set eyes on a girl around my own age. I still remember it now. The air changed in the party the minute they arrived, and I learned later on they were one of the old money families from Washington, The Kensingtons."

Pasquale exhales slowly and Domenico appears thoughtful.

"How do they know the Bachinis? I'm certain they're not the usual company that family keeps."

"I learned later that Claire and Anna grew up together. When Anna moved to Washington, she met Jared Kensington and subsequently lost touch with Claire. They met up one day when the Bachinis visited the capital and became friends again."

"I wonder why Jared Kensington wanted to make a friend of Sam Bachini. That's interesting."

Pasquale nods and I laugh softly. "It was obvious Mario was besotted with their daughter, Abigail. The best thing though was that Diana was devastated. A few days later I listened to them arguing and Mario was cruel and dismissive, telling Diana she would never be half the woman Abigail Kensington was, and if he had the choice, he would be with her and not a whore like Diana."

I turn and stare directly into Domenico's eyes and register nothing but dark intent and I say bravely, "I'm guessing Abigail Kensington is Mario's Achilles heel and the only woman he has loved and never had. The one that got away if you like. So, maybe she can be used somehow to cause a rift between them."

"Is that it?" Domenico sighs and appears disappointed, and Pasquale saves me from answering with a sudden laugh. "It's perfect."

"What is?" Domenico looks confused and Pasquale catches my eye and grins, which instantly changes my opinion of him.

"It fits perfectly with our plan. Three strikes and they are out. We just need to discover the third."

Domenico pours another coffee and appears thoughtful, and we wait for him to speak while he stares into the mug as if the answer lies there.

Then he says roughly, "I see your point. We stick with our plan, and I'll pass this one to Matteo. He's in a good position to uncover the facts about the Kensingtons and use them to our advantage. We don't have long before the will is read and so far, two out of three ain't bad."

He glances across at me and smiles, making me catch my breath at the beauty in his face as it relaxes a little. If anything, I am mesmerized by Domenico Ortega and can understand why Diana fell so hard for Mario. I understand the attraction because this man could do what the hell he likes with me and I would crave every delicious second of it.

As his velvet obsidian eyes burn deep into my soul, I will do anything to help him, even if it means destroying the one remaining person in the world who shares my blood.

CHAPTER 20

DOM

Flora has given us a gift and before we set off for the bank, I dash out a text to Matteo.

> Discover everything you can about Abigail Kensington. She is the person who will bring Mario down. Her father is Jared Kensington, a Washington billionaire. They are friends of the Bachinis. Remember, we don't have long.

He replies almost immediately.

> Consider it done.

Sighing, I pocket my phone and glare at my fellow diners. "Come. We must continue with our plan."
Pasquale nods and heads off to ready the cars and I can tell

Flora has many questions that she's afraid to voice, probably because I told her never to speak unless asked.

I say roughly, "This is our plan."

She starts and peers at me with a hint of worry in her beautiful eyes and I push away any softness inside me and say gruffly, "We are heading to the bank. I have Diana's account details and ID."

"But..." she makes to speak, and my dark glare makes her stop mid-sentence.

"Today you are Diana Corlietti. You will walk into the City Bank and demand to close your account. I have the new account number and details in a folder Pasquale has arranged. We will transfer the money that she stole from my father's account the day he died."

Flora appears shocked and whispers, "How do you know?"

"I know everything, Flora, and you would be wise to remember that."

I lean forward and stare into her eyes with a ferocity that makes her skin pale.

"The day my father died, my brother Leonardo became Don Ortega. He received documents that contained everything he needed, and he wasted no time in checking the resources. It appeared that my father's accounts were robbed earlier that day and all the money was gone. He discovered the money had been transferred to his widow, which was not against the law because she had joint control of his accounts."

I snarl. "That fucking bitch took our inheritance and we are taking it right back. We must act fast before she moves it again and so you will impersonate her and leave the bitch penniless."

"What if we're caught?" Flora says nervously and I snap. "Play your part well and nobody will find out."

I lean in and say harshly, "This is your opportunity to get your revenge. Take everything from your sister of any value to her and leave us to deal with the rest."

ORTEGA MAFIA – THE ENFORCER

"OK." She faces me with a bravery that impresses me and as she glances my way, I see a lot of Diana in her expression. There is a fierceness inside her telling me she will see this through, and I relax knowing she won't let me down.

I stand and reach for her hand, loving how it closes around mine as if it belongs there.

"Remember..." I say gruffly. "You are my father's widow, and I am your protection. They won't question that, and if Diana wants her money back, she will need to come through me first."

We head through my mansion and out into the courtyard where three black SUVs are waiting. The door to the middle one is open, and a soldier stands guarding it, who nods reverently, "Sir."

I nod and guide Flora into the car first before stepping in beside her. Then, as the door slams, the car in front moves off, closely followed by the rest of us. This is how we travel. As a pack, and I'm guessing none of this is new to Flora Corlietti. She was born into this life and knows how it works, which saves for lengthy explanations for the uninitiated.

As we pass through town, we are silent, both of us considering the next hour ahead. This could backfire on us spectacularly and I just pray Flora looks enough like her sister to fool the bank teller.

As the car stops outside City Bank, I register the interested looks from the passers-by as my men spill out onto the sidewalk and create a safe environment for us to exit into. I realize this is ostentatious and we draw more attention to ourselves than if we traveled like any other human being on the planet but here, in this town, hell even this state, I walk around with a huge fucking target on my back and by association so does Flora.

She is nervous beside me. I can tell that already and as she walks slightly in front, to anybody watching, we are people it's best to turn away from. The bodyguards, the menace that we wear well and the arrogant threatening glares we throw around like confetti, make people lower their eyes and look the other way.

This is how we protect ourselves and how it's always been, and I doubt that will change all the time I breathe.

The door to the bank opens and we head inside. Flora is slightly in front of me, walking with a straight back and purpose. We head straight to the desk, and it stuns me a little when she says in an identical voice to her sister, "I wish to close my account."

The teller doesn't react and just nods, turning to their computer screen.

"Do you have your bank details?" They say pleasantly and Flora removes the relevant details from the folder and passes them to the teller.

"Do you have your card, ma'am?"

Flora hands it over and I wonder how Pasquale does this. He's a master manipulator and it can't have been easy to arrange, but somehow, he has pulled off the impossible and duplicated everything needed for our plan to work.

As the teller taps away on the computer, only the slight raised eye and the nervous glance in our direction tells me this won't be as straightforward as we hoped and then she clears her throat and says apologetically, "I'm sorry madam, I will need my manager's authorization code to initiate the transaction."

Flora just nods as if she's bored already, and it strikes me how like her sister she is at this moment. The resemblance is astonishing, but it's soon apparent they are poles apart in personality when Flora grants you access to the frightened woman hiding behind the worried frown.

It only takes a few minutes for the manager to appear and cast a concerned glance in our direction, causing the sweat to appear on his brow when he is on the receiving end of my most menacing expression.

"Mrs. Ortega." He almost bows to Flora and hearing him use that name in reference to Diana makes my blood boil when I think of her marriage to my father. However, hearing him refer to Flora in this way deals me a strange sense of pride that I wasn't expecting. For some reason, I like thinking of her this way, and it shocks me a little.

"I trust there isn't a problem, um, Mr. Tav-i-st-ock."

Flora says sharply, peering at the manager's name badge and emphasizing every syllable of his name, causing him to glance again nervously in my direction.

I play along and consider him with a thoughtful gaze, telling him I now have his name and unless he plays along, things could get very uncomfortable for him and his family. I know I intimidate well. Hell, I've practised my craft all my life, and it has the desired effect when he coughs and taps in a code with no further questions and says with relief, "Account closed, Mrs. Ortega. May I ask if there was a problem regarding our service to you?"

He looks at Flora keenly and she snaps, "No, you may not."

She grabs the folder back from the teller and nods in my direction.

"Please check the funds have arrived in my new account."

I'm impressed with her acting because right now, even I believe Diana is standing before me and for some reason, it doesn't hurt as much as normal.

As I check the new account on my phone, I smile to myself because there it is. Five million dollars stolen from a thief right from under their nose.

"And the rest?" Flora says coolly, referencing the several savings accounts also currently residing at City Bank and, as I check every single one of them, it's as if we've won the jackpot when eye watering sums of money pop up in black figures on my phone. We have effectively cleaned Diana out and seized back control of the finances required to run our empire, but I can't relax until we are safely back at the mansion.

I say in a monotone voice, "It's all there."

Flora nods and stares at the manager with an expression that causes him to sweat, and she says imperiously, "I would appreciate your discretion in this matter, Mr. Tavistock. I have reason to believe that my late husband has many enemies who will stop at nothing to get their hands on his assets. I am withdrawing them to protect them, and nobody must discover any details about that, for all our sakes."

She waves her hand in my direction and says in a hard voice. "My stepson and his brothers are very protective of their family. I would hate to give them any reason to defend it. So, for your own protection, I would wipe all traces of our visit from your security footage and deny any knowledge of this meeting at all if anyone asks. It will be in your own interest to play dumb."

The manager looks as if he's about to pass out, but Flora just says politely, "Good day, Mr. Tavistock. Please send my regards to your family."

As she turns away, she catches my eye and the spark in hers does something to me I wasn't expecting. It hits me so hard I am stunned and as she walks away with a sway to her hips and a confidence that takes my breath away, I know in an instant that Flora Corlietti is more than a match for her sister and as it turns out, is also more than a match for me.

CHAPTER 21

FLORA

I am shaking inside. From the moment we walked into City Bank, I wished I was anywhere else. I was freaking terrified and yet when I placed myself in Diana's head; the fear melted away and supercharged me into someone even I don't recognize. It was so good. I felt so powerful. Flora was gone and Diana manifested in me, and I understood exactly how she would play it. I've watched her closely over the years and know how her mind works. She's used it often enough on me and I suppose I absorbed more of it than I'd like.

It was so good getting one over her. Knowing we had taken the money, I'm in no doubt she wanted all along. She's always craved wealth and power and probably targeted Don Ortega for that reason. He was an old fool and didn't stand a hope in hell of surviving Diana Corlietti.

It was always her intention to remove him from the picture and put Mario in his place as head of the Ortega family. It's obvious just from the way she acted since she slid between his sheets. The fact it happened sooner than she thought, probably had Diana and Mario rubbing their hands with delight because they didn't even need to kill the bastard themselves. Somebody else did it for them, which is why she acted fast to steal the money before his sons came to claim their inheritance and rightful positions as head of the family.

Now the money has gone she will be seeking revenge, which is why I set in place my own insurance policy by subtly threatening the manager.

We head straight for the waiting car and as the door slams behind us and we join the ever-present traffic, I sink back against the leather seat and close my eyes.

I'm aware of Domenico sitting silently beside me and there is so much tension surrounding us, I wonder what's running through his mind right now. Did I play my part as he intended, or did I overstep the mark? I'm worried about what will happen next because now I'm disposable. They have their money, and I am no longer any use to them. Will they let me go as he promised, or will I suffer an accident by their hands and sent back as a warning to my sister?

I'm afraid to look into his eyes because then I'll have my answer and he says in a dark voice, "Look at me, Flora."

My breath hitches and my heart thumps so hard I swear he can hear it. However, something is telling me I need to know and so tentatively, I open my eyes and glance in his direction and the anger and power in his eyes makes me tremble with an emotion I wasn't expecting — lust.

"How did that make you feel?"

His question takes me by surprise, and I say breathlessly, "As if I could take on the world."

I'm surprised when a lazy grin appears on his handsome face and his eyes sparkle with something I can't quite place.

"You liked threatening the manager?"

"I did." I'm ashamed to admit that, but it's the truth. I loved the power I had over him in that moment, and the way he cowered under my gaze made me feel invincible.

"That's my girl." His affection makes me smile, and he beckons me closer with his index finger.

I shift a little closer and am surprised when that same finger lifts my chin to his lips and he whispers, "As soon as we get home, I'm giving you a choice."

I wasn't expecting that and whisper, "What choice?"

He runs his thumb across my lower lip and says huskily, "I'll tell you after I show you what it's like to be mine."

"I don't understand." My voice is weak and shakes with desire, and all I really want is for him to put me out of my misery and kiss me long and hard. His breath dusts my lips, making me lean closer and my panties flood with the wet heat his touch creates, and he says huskily, "You have pleased me today, Flora. I wasn't expecting you to be so callous. So cruel and conniving. Qualities I love and admire so much it turns me on. Now you must deal with what that means for you."

"But..."

His thumb presses hard against my lips, effectively silencing me, and his eyes burn into my soul as he says roughly, "No more talking. Remember, I still control you and you are my prisoner until I say so. I have many uses for a woman like you, Flora, and I am figuring out what comes next."

He pulls away and, reaching in his pocket, takes out his phone and as he taps out a text, I sit back and contemplate the conversation.

More than anything I want to experience everything he just said, but there's something eating away at me that I can't shake. It cuts me deep and tears at my heart because when Domenico Ortega looks at me with desire, I'm in no doubt it's my sister he sees.

* * *

THE CAR PULLS to a stop outside his mansion and as the door opens and he exits, his rough hand pulls me with him into the sunlight. All around me is a wall built of menace as his men shield our arrival and close around us as we make the short journey to the large overbearing door.

My heart runs quicker than I can walk because it's what happens now that my mind is focusing on and as we step inside the impressive entrance, his men melt away as if they are wisps of black smoke with the ability to choke you to death.

Domenico says nothing and just pulls me along behind him at speed toward the huge staircase that dominates the center of the room. As I struggle to keep up, my throat dries and my pulse races because he is definitely not messing around.

As I thought, we head straight to his room and as he tugs me inside, he slams the door behind him and locks it with a wicked grin.

Then he turns and casts his wicked gaze the length of me and growls, "Clothes are no longer required. Strip."

He settles into a nearby chair and stares at me with a lust filled gaze as I hesitate, my face flaming with embarrassment, causing him to lean forward and snarl, "Now!"

My fingers shake as I reach behind me and tug on the zip, causing the dress to fall to the floor, the jacket having preceded it as my mind struggles to keep up. I shiver in the lace lingerie he obviously approves of, judging by the gleam in his eye and the growing bulge in his pants.

I falter and he growls, "All of it." Causing me to say fearfully, "I can't."

My words are at odds with my wishes because more than anything, I want this. But it's so cold. As if I'm a whore being paid for the pleasure, causing me to think back on a time when that was reality for me.

My eyes water with unshed tears as my past haunts me and

only his voice shakes me out of it as he growls, "Look at me, Flora."

I stare into his eyes that burn with desire and he says huskily, "You need to understand one thing."

"What?" I whisper fearfully and his voice softens and his eyes gleam with lust as he says huskily, "There is one word to describe what I think of you, Flora. That word is want. You are the most beautiful woman I have ever seen, and I want you to learn how much power you have over me. I am not using you for sex. I want you. I want to crawl inside your body and own your heart and mind. I want you to close your eyes and I'm the last thing you see and the first when they open. I want to fill your mind and body, and I want to own your soul. Above everything, I want you to understand how beautiful, sexy and amazing you are, and I want you to want me even just a little of how much I want you. But first we must banish those demons and teach you to own your own mind and body."

I'm stunned and don't understand what's happening and he interrupts with a soft, "You need to own yourself before I own your body. Stand before me proud of who you are knowing there is nobody I want more than you. Flora Corlietti. That's the woman I want, not a damaged imitation. I want your kindness, your innocence, and your softness. I want the perfect woman, not the tarnished one. I want to see you proud of who you are and own your past with no shame. So, strip for me, baby girl, and show me how much you want to be set free."

My eyes glisten with tears of gratitude because now I understand. Domenico is giving me the opportunity to own my past and make it mine. Not to be ashamed but to embrace it and rather than run from it and hide out with nuns, to understand it and use it to make me stronger.

As he settles back in his chair and stares at me through lust filled eyes, I reach behind my back and unclasp my bra. As it drops to the floor, his slight hiss empowers me and I run my fingers across my breasts, gasping as I squeeze my nipples between my fingers and thumbs. It feels so good to own my body and use it as a weapon on the powerful man sitting at my feet and as I hook my thumbs in the waistband of my silk panties, I stare deep into his glittering eyes as I drag them down my body and stand naked before him.

He doesn't move and I'm in no hurry and continue to caress my body and gasp and sigh as it responds to what I like. I tease my sex, an act that causes him to groan and feeling bolder, I head closer and start dancing, loving how sexy it makes me, knowing it's turning him on and yet he still hasn't touched me.

I stand with him between my legs and carry on the show like the sluttiest lap dancer and love how his pupils dilate and his breath quickens. I am so far gone I don't even recognize myself as I explore my own body, loving how he watches every move. Now I understand what it's like to control a powerful man, and I'm in no hurry to stop. Whatever happens after tonight, this will change me forever and, far from fearing what happens next, I can't fucking wait.

CHAPTER 22

DOM

This is pure fucking torture. I can't tear my eyes from this woman who has stepped out from the shadows and blinded me by her brilliance. She dazzles, unlike before when she hid behind a past that damaged her.

When she took on the role I demanded at the bank, she shone like the most exquisite diamond. She was breath-taking and if I want to hold on to that woman; I need to banish her inhibitions and the guilt she wears like chains around her soul, dragging it down and shrouding her in fear.

Now, as she dances before me, I am bewitched by her. I once believed Diana was everything I ever wanted in life, but I hadn't met her sister yet. She has all the qualities that drew me like a magnet toward her older sibling but appears to have none of the flaws that Diana wears like jagged scars on her tarnished soul with pride.

Flora is the woman I was meant to find. I am in no doubt about that and despite the urgent need I have to claim her; I recognize she needs to claim herself first.

So, as I stare in wonder while maintaining a stony expression, my heart thumps as I struggle to think of a way to keep her.

As she straddles my lap, the bulge in my pants is becoming quite a problem and the sweat dripping down my back tells me I won't keep my cool for long. I'm like a tiger waiting to pounce on its prey and I wonder if she knows how close I am to breaking. To leaning forward and going in for the kill. To consume, own and dominate. That is who I am, and this restraint is killing me almost as much as the need for the woman who appears to be somewhere else right now.

She bites her lower lip and has a glazed expression in her eyes as she sways and gyrates like the most exotic dancer in the world. Her long blonde curls dust her shoulders, spilling onto her breasts as she swings her hips. Her dazzling blue eyes are half closed as she appears to be in a trance and her ruby red lips glisten as she sucks them into a mouth I am keen to explore with my throbbing cock.

Her breasts aren't the biggest I've seen, but they are perfection, with her rosebud nipples standing erect to her soft touch. Her waist is small and her hips perfect as they splay out, making me long to slide between them into her gleaming pussy.

As she dances for me, I suppress the anger that is growing by the second for the two people who used her and made her past a bitter one. Images of disgusting men tearing her innocence from her makes me boil with rage and if I am sure of anything right now, it's that I will use my skills to make Mario and Diana's end a bloody torturous one. Because of Flora and because from now on she is the most important person in my life and so, for my own sanity, I hold up my hand and growl, "Enough."

Her eyes open and I note the worry that clouds them as she senses she has done something to anger or disappoint me.

I hate knowing I'm the cause of that and yet I need to create distance between us if my plan regarding Flora works to my advantage.

Softening my voice, I reach out and pull her naked body onto my lap and wrap my arms around her shivering body. Then I dip my head and kiss her slowly, in no hurry to rush into something I want to treasure. Not to take her in a moment of greed like the frantic fuck against the wall before we left for the bank, when I lost control for a second. Definitely not to act like every other man who has been there before me. The thought of which is like a painful hammer to my heart and as she sighs against my lips, it hurts so much knowing her past and not being able to change it.

I pull back and say huskily, "How do you feel now, baby girl?"

She gazes up and I smile, causing her to stare at me in total shock.

"You're smiling." She gasps and I shrug. "It happens. I have no control over it, but now you mention it, I'll remove it at once."

I scowl and her soft laugh flutters against my heart, searching for a crack to edge inside. "I like it when you smile."

She glances at me shyly and then surprises us both by reaching up and stroking my cheek with an angel's hands and then impulsively pressing her lips to mine and softly edging her tongue inside. It takes a superhuman effort on my part to hold back as I give her the freedom to explore me at her will and as our tongues entwine and dance like lovers, I don't believe I've ever been this happy in my life.

An unfamiliar warm sensation is spreading through my body and softening the hard edges that have always lived inside me. Her soft lips on mine and her naked skin grazing against the fabric of my clothing is causing friction that will probably test every inch of my resolve, but I hold back and let her explore with no fear of what I can do.

Her fingers inch inside my half open silk shirt and just feeling them caress my body is complete torture. She is relentless as she kisses me softly as she slides her hand across my chest and her small moans of desire are like green fucking lights exploding in my head. She shifts closer and then pulls back and stares at me through lust filled eyes and I say softly, "You never answered my question."

She smiles, and it's as if the sun comes out as she whispers, "I feel happy and I have you to thank for that."

"Because…" I arch my brow and she giggles. "It's as if I'm safe with you, which is strange considering I'm your prisoner."

"You are." I grin, causing her to giggle again and I reach up and twirl my finger around her curls, loving how soft they are against my skin. Images of them sliding against my naked flesh like the finest silk make me groan inside because I am starting to hate this soft approach. I am a hunter and take what I want without considering my victim at all, and this is a first for me. A lesson I'm learning the painful way.

"Domenico."

Hearing my name on her lips makes me smile and I say gruffly, "Call me Dom."

"OK."

She smiles shyly. "Dom, um, I'm a little confused."

"Of what?"

I keep my tone devoid of any emotion because the last thing I need is to let her peer inside my soul and see how weak I already am where it concerns her.

"I thought we would um…"

"Fuck." I state the obvious, causing her to blush the color of the red flag that should be warning her to stop.

"We fuck when I say we fuck."

I bark back, causing her eyes to widen and a little of the happiness to die inside them.

"I say when, where, and how. You do what I tell you and never question me."

"Oh." She glances down and I hate bursting the bubble that we created, but she needs to fear me; to know what I'm capable of because until I know for certain that Flora wants me even a tiny bit of how much I want her, she will never learn that the weakness inside me is her.

CHAPTER 23

FLORA

I am crushed. He has kicked me back down and is currently standing on my heart. I thought we had something special for a moment. The way he looked at me with desire and encouraged me to be bold, to love myself knowing he wanted me. Now he has pushed me away and it can only be because he realized I'm not my sister. In his moments of tenderness, it's Diana he sees. Her he's talking to and touching, kissing, loving. Not me. Not the whore my sister made me, and that is the hardest lesson to learn.

I want him.

I want the tender man who has protective power surrounding him like a force field. To be loved by a man like that would be the best gift ever, and yet I'm merely a carbon copy of the one woman he truly loves. A stop gap until he wins her back. A pale imitation who doesn't measure up and the fact he pushed me away tells me I'm right, so I retreat and wait for his next step.

"Come." He shifts me off his lap and grabs my hand and I follow him into the bathroom, thinking I've failed somehow.

He points to the bench where I sit meekly waiting for

instruction and as he strips off his clothes, I hate that I want him even more.

Domenico Ortega is possibly the most handsome man I have ever met. His dark close-cropped hair frames the most beautiful face I have ever seen on a man. The dark stubble grazing his jaw tells of an alpha male who likes to control and his dark brown eyes glitter with a dominance that is turning me on against my better judgment.

As he tears off his shirt, my eyes feast on a body that appears to be carved from marble. The dark hair mixes with tribal ink and I physically ache to trace a path around every stroke of genius that scripts this man's body. As he drops his pants, the dark hair that frames his huge cock makes my mouth water and the strong legs that make him stand tall and powerful are in perfect symmetry with the rest of his insanely muscular body.

Who wouldn't want a man like Domenico Ortega and I'm the fool who has pushed aside his indifference to clamor for just one taste of it? He stated the obvious back in his bedroom. I am his prisoner in every way possible because even if he opened the door wide and told me to leave, I would be thinking up excuses to stay, even though I realize he prefers another.

He turns on the shower and the hot steamy water soon fills the room and I'm surprised when he says abruptly, "Inside."

He points to the shower, and I need no further invitation to stand under the steaming water and let it bathe me in the only warmth I'm ever likely to get from this man. As the spray hits my body, I close my eyes and try to block him out because he is doing strange things to my heart that I simply can't cope with right now.

Then, from out of the fog that swirls around the room, I hear a soft, "Let me help you."

My eyes snap open and I swallow hard because standing

before me is a god among men. I'm surprised to see him lathering up his hand and even more surprised when he runs that strong hand over my breasts, causing me to gasp in surprise.

"What are you doing?"

"Caring for you."

"Why?"

I'm a little taken aback by this because nobody has cared for me in a very long time and the tears burn as I struggle to deal with this situation.

His voice is low and sexy as he massages the soap into my skin. "I want you to feel safe with me. To push away your fear and dispose of any embarrassment."

"Why?" I gasp as he moves lower, the simple act so sensuous I never want it to end.

"Because you're mine, Flora. You don't realize what you did when you walked through my door. When I saw you fighting Senator Billings and when you gazed into my eyes for the first time. I felt it and that's a huge problem for you because until you fall in love with me, you will never be free."

Any sane person would be thinking up ways to escape an obvious madman, but I'm fast realizing where it concerns Domenico Ortega, I have stepped into insanity. It's obvious he's confusing me with Diana, and that makes me sadder than I expected.

As he gently rubs the soap into my skin, I am conflicted. On the one hand I'm loving his attention, every delicious second of it but on the other, I accept it's Diana standing forefront in his mind and I'm the imposter who is hiding behind her, desperate to experience a little of what it's like when a man wants a woman, hell *loves* a woman because this touch is pure love.

He spins me around and carries on soaping my back, his strong fingers running around my neck, reminding me how fragile my life is at his hands. With one swift move, those strong arms could break me. Slide around my neck and snap it in two. Then again, that would be the easy way out of madness because the damage he is inflicting on my heart is far more devastating, especially when whatever this is ends and I'm no longer required. I'm not sure I'll ever get over my encounter with him and will probably be banging on that convent door and begging them to throw away the key.

It almost makes me jump when soft lips burn against my skin as he kisses the back of my neck and his strong arms fold around me, his large hand splaying out across my abdomen as he pulls me in hard against his body, his huge cock pressing against my ass.

The water rains down on us both as he sucks gently at my skin, causing a soft moan to escape and get swallowed up by the noise from the jets of water crying a river around me.

I hold my breath because I don't want to give him any cause to stop and as he dips his hand lower and gently teases my clit, I moan again as my legs part voluntarily, desperate for more.

I arch back against him and shiver when his finger enters me, pushing in deep and searching for my G spot. I push down hard, desperate for more as he continues to kiss my neck and invade me inside with just one finger, making me ache for the whole of him. It's almost unbearable as he continues to tease and torture me in the most delightful way, and I wonder why he is doing this at all. He could have fucked me by now; we both know that, but for some reason, he is dragging out the inevitable and I'm not certain why.

"Do you like this, baby girl?" He whispers against my ear, and I nod, saying huskily, "Yes."

His low laugh confuses me a little and I almost groan with disappointment when he withdraws his finger and says with some satisfaction. "Good. When you're finished, I'll be waiting in the bedroom. Make the most of the time you have alone. There won't be a lot of that all the time I'm around."

As he makes to leave, I blurt out, "Why are you doing this?"

A low chuckle is his answer as he steps from the shower, grabbing a towel and tying it around his waist. "I told you, Flora. You need to learn to trust and feel safe with me."

He flashes a wicked grin in my direction as he leaves the bathroom and I watch him go with a thumping heart. *Feel safe with him.* That statement almost makes me laugh because how can I ever feel safe with a man who could ruin my life the moment he gets bored and sends me back to hell?

CHAPTER 24

DOM

I'm not sure when I became Prince fucking Charming, but it's not sitting well with me. It's fucking torture because more than anything I have a primal need to be inside Flora and stay there. Just imagining how delicious that would be makes me groan and rub my cock through the towel, knowing I would probably embarrass myself and come as soon as I make it inside.

I briefly wonder whether to head to my club and fuck a whore to take away the edge, but I already know that will never happen. Not all the time Flora is here, waiting for my next move and probably wondering how she got so unlucky.

I can tell she wants me, desires me and is confused by my hesitation. I also know she thinks I'm in love with her sister. I see it in her eyes, and she couldn't be more wrong. I *hate* her sister. Detest her and want to end her life, but in bringing Diana down I am using her own flesh and blood against her.

What started out as revenge has turned into something I wasn't expecting, and I am trying so hard to play this situation the right way. To make Flora fall in love with me because everything I desired in her sister is what Flora has in abundance, with none of the vitriol.

I had to remove myself from the situation for my own sanity and as I sit on the bed, I reach for my phone that has lit up on the bedside table.

There's a simple message from Pasquale that immediately commands my attention.

> You have a visitor.

I waste no time in calling him and he answers almost immediately.

"*Sir.*"

"Who is it?" I growl, irritated that I'm even having this conversation.

"*Miss Gray.*"

"What the fuck does she want?" I hiss through gritted teeth and his reply has me standing in a heartbeat.

"*Your assistance.*"

"I'm on my way."

As I cut the call, I'm annoyed that she dared come to my home at all. More than anything, I hate that woman, but the fact I have her employee locked up in my bedroom tells me I need to deal with this shit, so it doesn't come back to bite me.

I briefly wonder whether to tell Flora I'm stepping out for a bit, a thought that makes me smile because when did I ever let another person know what I was doing? The fact I like it tells me I'm falling faster than is good for me because having Flora in my life is smoothing away a few of my hard edges and giving me a reason for living for once.

As I dress, it strikes me how good it is knowing I'm so close to securing the one piece missing from my life. Someone to share it with and I will not fuck this up. Whatever happens next, I know only one thing. When Flora stepped unwittingly into my life, she sacrificed her own to me.

It doesn't take me long to dress and as I slide the smooth steel of my revolver into my jacket, it's as if an old friend walks beside me. I can't count the number of times this particular friend has saved my life and claimed the ones of my enemies. I have no fear of using it and wear it against my body with pride. It's who I am—what I am and that will never change, despite the fluttering emotion daring to raise its head inside me.

Flora brings out my softer side that was kicked into touch a few years ago by her sister. I thought she was the one. The perfect woman and the one I had been searching for all my life. She played me though, along with every member of the Ortega family, which is why I hate her so much. She edged her way inside our lives and blew us apart from within. Now it's my turn, but first I need to discover why Desdemona Gray has the audacity to show her face at my door.

As I leave the room, I lock it behind me, knowing that Flora will be kept safe inside until I pick up where we left off. Despite my feelings toward her, the situation hasn't changed because she will remain my prisoner until she falls in love with me. Until she no longer glances at the exit with hope and until she gives me her heart in return, however long it takes.

* * *

ANY SOFTNESS inside me is left behind and as I head to the room I receive visitors in, I sharpen my mood. I fucking hate and detest Desdemona Gray. I always have because of everything she represents. A cold, callous, calculating woman who uses sex to drive her ambition. Some may call me a hypocrite because I do the same and use women for sex and nothing else. I don't let them inside because the only time I did, the thief ran off with my heart, causing me to lock down and maintain a cruel edge that I need to keep me from crumbling.

I have sharpened my emotions not to let anyone in and am considered a bastard by everyone I have ever met. Now I find myself with an interesting predicament because, for the first time since Diana, I feel my guard shifting and letting a chink of light inside my dark heart.

Pasquale meets me at the foot of the staircase and says in a low whisper, "It appears that our gallery owner is a little on edge."

I raise my eyes. "Do you know why?"

He shakes his head. "She's nervous. Uncharacteristically so."

"What has she said?"

"She turned up, demanding to see you. Told me she had information you would want, but she needed protection in return."

My interest sits up and rubs its hands because I love a desperate visitor and look forward to using her despair to my advantage."

"Sounds like fun." I grin as Pasquale's eyes flash with pleasure.

We are so alike. We love using a desperate situation to our advantage and knowing the woman waiting for me, I'm positive she will make for interesting listening.

We reach the small intimidating room I use for my guests and before I head inside, I say in a low voice, "Ask Gretchen to prepare breakfast in the dining room—for two."

Pasquale nods and dashes off a quick text and as I turn the handle, I prepare to get rid of the woman inside as quickly as possible.

"Domenico."

She stands and says my name with an urgency that interests me because she is normally calm and controlled as she hides behind a hidden agenda.

"Desdemona."

I nod abruptly and point to the seat she rose from.

As she sits down, I note her pale skin and trembling lips. Her eyes darting around the room as if she's afraid of something.

It's interesting watching a normally controlled woman crash and burn before your eyes, knowing you're not the cause and I say nothing and just regard her through hooded eyes, waiting for the reason she's here to raise its ugly head.

She shifts awkwardly on her seat and glances around with her nerves fully out on display. This room has a lot to do with stirring up nerves. Charcoal gray paneling draws it in closer. Low lighting creates many shadows to hide in and the uncomfortable hard chairs make a person sit straight and rigid, any comfort firmly left outside the door. There are no windows, just subdued lighting that offers no comfort. It's not seductive in this room, it's a threat that you make it out alive only if I say so.

The paintings on the wall mock me almost as much as they intimidate my visitors. My hated father and two brothers glare down from the walls, reminding me of how much I hate them. On a silver frame on the window ledge is a family portrait, taken when life wasn't so empty. When I had a mother and a sister who were the only light in our lives.

Once again, the guilt tears at my heart when I think of Eliza and her fate, just because of who she was. She ran from a father who only saw her for the opportunity she gave him to sharpen his empire and expand into territory he didn't control. Blown to pieces by a vendetta we still have no knowledge of and as I sit surrounded by the ghosts from my past, it sets my mood accordingly and I glower at Desdemona Gray, offering her no warm welcome.

"I need your help."

She's straight to the point and I regard her through obsidian eyes, waiting for the reason.

"My assistant. Flora Corlietti."

"What about her?" I snap because at the mention of Flora's name, my hackles rose immediately.

"I need her back."

"Nothing to do with me."

I lean back and regard her with a blank expression, and her voice falters as she whispers, "Please. I know she's here. Let her leave with me and do us all a favor."

I'm curious and lean forward. "What are the reasons behind your request?"

She shifts in her seat and says with a slight tremble to her voice. "I received a phone call two hours ago. It was a woman who sounded scared."

I feel my chest constricting as I prepare myself for what I suspect is coming and Desdemona's voice quivers as she whispers, "She told me that Flora was caught up in the murder of Senator Billings."

Her voice cracks as she says in a rush. "I would never have let her accompany him if I knew what that man was into."

This is news and my ears prick up. "And what exactly was he into?"

Desdemona shivers. "The caller told me that Senator Billings was involved in satanic rituals. He took innocent young women and performed disgusting acts on them, along with his club members."

I say nothing and let her speak. "The caller told me she had escaped from him and knew what his intentions were regarding Flora. That he was involved in serious fucked up shit and was found dead minus his heart on his way home from your gala."

She twists her fingers in her lap and whispers, almost as if she is afraid his ghost is in the room. "Flora was his intended next victim. Apparently, he takes vulnerable women to events like yours and then slips something into their drink to make them willing. He leaves and heads to a house outside of town that the men use for their disgusting club. Inside, they are waiting dressed in satanic robes and the victim is brutally assaulted and then sacrificed on an altar of stone."

I'm not sure if she's feeding me shit, but something is telling me it could be true. The senator is well known in my dark world and has been called on several times to return a favor for silence on his dubious extra-marital activities and I wonder if it goes deeper than I first thought.

Desdemona's voice shakes as she whispers, "I was told to come here and not leave without Flora. If anything happened to her, the caller would implicate me in the senator's death, telling the authorities I was complicit in supplying him with fresh victims."

"Is she right? Did you supply the senator with unwilling women?"

My voice is gruff, and she says quickly, "We had an understanding. Art for willing company. Nothing more than that, and I have no reason to think he harmed any of the girls I arranged for him."

"Tell me about your arrangement."

I lean back and set my expression to bastard, and she shifts awkwardly in her seat.

"You know how it works, Dom. We all scratch each other's back and exist within blurred guidelines. My girls know the score. An evening sucking up to the senator in return for a cut of the commission. If I have no assistant to do the job, I recruit a whore. It's purely business and everyone knows where they stand. Nobody is hurt and we all get what we want. Hell, you've even taken advantage of that yourself, if I remember. A sexual act for a painting, a sculpture, or information."

She leans forward and for the first time since entering this room, a little of the fire inside her flares up and she hisses, "You are no different to the rest of us, but satanic shit is something else. Whatever you're into, I need my assistant back and if you want a replacement, it can be arranged. Hell, I'll even offer my own services in return for setting her free because unless I pack her onto the next flight out of here, my whole business, hell, my life, is under threat."

I can tell Desdemona is scared and whoever called her has done a good job of scaring the shit out of her, and I already know the answer to my next question before the words spill from my lips.

"Who called you?"

A simple enough question that makes my guest blanch as she whispers, "Your stepmother. Diana Ortega."

CHAPTER 25

FLORA

As soon as Dom left, I could breathe again. The minute the door closed, I sank back against the marble wall of the shower and let the breath I was holding out in a sigh of relief.

What was I thinking back there?

I wanted him so badly I was prepared to step away from my principles and let him control me. Own me and dominate me. My mind is fucked because I don't recognize myself anymore.

Since I arrived, this is the first moment I've had to catch a breath and take stock of my situation and as I step from the shower and wrap myself in a large fluffy towel, I sit on the bench and consider my options and arrive at only one conclusion.

I need to escape, and fast but how? This place is a fortress. I've lived in one most of my life and know how it works. I will only leave if he says so, and from the look in his eyes when he casts them over me, I'm going nowhere.

He wants Diana, not me, and I must keep reminding myself of that. However, when he gazes at me with a lazy, lustful intent, it's hard to remember that. When his rough fingers drag across my skin and his loaded gaze falls on me, I push away the knowledge it's another woman he sees.

How can I want a man like that? Where is my self-respect? Now he is away from me, the fog clears and reminds me how serious this situation is. The man I came here with is dead—murdered after being publicly escorted from the premises and sent home in disgrace. A home he never made it back to.

Then I was forced into committing a serious crime, hell fraud and stealing my own sister's millions from under her nose. In less than twenty-four hours I have sunk as low as a person can and loved every second of it. It excites me. The danger, the thrill and the adrenalin rush, and I want more. More of this life and more of him. The man who encouraged me to step outside my comfort zone and fly.

As I glance at the bathroom door leading into the bedroom, I picture him sitting there waiting for me. Is this it? Will he expect me to open my legs and allow him inside? Is he about to drive the final nail into my coffin and ruin me forever?

For some inexplicable reason, I hope I'm right and with a sigh, I step across to the mirror and regard the conflicted woman staring back at me. I am fucked whatever happens, so I suppose I may as well have some fun along the way. Ironic really to think of this as fun when it really is the opposite of that. I am being held here as a cruel man's prisoner and I should be fucking terrified.

With a deep sigh, I reach for a toothbrush in the cupboard behind the mirror and clean my teeth, loving the freshness that lingers in my mouth as I anticipate the next step.

As I finish up and take a deep breath, I head for the door, clutching the towel as a flimsy defense against a man who I know could eat me alive.

However, as I step through the door, I immediately note the room is empty and I'm not sure if it's relief or disappointment that I'm experiencing now.

As I glance around, I wonder if he's lurking somewhere in the shadows, watching me, preparing to pounce when I least expect it. However, on further investigation I can tell I'm alone and I should be happy about that but strangely, I'm not. Where is he?

I'm uncertain what to do now and just perch on the edge of the bed and figure out my choices. It doesn't take me long to realize I have none and so, with a sigh, I stand and head to the other door in the room that I believe leads to his closet.

As I walk inside, the scent of leather and sandalwood hits me and I take a deep breath. It smells like him. Strong, powerful and sexy; all the qualities I should turn away from and head toward kindness, respectability and ordinary.

I already know I'm screwed when that thought terrifies me and as I filter through his shirts, I love the soft fabric, imagining it caressing my naked body.

The towel drops as I give into temptation and as the folds of the material close around my body, I picture the man himself in its place. How I long to experience what it would be like with him. Domenico Ortega. Possibly the sexiest man I have ever laid eyes on, but definitely not the most frightening one. No, that honor is reserved for Mario Bachini, the most abhorrent human being on the planet and so rather than test the door to freedom, I reapply my chains and wait for the man who holds the key.

Footsteps head toward the door and I begin to shake. My head throbs with pressure as I lie naked on the bed that consists of only a silk covered mattress. Panic surrounds me; swirls around me like an avenging angel as I consider my position. Why are they doing this —to me?

The footsteps stop outside the door and my throat dries. I can't even swallow in case I choke on the bile that's never far away. I shiver as the breeze from the fan above my head chases the heat of oppres-

sion away and, if anything, I hope it will be quick and there are no others to take his place.

The door edges open and a low laugh makes my skin crawl.

"Well, what do we have here?"

The accent is a slow drawl, Texan perhaps. I've heard them all this past year and I wonder why I'm so interested.

I remain still and focus on the fan spinning around, just like the nerves inside my body.

I hear a belt ripped from pants and the heavy breathing of a man who is intent on only one thing. Me.

The sound of fabric hitting the floor and a zipper unfastening. That's what I focus on to drive away the fear that threatens to end my life in a heart attack.

"Good girl." The slightly slurred drawl of a man who is about to ruin me makes my skin crawl and my heart begins to thump as if it's attempting to run from the situation. I'm no stranger to this, hell I wish I was, but every time it happens, the fear only gets more intense.

The man stands at the foot of the bed, and I try not to look. It's easier that way and as he grips my ankles and pulls my legs wider, I squeeze my eyes tightly shut, trying to retreat to the happy place in my mind. Sad to know that happy place is a mafia mansion surrounded by men disguised by shade. At least I was safe there, or so I believed.

"Perfect." His excited whisper makes my skin crawl and as the bed dips, I pray this won't take long. It doesn't.

He wastes no time in enjoying what he paid for. Ripping through my body with no regard for my comfort. The bed banging against the wall as he destroys what is left of my soul.

At least he doesn't strike me, that's the only plus I can get from this situation and as he finishes up after leaving me broken and ruined, I fight against the ever-present tears that reinforce my life may as well be over.

"Thanks darlin', I'll give you a good report."

He dresses quickly, anxious to get on with his day and as he heads outside, I relish the sound of his footsteps walking away from me, knowing that it won't be long before others take their place.

By the time the door opens, I have scrubbed every inch of my body with soap that smells of sin and depravation and my heart drops when my sister stands before me, holding a glass of water along with a contraceptive pill.

"Chuck seemed pleased." She says, as if discussing a successful day at the office and I suppose it was—for her. For them.

As I silently take the glass and pill from her hand, my heart hardens against the people who hold me captive and use me as a golden goose. Not that Diana is averse to taking my place. If anything, she gets off on it.

She glances at the watch strapped to her dainty wrist. "The party starts in two hours. Maybe get some sleep. I'll send some food up; you'll need your strength."

"Please Diana."

Her eyes narrow at the plaintive whisper in my voice and the tears gathering in my eyes. "Please what?" Her voice is rasping, telling me not to even go there but I must try. Surely somewhere deep inside her heart our blood counts for something.

"Let me go." I whisper and may as well have saved my breath because I'm rewarded with a stinging slap across my cheek and note the fury on her face.

"You ungrateful bitch." She hisses. "After everything Mario has done for us. You want to walk away and not pay him back for giving us a home and keeping us off the streets?

"I could get a job." My voice sounds pathetic as I state the obvious, and her low laugh of derision makes my heart sink.

"You have a job, and you should be grateful we keep you safe. It's not the same as on the streets. There's a different type of customer that prowls them."

She grabs my shoulders and shakes me, the fury blazing from her eyes as she hisses, "Why are you so ungrateful? I've done everything possible to care for you, sister, and this is how you repay me. If you speak any more about leaving, I'll let Mario deal with you."

At the sound of his name, the blood freezes in my veins and, terrified, I gasp, "Please no."

Her eyes narrow and a sinister smile settles on her lips. "Then never ask to leave again. Just lie back and know that this is the best it gets for both of us."

As she casts a derisive glance in my direction, she heads for the door, and I almost consider raising the lamp beside my bed and bringing it down on her evil head. Then again, my chance would be a fleeting one because the only way out of here is past the man who guards his possessions so securely and makes certain the only way to freedom is through him.

As she leaves and I hear the key turn in the lock, I fight back the tears, knowing if I have any chance of surviving this, I must wait patiently for the moment to present itself. The first chance I get I'm running and it's up to me to make sure it's to a place they will never find me.

CHAPTER 26

DOM

Desdemona has surprised me. I never had her down as vulnerable before, but whatever she has heard is scaring the shit out of her.

She is waiting for my decision, and I swear she's not even breathing as her eyes stare straight at me and the blood has drained from her skin.

"No." I bark out, causing her to shake and say wildly, "Please, you must let Flora go."

"Why should I?" I lean forward and snarl. "This is not my problem. You were happy enough to send her off with a fucking rapist in the name of business. You knew what that man was capable of and yet you didn't give Flora a second thought. All you cared about was selling a fucking painting, so no, Miss. Gray. Request denied."

I stand and frown down on the woman who appears to be in shock and say through gritted teeth. "Now fuck off out of my home and never come back."

I'm surprised when she falls to her knees and sobs, "Please, I'll do anything. Don't turn me away. I'm well…" She peers up at me, the tears pouring down her face as she whispers, "I'm afraid."

"Of what, exactly?"

I fold my arms and appear disinterested, and she gulps, "Your stepmother."

"You don't even know the bitch." I snap angrily and she shakes her head.

"I wish that was true."

My heart thumps as she gulps, "I met Diana a long time ago. Our paths crossed through a mutual acquaintance. Even then, I learned not to cross her."

"Why not?" Now I'm interested and she shivers, her head bowed as she kneels before me.

"She was at a party I went to, accompanying a man who she introduced as her stepbrother, but from the looks of it, they were a lot more than that."

My blood boils as I think of the people who ruined my life and I hiss, "What happened?"

"Nothing, not really, but there were whispers about their involvement in mafia."

"Why should that terrify you? You've danced with the devil for years."

She shakes her head. "There is mafia and there's them."

I kind of get what she means because mainly when you come from a mafia family you abide by some kind of fucked up code. I'm guessing Mario Bachini writes his own and Diana is so twisted she goes along with it.

Desdemona shivers. "The man I was with that night was doing business with them. He told me he was in deep and couldn't work a way out of it without cutting Mario into a share of his business. I've never seen a man so afraid and rightly so."

"Why?"

"He was murdered that same night on his way home from my gallery. His heart had been cut out, just like the senator."

I sit down, the disgust sliding through my veins like a river of damnation.

Desdemona looks up and pleads, "Help me, Domenico. They want Flora back. Apparently, she's family and if I had known that from the start, I would never have employed her in the first place."

"Why not?" I'm irritated beyond belief, and Desdemona says pitifully, "Because I want nothing to do with those murdering bastards. If I never hear of or see them again, I will consider my life well lived."

"What did my stepmother say to you?"

Desdemona's voice breaks. "That if Flora wasn't on that plane later today, she would hold me responsible."

"That's it?"

I laugh out loud and the woman on her knees openly sobs. "Please, if I don't send Flora back, I've no doubt I'll end up like Senator Billings. That woman is a murdering bitch tied to an even bigger murdering bastard. Don't make me a target, I beg of you, for old time's sake."

I've had enough of her whining and stand, casting a derisive gaze over the cowering, broken woman at my feet and snarl, "Then you shouldn't have played with the bad boys if you can't keep up. Now I'll say it again, get your fucking ass out of my home and never even look in my direction again. If you think I'd ever send Flora back to those deranged bastards, you don't know me at all. She stays here—with me and you can tell that to my bitch of a stepmother. In fact, tell her if she wants her darling sister to come and get her personally."

As I leave the room, Desdemona's pitiful sobs accompany me, and Pasquale straightens up as I head through the door.

"Anything I should know?" He appears mildly interested and I say with a sigh, "The usual family shit concerning my stepmother. Show the unwelcome whore out and make sure she knows not to return."

Pasquale nods and heads into the room, leaving me to head back to the only place that interests me right now. Inside my prisoner.

*　*　*

The room is in darkness and dressed in anticipation. I can see Flora curled up in a ball inside my bed, apparently asleep. The fact she is breathing rapidly, and small cries head my way, tells me she's dreaming and it's not a pleasant one. I silently approach the bed and gaze down at a woman that, for some reason, I yearn to protect. I'm not sure why and merely put it down to the infatuation I have with her sister, or should I say, had. That infatuation is now firmly focused on this woman and as she shivers and cries out in her sleep, I waste no time in pulling her into my arms, causing her to wake with a start.

I hold her close to my body, loving how soft she feels, and stroke her hair, whispering, "You were dreaming."

She sags in my arms, and I kiss the top of her head gently, causing her to shift a little closer. It's so good to hold her, to care for her, something I can't ever remember doing, even with Diana. It was a different kind of need I had for her. A greedy desperation to experience something other than pain for once in my miserable life. With Flora, though, it's different. I want to reach out and seize her pain and crush it in my fist, to set her free and place a smile on her pretty face.

"Do you want to tell me about it?" I whisper huskily, still stroking her hair.

She sighs. "It's ok, just painful memories that I'd rather not talk about."

Hearing those words drive a dagger into my heart and I growl, "I want you to tell me everything."

"You won't like it."

I shake my head. "Maybe not, but I want to know, anyway. I deal with a lot of shit in my life, Flora, and now I want to deal with yours."

She pulls back and, seeing her eyes sparkling in the dim lighting of the room, rips the breath from inside me because I don't believe I have ever seen a woman as beautiful as the one in my arms.

"Why?" She smiles and, reaching up, strokes my face gently and as I lean into her hand, I say huskily, "Because you need someone to fight for you. To have your best interests at heart and to keep you safe."

"Why do you want to be the one to do that?"

She can't disguise the pleasure in her voice and the way her eyes lit up when I spoke. I'm shocked to experience a softening in my heart that I wasn't expecting as I hold this beauty in my arms. She is so vulnerable, so soft and delicate and for a man like me it's kryptonite and I whisper, "Because you need me."

She stares in wonder and, to my surprise, leans forward and gently touches my lips with hers. It takes me by surprise because usually any woman in my arms is there for a price and never looks at me the way Flora did just then. I recognized the yearning in her eyes that I know a lot about. She is as lost as I am, and I suppose that's why she appeals to me so much.

As her lips press against mine, it focuses my entire mind on her.

I freeze, reluctant to do anything to disturb this incredible moment and as she slides her hand inside my open shirt, she whispers, "I've never wanted to make love as much as I want to now."

Love. The one word that escapes anyone in my position and I reach out and grab it quickly before it disappears into the dense fog surrounding my soul. Just once I give into the desire to experience something so pure, I never believed it would happen to me.

"Does that shock you?" She whispers against my lips, and I laugh softly. "A little."

"Good." Her soft giggle dives deep inside my heart, and I wonder what she will do next. For some reason it has to come from her because the last thing I want is to scare this fragile creature away and as she gazes into my eyes, she blushes a little as she whispers, "Please Dom, show me what it's like, just once."

CHAPTER 27

FLORA

I don't even recognize myself anymore. Who is this wanton harlot who is begging to be fucked?

My vow of celibacy lies discarded at my feet, laughing up at me as I plead with the man in my arms to give me something I've never had. Love.

I've been fucked countless times and hated every second of it. However, somewhere in the far recesses of my mind, I always hoped that one day things would change for me. That somebody would see the girl, not the body and definitely not the whore. As soon as I met Domenico Ortega, I knew I wanted it to be him. Whatever happens after is something I will have to deal with, but now, in this delicious moment, I want to be normal for once in my life and experience what everyone else takes for granted.

I wait for his reaction, fully expecting him to laugh in my face, but I'm surprised when he smiles and his eyes glitter with an emotion I can't quite place.

Then he reaches out and unbuttons the shirt I dressed in and as the fabric slides off my shoulder, he whispers, "You are so beautiful, Flora."

My nipples stand erect as they crave his touch already, and I watch with a hunger that scares me a little as he leans back and removes his own shirt, revealing the warrior that hides behind.

I shiver as he stands and unfastens his belt, the memory of similar actions making my heart beat a little faster and he must sense my fear because he whispers, "I won't hurt you. I won't do anything you don't want me to. Say stop at any time and I will, no questions asked. Do you understand the rules, baby girl?"

The rules. Not really. Not these rules. I understand the ones that were drummed into me, courtesy of Mario and Diana. The ones where I put up, shut up and spread my legs. The one where I don't question and accept they are looking after me and to be grateful for that. Understand that the drugs they fed me were for my own comfort and to help keep me safe and the rule where I was their prisoner with no hope of release.

However, these rules are ones I can agree to, so I nod my head and prepare to discover what desire feels like.

As Dom's cock springs free, I can't look away and as he stands before me naked and so buff, I can't stop drooling over him, I reach out and tentatively touch the hard cock of a man who I'm guessing knows exactly what to do with it.

I glance up, almost as if I need permission, and say breathlessly, "May I?"

He touches the top of my head and nods. "This is all for you, baby. You're calling the shots now."

For some reason that makes me smile because when have I ever called the shots and as I dip my head, I press my lips against the throbbing phallus and his low hiss gives me all the power I need to open my mouth and slide it home.

As his cock fills my mouth, I close my eyes and relish the taste of him. Smooth, like velvet and the most delicious treat. I cup his balls and roll them around my hands, sucking gently to give him as much pleasure as I can possibly give.

He stands rigid before me and I take comfort from that, encouraging me to be bolder and suck harder, moving him gently in and out of my hungry lips.

I love the way it throbs in my mouth as he groans and says with a tortured sigh, "Carry on and it will be over before it began."

It makes me smile against the soft stretched skin and, disregarding his words, I carry on with my pleasure. Back and forth, sucking, licking and teasing, I give Domenico Ortega the blow job of his life.

As his salty cum spurts down my throat, I love every delicious drop of it coating me inside, knowing a part of him is inside my body at least. The fact he comes so hard tells me I did it right for him and that gives me a certain kind of satisfaction that I wasn't really expecting.

I pull back and run my finger around the outside of my wet lips, coating it in his juices before inserting it in my mouth, gazing at him as I suck the residue from my finger, causing him to growl, "Fuck me, can you be any more perfect?"

The way his eyes flash with danger excites me even more and I know I've driven him to edge and whatever happens now is all my fault and as he leans down and pushes me back against the silk sheets, I know that my wish is about to come true.

"I want to f…" he checks himself and smiles, "Make love to you, Flora. Is that ok with you?"

I nod shyly, loving the way those words make me feel and as he stares into my eyes and gently presses light kisses on my forehead, traveling down my face until they rest on my lips, it's as if I'm in heaven right now.

This is soft, sensual and the perfect beginning. If anything shocks me, it's that I want this to be the beginning of something, not the end.

He sucks my lip inside his mouth and bites down gently, causing me to moan softly as I wait for more. Then he travels down to my breasts, sucking each one into his wicked mouth, gently teasing the nipple until it throbs for his touch. His fingers fall between my legs and caress my clit, rubbing it softly, coaxing it to life. The wetness between my legs tells me something new. I want this. I ache for him and as his finger edges inside me, I cry out as a wave of longing shoots through my soul.

"I want to be inside you so badly, baby."

His low tortured murmur makes me whisper, "So, what are you waiting for?"

I'm surprised when he reaches across to the table and removes a condom from the drawer and as he rolls it quickly onto his cock, he says with a growl, "Until I prove to you I'm clean, I'll protect you."

My eyes widen because condoms have never been allowed to feature in my life. I was fed the contraceptive pill every day with no regard for my health at all. When I questioned it, Diana told me the men preferred unrestricted access, and I didn't have a say in it and so this gentle act of protection for my sake causes the tears to trickle down my face.

A strong thumb wipes them away and a husky voice whispers, "Do you want me to stop, baby girl?"

"No." I smile through my tears. "That's the last thing I want."

Just that simple consideration tells me things have now changed between us because he never gave that a thought when he fucked me hard against the wall.

As he positions his cock at my entrance, I swear I hold my breath and he growls, "I want the whole of you, Flora. I want to worship every inch of your body, but you must excuse me because the need to be inside you is putting all that on hold."

"I agree." I say with a soft sigh. "Fill me, Dom, make me your prisoner in every way. I'm begging you."

With a low groan, he slides in home, and I cry out as his large cock grazes against my slick walls. Knowing he's inside me is overwhelming, causing emotion to flare up inside me, giving me hope. His low hiss and 'Fuck me' makes me smile and as he pushes in deeper, my legs wrap around him and I cry out, "That is so good."

It's as if my words unleash the beast inside him as he powers in and out so hard he grabs my hair and holds it in his hand as he fucks me good and proper.

So, this is what it's like to be wanted. To be owned and to be, dare I say it, loved. It's undeniable the strong emotions he drags from inside me and I have never known a man so be so emotional during sex. He roars my name and worships my body, whispering sweet words in my ears before filthy ones take their place. He's like a wild animal as he marks his territory, and I am in no doubt about that at all.

I am his.

I knew that the minute I met him, although the thought of that terrified me then. Now it excites me way more than is healthy and as I claw his back like a wild animal, the sweat drips down between our bodies, merging us together as if it's eternal glue.

CHAPTER 28

DOM

What just happened? I'm lying on my back after the most intense orgasm of my life, with Flora's soft head resting on my chest, her fingers rubbing circles around the ink, gently pressing light kisses to my skin.

I'm not one for emotion but I'm buckling under it now as I hold on tight to the most perfect woman I have ever met in my life.

She turns and peers up at me from under her long, sexy lashes and as our eyes meet, she smiles sweetly. "Thank you."

"For what?"

I can't stop smiling and she giggles softly, "For showing me how good it can be."

Her words remind me of her past, which dampens my mood and with a sigh, I pull her face to mine and say gruffly, "Whatever happened before this moment stays in the past. Unless you want to talk about it, I won't ask."

I hate that her eyes fill with tears, and she whispers, "It's not a past I'm proud of, or even wanted."

She sighs. "I'm guessing we both have skeletons in our closets and must accept that."

She appears worried and I say huskily, "What's bothering you?"

"It's nothing." She lowers her eyes, and I grip her face tightly in my hand and force her to look at me. "I disagree. Tell me, you mustn't keep any secrets from me—ever."

For some reason, her eyes fill with tears and as they spill down her face, I lean in and lick them away, causing her to gasp and stutter, "I'm not sorry for begging you to make love to me but I can't shake the feeling that I'm not the person you see when you look at me."

Her words anger me far more than she probably intended them to, and I fist her hair, my grip tight and painful, causing her eyes to glitter with startled tears caused by pain.

"You think I see your sister?" I growl, hurt that she could even contemplate I would look at her sister the way I look at her.

Her slight nod sends me into a blind rage, and I hiss, "I hate that fucking bitch. But you, Flora…" I break off and relax my hold, pulling her fiercely toward me and cupping my hand protectively around the back of her head, tugging her against my chest as if comforting a broken woman.

"You mean everything to me, and until you feel the same, I'm the big bad wolf in your life who will never let you go."

I hate knowing that thought even entered her pretty little head and as she relaxes against me, I hope I've done enough to push it off the metaphorical cliff.

Love Diana? Not fucking likely.

As we lie entwined on my silken sheets, it strikes me that I've never had this. When I fucked women, they left soon after. There were no hugs, cuddles, or whispered words of affection. When I fucked Diana, it was usually a hurried affair against a wall or in a wooded area against a tree. There was none of this. It was just a dirty affair that probably only stood for one thing in Diana's mind. Control.

Rather than think about that woman, I say roughly, "Come. We need to shower. Gretchen has prepared food for us. We must eat."

Flora looks up in surprise and laughs. "I kind of forgot about food, but now you mention it."

She brushes her hair from her face and grins and just like that, a powerful emotion nearly knocks me senseless. Is this what love is like? Is this what I yearned for as a kid and heard of but never saw first-hand? More than anything, it pains me to step outside this bed because it will destroy the intimacy of the moment. Burst the bubble we have created and wrapped around us while we pretend that everything in our life is normal.

Feeling slightly bemused, I lead Flora to the shower, by holding her hand and gently pulling her after me and as we cling together under the raining jets, I hold her so tightly it even worries me. How has she become so necessary in my life so quickly? Is it because of her sister? Was she not far off the mark?

Part of me shoots that down in flames, yet there's also a part of me that knows why I fell in love so quickly with Diana. She was the woman I couldn't have. The one person who seemed to get me. To soothe rather than slay, and she was so good at that. She made me believe I was the most important person in her life, and I would have done anything to catch that feeling and keep it.

When I discovered she was doing the same to my brothers and yet chose to marry my father, we stepped back and saw through the light she blinded us with. We saw our enemy and I don't consider her anything but that now.

My thoughts turn to Flora and her needs. Since coming to Vegas and taking over my father's business interests, I have been the focus of attention for every well-meaning business in town. Subsequently, I am gifted many items in the hope of a favor or two and the designer outfits that hang in my his and hers closets are the result of that.

I've never had a need for the women's clothes before and yet for some reason I don't like the idea of Flora wearing them. I want to mark her and drench her with my scent in a primal instinct to claim what's mine. Those gifts belong to a past that has no business in my future, so I wrap my robe around her and tie it tightly, saying gruffly. "We'll arrange some clothes. You're moving in."

"Excuse me." She blinks in astonishment and seeing her pretty face flushed with the steam from the shower and the aftermath of sex, makes my heart physically ache.

"You heard me." My voice is gruff and scratchy because I won't allow her to leave, go anywhere away from me and what I want us to be, and she had better get with the program because my perfect life will be provided by this woman.

"I have an apartment. I have clothes. I have a life." Her voice raises indignantly, and I growl. "Had, Flora. You had all those things and look where it got you. You have been used all your life and allowed it to happen."

"You fucking bastard." Her hand slaps me hard around the face before I know what's happening, and her eyes flash as she screams. "I *allowed* it to happen! Allowed it! You know shit, Dom. You know nothing about my life, about how I begged to be set free, tried several times and have the scars to prove it."

"What scars?" I hiss, leaning closer, my earlier mood punched hard against the darkened walls of my room.

"This scar!" she screams and raises her hair, turning slightly and revealing a long-jagged scar to the side of her neck. She opens her robe and lifts her leg and points to one running inside her thigh, stopping short of her pussy.

"This one too. The one Mario gave me when I tried to escape one day. The one on my neck was when I tried again, and he strangled me before slicing a chunk of my skin." I stare at her in shock as she shouts, "Then there are the bruises, the bites, the scratches and the blood that has long since dried. The hair that was cut off and my head shaved. The nights I spent chained to his bed while he raped me on repeat. The nights I was locked in a cupboard while Diana and Mario fucked in the same room. The times the men they sold me to beat me to within an inch of my life and the drugs they fed me to keep me willing. You know nothing about how hard I tried to escape, and you know what, you don't deserve to, so fuck you, Domenico Ortega. You're exactly like them in keeping me your prisoner."

The rage blinds me as I lash out and grabbing her throat, I hold her hard against the wall and roar, "I am *nothing* like them. I fucking love you, Flora Corlietti, and the only reason you're here is so I can protect you and keep you safe."

As soon as the words leave my mouth, she stares at me in shock, and I can't believe I actually voiced them out loud. Hearing her speak of the horrors she's endured sent me into a violent rage that once again she bore the brunt of. Picturing those men defiling this beauty and Mario and Diana allowing it to happen makes me into one big fucking murdering bastard. What Diana did to me is nothing to what she did to her own blood, and I'm the bastard who just added to her pain.

With a roar, I pull Flora toward me and crush my lips to hers in a blind desire to wipe those words from existence. It hurts too much to picture her life and yet despite everything, she came out on the right side. As she kisses me back with a hunger that settles my heart, I vow to make it my life's work to make hers a happy one. To wash away the sins of her past and set us both free.

Panting for breath and flushed from emotion, we spring apart and just stare. Her alabaster skin is flushed, and her eyes sparkle and to my surprise she whispers, "You said you love me."

"What of it?" I turn away because to love is showing weakness and as she grips my hand, she turns me back to face her. "I want to love you, Dom." she says in a sad voice that cuts me deep.

"I want to know what it's like. To be the center of someone's world and make them the center of mine. To grow together and make plans—together."

She looks worried. "But this isn't love, not really, not yet. I want it to be. I *think* it could be, but how can it be? We've only just met."

Reaching out, I stroke her face that is fast becoming my favorite thing to do and whisper, "You're wrong, baby girl. In my heart I've been waiting for you all my life, which is why I am so scared of you walking away from me."

Now I've exposed my heart to this woman, I feel like a pitiful fool and yet the expression in her eyes makes me catch my breath.

"I'll stay." She says softly, seductively and calmly. "I will stay because I want to, and not because you are forcing me to."

She steps closer and this time her hand traces a light path down my face and as she cups my face in both hands, she kisses me long, luxuriously and slow. A sweet kiss of acceptance. A kiss of new beginnings and promises. To seal the deal we made in extreme anger, borne out of desperation. Flora accepts me for who I am, and I feel exactly the same.

CHAPTER 29

FLORA

I love this house. As I head toward the dining hall, I hope there is lots of food because I'm so hungry, I may pass out from lack of it right now. Either that or Dom's declaration of love back there. I never expected that. Lust maybe, but never love. He is silent beside me and is probably regretting even saying it, but in moments of passion the truth has a habit of coming out.

It warms my soul for once in my life, knowing that somebody wants me despite my past.

To break the silence, I say reverently, "You have an amazing home, Dom."

I'm not kidding either because I am overawed by the wealth here. The paintings that stare down from the walls wouldn't be out of place in an exhibition of masters. The sculptures on pedestals make it feel as if I'm walking around a museum and the antique furniture that gleams as we pass appears centuries old with so many stories to tell absorbed into their polished wood.

"It's all shit." He growls, making me say indignantly, "It most definitely isn't shit. I know my art and this stuff alone must have cost millions."

"If you're impressed by money, prepare to be dazzled." He laughs bitterly. "All of it earned by blood, ruining lives and bringing pain and misery into the world. Not so attractive now, is it?"

He appears in a strange mood and I'm guessing he's already regretting letting me poke inside his heart back there, and I shrug.

"Well, I love it, blood and all."

He turns and regards me through glittering eyes and just like that, I want him again.

He stops and pushes me against one of the huge paintings hanging on the paneled wall and holds my wrists above my head, so the robe falls open to the waist, my bare breasts exposed to anyone who cares to walk by.

"Would you like me to fuck you against this masterpiece? Would that turn you on? It can be arranged."

The desire lighting his eyes is like a flame to a moth and I say with a catch to my voice, "If you insist."

He leans in and bites down hard on my lip, causing me to groan out loud and only approaching footsteps cause him to pull back and wrap the robe firmly around my body.

I am pulled beside him the minute someone rounds the corner, and I recognize the man who stood beside him at the gala. Like Dom, this man has one hundred bastard tattooed in invisible ink on his forehead, and I watch as his dark amused eyes take in the scene.

He nods to me with respect and says lightly, "We need to talk after your meal."

Dom nods. "I'll call you when we're done." As the man makes to pass, Dom says quickly, "Pasquale, arrange for the closet to be filled next to mine. Miss. Corlietti is moving in. Arrange it."

The amused grin of his soldier tells me this man knows his boss on a more personal level than most, and he nods. "Consider it done."

As he moves off, Dom grips my hand in his and says tightly, "We should eat. You are a delicious distraction, baby girl, but we need our strength to continue this conversation in the bedroom."

He winks, which disarms me a little because the wickedness in this man is like paraffin on a flame to me. As I follow him inside a huge dining room, I note the immense table that stretches the length of the room and gasp, noting that it's set for two at one end.

"Why is this table so big?" I stare around me in amazement and Dom shrugs. "So I can fuck you on it and you won't fall off." It makes me laugh out loud and as he does the same, I stare in astonishment as it transforms his features. Gone is the scowling, dominant male and in his place is a sexy, handsome man who is very attractive to me right now.

Shaking his head, he pulls me after him and holds out my chair before taking the one by my side. As he pours me some coffee, I could be excused from believing everything about this situation is normal.

"Tell me about your life." I say before shoveling a mouthful of scrambled egg into it.

"You understand my life, Flora. I'm guessing your parents introduced you to it the day you were born."

"I guess." When I think of what that involves it saddens me because I know what it's like for the sons of the dons and their soldiers. A long hard lesson in loyalty and family. How to kill a man slowly and painfully and never get caught. Master the art of guns and knives and study intimidation. Yes, I know only too well what his life is like, and it hurts me inside.

"What about you, Flora? How come your parents aren't around?"

He eats but watches me through dark eyes, showcasing a thirst for knowledge of every detail of my life.

"I'd rather eat first because I don't want to lose my appetite." I say bitterly and he nods, knowing immediately what I will probably reveal.

For a while, we just eat. So ravenous it's really the most important thing right now and as soon as we can't eat another mouthful, he pours me another coffee and says firmly, "So, your parents."

"Dead." I shrug off any emotion that the word brings. "My mother was murdered by the don's wife when she caught her screwing her husband. Apparently, it wasn't the first time either. Then her husband did the same to her and started a war with Mrs. Matasso's family. My father stayed to fight that war and, by all accounts, ended up with a bullet in his brain as a thank you."

"What was that name?" Dom's eyes flash as he leans forward and I say with a shrug, Matasso. Giselle Matasso was the daughter of Don Vieri, and he wasn't too happy that his princess was murdered in cold blood."

"Is that what you think?"

Dom stares at me hard. "Who told you that?"

My heart drops like a leaded brick as I say faintly, "Diana."

Dom reaches for my hand and squeezes it gently. "Giselle and Carlos Matasso are alive and well and so, I believe, is your father."

The room spins as his words register and I'm only aware I'm still breathing when he holds a glass of water to my lips and says roughly, "Drink."

As the cool liquid slips down my throat, it brings me back to my senses and I say in shock. "What are you talking about? He can't be. How do you even know?"

Dom regards me with pity in his eyes and says gently, "I heard from the Don only last week when my father died. He sent his condolences and offered me his support. They have always been friends of the family and Pasquale knows your father well."

"I don't understand." I am so confused, and Dom lifts his phone and says curtly, "Could you come in here, please?"

He places it on the table and says with concern. "Pasquale will tell you everything. I can arrange for your father to meet you; he will have the answers."

I'm in shock and as Pasquale enters and takes the seat opposite me, Dom fills him in, and I can almost touch his pity from where I'm sitting.

"What do you want to know?" Pasquale says kindly and I glance at Dom, who nods reassuringly.

"Dom says you know my father, Ben Corlietti."

"I do. We work in the same field and often swap intelligence."

"Then he's alive."

"Of course." Pasquale appears concerned and I say pityingly, "Then why didn't he find me?"

As my question hangs in the room, I feel so betrayed. My father never came for me. He must have known we were alive, where we were and if he had come for us when my grandmother died, we would never have met Mario.

Dom's hand slips into mine and squeezes it reassuringly. "He must have had his reasons."

"And my mother? Is she also alive?"

My voice is rough and both men glance at me with pity, causing me to stand.

"I can't deal with this. I want to see him."

I glare at Pasquale. "Call him."

Dom nods and Pasquale stands.

"I'll call him now."

As he leaves the room, the fire dances inside me, burning away the pain, leaving me ready to do battle and demand an explanation. I'm aware of Dom watching me and snap. "It's as if they betrayed me."

The tears burn and I'm grateful when his strong arm wraps around me and pulls me against his hard chest. He drops a light kiss on the top of my head and whispers, "I've got you, Flora. I'm here and on your side. Always."

It's so good knowing that and as I cling to him, I harden my heart because there can be no acceptable reason why my father abandoned us.

CHAPTER 30

DOM

Flora is in shock, and I don't blame her because discovering your life is built on a lie is hard for anyone to take. As I guide her back to my bedroom, sex is the furthest thing from my mind and as I walk into my closet, she follows me inside.

"What now?" She slumps onto the bench in the middle of the dark paneled space that has every single item of clothing a man like me needs. Mainly, several black handmade suits and silk shirts. Gym gear and t-shirts and the odd dress shirt and tuxedo.

My watch collection is impressive, and I have several belts all lined up like soldiers. I have everything money can buy, but I would give it all up to spend a life in love with the dejected woman whose whole world has imploded in a spectacular way.

Grabbing a sweater from the shelf, I hold it out to Flora and say gruffly, "Here. This should fall to your knees. Your clothes should arrive later today, but you may be more comfortable in this than the robe."

She nods gratefully and as the robe drops to the floor

revealing her perfect body, I push away my desire because sex is definitely not what she needs right now.

More of a distraction than anything, I reach for her hand and smile.

"Let's get some fresh air. I think we could use some."

"In bare feet." She peers down at hers and I smile.

"There are some boots by the garden door. I'm sure you will find a suitable pair among them."

As we head downstairs, Flora is quiet beside me, and I almost wish I'd said nothing because I hate seeing her in pain.

We head to the garden door in silence, both of us with too many thoughts swirling around our head in this fast-moving situation.

After searching for a suitable pair of boots for Flora, we head outside and take a deep breath of fresh air and as we head to the lake at the far corner of my estate, it feels good to be away from the toxic air of the mansion.

"You're a lucky man." Flora says wistfully and I smile, gripping her hand tightly. "I am."

Raising it to my lips, I kiss it reverently, wondering indeed how I got so lucky.

"This place is perfect. Although it's a fortress you wouldn't know it standing here."

She peers into the distance and all we can see is nature stretching out before us, carefully constructed by the best landscaping designer in the business to disguise the security that is just about everywhere.

"I want you to be safe here, baby girl."

I really mean that and Flora smiles, and it's good to note a little happiness in her expression.

"I do. I shouldn't, but for some reason I always accepted I'd be safe here. Ironic really, when at first you wanted to kill me." Her soft laugh makes me smile and takes me back to the moment I first laid eyes on her.

"You're right, I did want to kill you, but it wasn't you, baby. You know that."

"Diana." She shivers, reminding how that name burns like acid on your tongue.

"I'm so afraid of her, Dom."

I wrap my arm around her and pull her close to my side and attempt to unlock another piece of Flora's missing past.

"How did you escape them?"

"I took a chance." She sighs heavily and her pinched face tells me this is not going to be a happy tale.

"Mario had arranged a road trip, as he called it. It meant we were being shipped out to a house somewhere in the middle of nowhere to entertain paying customers."

I was right. This is not a happy tale, but I grit my teeth and say nothing.

"When we got there, I was locked in a room with about six other women, all there for the same reason. Diana was with Mario as usual, no doubt arranging her own private party with the most powerful man there."

She sighs heavily. "Unlike me, the girls were willing, excited even, anticipating a huge pay out and enough drugs to feed their habit. You see, that's what Mario loved. Drugs, women, and alcohol mixed with depraved sexual acts that would make a whore blush."

I'm not sure I want to hear any more of this sadistic story, but Flora says in a dull voice. "One by one, we were selected to wait in a room upstairs. Apparently, the men weren't keen on being seen by others and wanted privacy to carry out their sordid act with no witnesses. It didn't bode well. While I was waiting, I paced around and heard a commotion in the room next door. It sounded as if there were several people in there and then my door opened and a man ran inside, sweating like a pig. I asked what was wrong, and he told me to shut the fuck up and pretend he was here all along. I watched him snort some cocaine; he was agitated and didn't even appear to remember I was there. In his haste, he had left the door open and when he went to the bathroom, I seized the opportunity and ventured outside."

She shivers at the memory and whispers, "As I passed the room, I saw one of the girls had collapsed on the floor. At first, I thought she was unconscious, but when I went to help her, I could tell she was dead."

"How?" I growl and Flora says sadly, "There was a needle sticking out of her arm. I'm guessing they tried to drug her, and she reacted to that. I could tell she was gone. Her empty eyes stared up at me and there was no pulse or heartbeat. Then I noticed she was wearing a wig, and I spied her purse on the floor by the bed. I hate saying this, but I wasted no time and grabbed her wig and pulled it over my hair and took her purse. Then I edged my way downstairs, thanking God everyone was busy partying and paying no attention. I made my way into a room on the ground floor and escaped through the window, heading for the bushes before anyone could notice me."

She looks so proud of her escape my heart fills with pride for my brave girl and she laughs softly. "I walked to the nearest town. It took me hours, but I have never felt so free. I kept to the shadows and if a car approached, I hid until it passed. When I reached the town, I went directly to the bus station and hopped on the first bus out of town. Luckily, there was money in the girl's purse, and I used it to buy my ticket to freedom."

She turns and grins and for some reason, a surge of love washes over me as I register the excitement in her eyes.

She laughs softly. "I did it. I pretended to be Maisy Edwards and headed to Vegas. I was certain nobody would discover me here and my first stop when I arrived was the convent. You know what happened there and when I left, I used Maisy's name to rent an apartment and look for work, which I found in the Barrington gallery working with Desdemona Gray."

We reach the lake and I pull her down onto the grassy bank and sling my arm around her shoulder, loving how she rests her head on my shoulder. "This is nice." She says sweetly, and I squeeze her a little tighter. "It is."

My thoughts return to her story, and I say with confusion, "Then why give your name as Flora Corlietti on my guest list if you were known as Maisy Edwards?"

"Because Desdemona did some checking and told me that apparently, I was dead."

She shivers. "Turns out my new employer wasn't shy of turning my problem to her advantage and she told me she would protect me; it would be our secret. She said it would be better to use my own name in case the authorities thought I had something to do with Maisy's death and I could hide out in Vegas and start again."

I remember the phone call that Desdemona received from Diana and wonder if I should tell Flora about it. However, I decide against it because she has dealt with so much already in such a short space of time and if she knew that Diana discovered where she is, she would be on the next bus out of here, protection or not.

We must sit by the lake for well over an hour, just kissing, talking, and making plans. I can't remember the last time, if ever, that I felt like this. I'm so happy, so free and at this moment in time I am sure nothing on earth can break us apart.

As it turns out, I was completely wrong about that.

CHAPTER 31

FLORA

I have never been so happy. Being here with Dom is surprising in the best possible way. If anything, I fall in love with him at the edge of the lake and when he stands and tugs me with him, I know exactly where I want to go next.

We head back to the mansion with our arms around each other and chat like any normal human beings. As we approach the garden door, Pasquale is there to meet us and something about the expression on his face makes my heart stop beating.

"Boss."

He addresses Dom and there is a dark expression on his face as he says in a low voice, "You have a visitor."

"Who is it?"

Dom doesn't release me from his arms and Pasquale winces as he says in a low voice, "Your stepmother."

If Dom wasn't holding me up right now, I would have fallen and my legs almost give out on me as he hisses, "What the fuck? Who let her in?"

"She's in the visitor's room. Enrico is guarding her with Vittori and Ryan on the outside."

Dom glances at me and the retribution that flares in his eyes gives me hope at least, and he nods toward Pasquale. "Take her to my room and stay with her. Lock the door and only open it for me."

"No!" I glare at him furiously. "I want to see her. I'm not afraid of her anymore."

"It doesn't look like that." He says with an arch of his brow, and I attempt to stop my voice from shaking as I whisper, "Please, Dom. I need to face my fears."

He nods and says with a grim determination. "Then we settle this together. I won't let her hurt you again."

Pasquale falls into step behind us and as we approach the house, my nerves are rattling as I prepare to face my demons.

Dom leads us to a door not far from the entrance and I note the two soldiers standing on guard outside and shiver. Their menacing expressions tell me this is serious and as Dom approaches, he nods, and the door opens as if by magic. I'm grateful for his strong hand holding mine as we head inside the room as one unit and I see her standing by the window, looking as if she's come for tea, not to wreck my life.

"Flora." She stumbles toward me, her arms outstretched as if she's fearful for me and needs to check I'm ok. "I was so worried. Where have you been? What happened to you? It's all my fault."

Before she can reach me, Dom pulls me behind his massive body and snarls, "Back off, bitch. Flora doesn't want to see you and neither, as it happens, do I."

She stops short and stares at us with confusion swirling in her large, baby blue eyes. As actresses go, Diana has always been an outstanding one, and she wipes a tear away and whispers, "Dom. It's me, Diana. You know how I feel about you. Please don't use my sister to get revenge on me."

She blinks as if she's innocent as fuck and says in a soft

voice, "What happened between us was special. You may not believe me, but it was always you. Your father, he, well, he forced me to marry him, and I was scared, not only for myself but also for you."

Dom openly laughs and snarls, "It was always me you say. What about my two brothers, oh and my father as well? You are convincing, but you forget I know you, Diana, and this is all an act, as much as your concern for your sister."

"I love my sister." Her voice is fierce and to any stranger listening, they would think Dom was being cruel and heartless, but we both understand what this woman is capable of, and her words are wasted on us.

I step from behind my protector and say sadly, "Please leave. You are no longer my sister. What you did to me was inexcusable and I will never forgive you."

Diana peers around in confusion and then takes a step back, her hand flying to her throat. "No! Please tell me it's not true."

"What isn't true?" Dom laughs out loud.

"The two of you—together."

Dom shakes his head and pulls me closer. "Your eyes don't deceive you. I found a better woman that's worth my attention and there is no place for you in our lives, so turn around and get the fuck out of my house."

The rage inside me is about to rain retribution down like bullets and suddenly, she softens her voice and tears fall down her cheeks like diamonds.

"Please help me."

She glances around her and whispers, "I need your help, Dom. Mario is behind everything. He is blackmailing me to take over your father's business, and I have no choice but to play along."

She gazes between us and sobs, "I never wanted to involve you, Flora. Mario forced me to include you in his wicked world. Please help me escape. You did it; you could help me too."

I make to speak, and Dom claps loudly and snorts. "You almost had me fooled there, but I shouldn't be surprised, you always were a master at that."

I watch in fascination as her eyes narrow and she hisses, "I want to speak to you alone, Dom."

"No!" I object, and she laughs derisively.

"Look at you, Flora, desperate to be relevant. You were *never* relevant, always controlled by someone, and that hasn't changed. Do you really think Dom wants you?"

She laughs in my face. "It's *me* he wants. Has always wanted and you are the poor imitation who will do until he works out a way to make that happen and for your information, unless you haul your ass back home with me, you're heading straight to jail for murder."

I step back and her eyes gleam as she throws threats like punches. "If you think I'm leaving you here with him, you're mistaken. There's a cab waiting and if I'm not in it, Mario is waiting to report me missing. He also has everything he needs to file charges against you, Flora, for the murder of Maisy Edwards."

She turns to Dom. "The same goes for you. I know you both stole my money and I want it back. You have twenty-four hours to return it, and if you fail, you will be arrested for the murder of Senator Billings. We have enough evidence to send you down for life, so nice try people, but I win."

I am so afraid because I know my sister, and these are not empty threats. Then Dom steps forward with a menacing glare and snaps, "Nothing you say or do can change our minds. You have fuck all against us and like your heart your threats are empty. So, fuck off, darlin' and tell your puppet master to watch his back."

Without another word, Dom pulls me out of the room and snarls to Pasquale, "Throw the bitch out."

Diana shouts after us, "You'll regret this, Dom. Twenty-four hours. That's all you've got and don't say I didn't warn you."

As the door slams behind her, my heart bangs mercilessly inside me as Dom pulls me up the stairs with him, angrier than I have ever seen him before.

CHAPTER 32

DOM

I am furious. Both with myself, my staff and Diana. How dare she come into my home and threaten us? She has the nerve of the devil and would probably even try her luck with him.

When she threw her threats out in the open, it made my blood boil and more than anything, I want to end this once and for all and watch her and that despicable man she follows like a puppy dog get what they deserve at my hand.

Flora is shocked. I noticed that the moment she set eyes on her sister and the thought of sending her back to those sadists is a joke. Not fucking likely. Not happening and as soon as we reach the bedroom, I pull Flora down onto the bed and wrap my arms around her as if I'll never let her go.

"Did that really happen?" Flora says fearfully and I hiss, "Unfortunately it did."

"What if she's right? We could go to prison."

I hate the fear in her voice and snap, "That will never happen. Trust me, baby, I will make it all go away."

"How?"

"By calling in favors; you know how it works."

She falls silent and I hate what I must do next, but I have no choice.

"Listen, baby." I pull her face to mine and kiss her lightly on the lips. "There's something I want you to hear before I sort this shit out."

"What is it?" Her eyes are wide and fearful, and I relax my frown and whisper, "When I look at you, I see the woman I love. Flora Corlietti. Not her damaged sister, Diana. Do you understand that?"

The relief in her expression is the only answer I need, and she whispers, "Thank you. That's good to know."

I say with a rough edge to my voice. "That woman is nothing like I imagined her to be. I fell in love with the idea, not the person. You, however, you are all those things I was looking for and a lot more besides and if you can bear the pain being with me brings, I will fight to the death to make you happy, whoever stands in our way."

"You want me to stay?"

"Of course, I fucking want you to stay. Not as my prisoner, though." I laugh softly. "You see, Flora, I want you in my life as my lover, my best friend, and the mother of my future children. To make your life a happy one and torture your demons for pleasure. Nothing will hurt you all the time I am by your side, but you need to put your trust in me. Can you do that, baby girl? Can you give your soul to the devil in return for that?"

Her smile tells me what I needed before the words confirm it and she says shyly, "I'm going nowhere, Dom. You see, I never expected to fall so madly for a man who chained me to a dungeon wall within minutes of meeting me. Who imprisoned me in his bedroom and yet was the perfect gentleman despite that. My only concern was you wanted my sister, not me, but you've already smashed that fear into dust at my feet. If we can get through this, we can get through anything all the time we have each other's backs."

"Then it should be easy." I wink, causing her to giggle. "Now we need to rid ourselves of the two people who deserve everything coming to them."

I almost don't get to finish my sentence before Flora leans forward and presses her lips to mine. This time there's an urgency inside her that I can't ignore.

As she slides off my shirt, I pull the sweater over her head and love how her skin feels under my rough hand. With the other hand I push down my pants and kick them to the floor before lowering Flora back on the bed and kissing her with a hunger that never goes away.

Then I gently worship her body with light kisses, traveling down until I reach Nirvana.

As I reach her pussy, I take a long, leisurely swipe and love the taste of the woman who has attacked my heart like a wrecking ball. Her soft gasps of pleasure spur me on and as I tease, coax and lick her orgasm out from inside her, I relish the scream of ecstasy that explodes on my tongue. I make short work of sheathing my throbbing cock and waste no time in thrusting inside the wet heat that I created, loving how tight she is as she squeezes my cock gently, causing a burst of pleasure to vibrate through my entire body.

Her legs wrap around my waist, and she pulls me in deeper and as I push in mercilessly, I stare into her eyes, pledging my whole heart to this incredible woman in my arms. Somehow, this feels different. Almost like a pledge, a promise and a contract we are drawing up. This is the rest of our lives and now I've found her, I'm not letting anyone get in the way of that.

* * *

LATER THAT AFTERNOON, Flora's closet order arrives and as I leave her to enjoy unpacking it, I head to my den. I have work to do, and it won't wait any longer.

The first thing I do is call my brother Leonardo, and he answers almost immediately.

"Dom."

"Leo."

I sigh. "I had a visitor earlier today."

"An unwelcome one, I take it."

"Our stepmother."

His sharp intake of breath reveals his feelings on that, and he says darkly, *"Interesting. I take it she wants her money back."*

He says with interest. *"What was her trump card?"*

"Murder charges. One for me concerning Senator Billings and one against her sister if she didn't return with her."

"She's still there?"

"She's going nowhere."

I hate his sigh of exasperation and hate the words from his lips even more as he says roughly, *"She's not Diana."*

"You're fucking right about that. Flora is nothing like her damaged sister and she's going nowhere."

"What murder charge have they got on her?"

I fill him in, and he growls, *"Fucking bitch. Using her own sister. How low can she go?"*

He says quickly, *"What are your thoughts on Eliza?"*

"In what respect?"

"The reason she ran."

Despite my own reservations, I snarl, "That she wanted her freedom. Didn't like being told what to do; was a spoiled brat."

"So, what our father and Diana told you."

His words silence me and as I think about it and knowing what they are capable of, my world collapses under the weight of responsibility.

189

"You think they did something to her?"

"I do."

Leo hisses, *"It's probable that our sister died running from them. There's also the explosion that killed them both. What do you know about that?"*

"That it worked."

The silence stretches between us as we contemplate something that never occurred to us and Leo snarls, *"I'll do some digging. If we are going to win against them, we need to line up our soldiers. The money was the first step. Now we need to discover their weakness."*

"Have you heard from Matteo? He was already searching for Mario's weakness."

"He's working on it as we speak."

"And the will. Have you managed to get a copy?"

There's a brief silence before he says abruptly, *"I'm working on it. Leave it with us, you have the money and her sister and it's up to us to play our part too. Stay strong and inform me of anything that comes up."*

"Will do."

He hesitates and for some reason I am reluctant to end the call and he says with a slight edge to his voice, *"Dom, I..."*

"I know."

"You do?" He sighs heavily. *"We were played, every fucking one of us, but we're so pig-headed none of us will admit that. For the record, I have no hatred toward either of you now. I've cooled down and realize where the blame lies."*

There's a brief silence before he says, *"This woman, Flora."*

"What about her?" I growl and he laughs softly.

"Keep her. She's good for you."

"You don't need to tell me what I already know."

This time I do cut the call, but it leaves me with a smile on my face. It's as if the storm clouds are clearing and I watch the light filtering in. Suddenly, my life isn't as lonely as it once was.

I have my brothers back and now the most amazing woman on the planet. It's as if everything I wanted is coming good and yet there's one knife twisting in my heart that will probably never go away. My sister and the real reason she ran straight into hell.

CHAPTER 33

FLORA

I'm like a kid in a candy store. This stuff must have cost hundreds of thousands of dollars because there is a huge box from every designer going and it's all in my size.

As I unwrap tissue filled boxes and draw out beautiful silk dresses and soft cashmere sweaters, I sigh with pleasure, trying it on like a kid playing dress up.

Designer shoes made from soft Italian leather that match silk cocktail dresses and floor-length evening gowns. Handbags of every shape and color and jewelry so beautiful it takes my breath away.

I am surrounded by luxury and living every woman's dream and as distractions go, I can't fault this one. Dom asked me to trust him and I'm doing exactly that because I no longer want to think of the trouble we could be in all the time I'm safe in Dom's home.

It takes me three hours to organize my closet and I've never spent so long looking at clothes. I've never had money to buy nice things. Most of the dollars I earned at the gallery paid for my apartment and food. This is extreme wealth and I'm struggling to deal with that and when Dom finds me, I am trying on the most amazing lingerie that I have ever seen.

As I spin around admiring myself in the floor-length mirror, I catch his reflection as he leans against the door, regarding me with a wicked glint in his eye.

Our eyes meet and as I turn, he drags his gaze the length of me and I know exactly where his mind is.

"Do you like it?" I smile and turn, loving the lust that sparkles in his eyes.

"What do you think?"

I watch as he shifts off the wall and heads further into the room, stopping to grab a silk scarf from the floor.

"What…?"

I make to speak, and he presses his finger to his lips, effectively silencing me and spins me around, so my back is to him and binds my wrists behind my back with the scarf.

Then he pushes me against the mirror and with one hand around my neck, he lifts my face to see him in the reflection. The slightly crazed look in his eyes turns me on and as I hear the zipper on his pants lower, I catch my breath as his cock teases my entrance and he growls, "Watch me fuck you, baby."

He pushes me harder against the mirror, my breasts pushed against the glass dressed in the finest silk. I note the flush to my face and the desire burning in my eyes as he edges inside with nothing between us.

"You're…"

I make to speak, and he grins. "Bareback."

He pushes in hard, causing me to hit the mirror and then lifts my face to watch him as he thrusts in deeper and faster, fucking me from behind. It's so erotic. I'm dressed in nothing but scraps of silk that are held together with fine lace, the man behind me wearing a designer suit unzipped for only one purpose. It's as if he's using me and yet I know it's nothing like that. He wants me, any way he can get it, and his tortured groans add to mine as he hammers me to the glass.

The white heat that explodes around me causes me to scream his name and as he fists my hair and comes hard, I love his thick, sticky cum, filling my drenched pussy. Some would say this is fucking, not making love, but I disagree. This is our kind of love, and I wouldn't want it any other way.

* * *

THE CLOSET IS RUINED. For the next hour, Dom fucks me on the floor, against the wall, on a bed of designer clothes and bent over the velvet covered bench. I straddle him, suck his cock and dance for him, and it's as if we're in our own private room in a sex club. Nothing else exists outside this room. This is our time to seal a deal that will be sealed many more times before we're done. I can't get enough of him and it's obvious he feels the same, and it's only when his phone vibrates that he stops and groans.

"Sorry baby, duty calls." He pulls on his pants that are lying in a crumpled heap on the floor and throws me a wicked grin.

"Maybe you should clean up and then call Gretchen and ask her to feed you."

"What about you?" I smile provocatively from my position on the floor, my legs up on the bench crossed at the ankles, completely naked except for the diamond necklace he insisted on me wearing while he fucked me.

"I'll grab something on the go."

"You're leaving?" Now I'm anxious and pull myself up, reaching for a silk robe that we robbed of its tie.

"Just work, baby. I have a meeting arranged at my casino. I won't be late, but I'll leave you well guarded. Enjoy the rest while you can get it. I'm keen to carry on with this closet warming party on my return."

He grins and heads out of the door, leaving me with an emptiness inside that I wasn't expecting. However, as I glance around the white marbled interior of a room fit for a princess, a warm tingle spreads through me. It feels like home. *He* feels like home and if this is going to work, I need to make this my home.

* * *

It takes me another hour to clean up, shower and then pull on some sweatpants and a sweatshirt, pushing my feet into sliders and heading off to find Gretchen. There's no need to dress up, so I may as well be comfortable.

Wandering the hallway of Dom's fabulous mansion is an experience I never thought I'd be doing, and I stare in awe at the amazing art and objects that decorate a space that must have cost millions to produce.

I've always been impressed with history. I'm not sure where this love of mine came from. Probably because I have been surrounded by it all my life. I grew up in a house much like this one. The Matasso mansion, where my father served his master well and was rewarded with an apartment for his family. It turns out the Don had an ulterior motive where that was concerned, and the knowledge that he shared an intimacy with my mother is a difficult memory to deal with.

I used to listen to the arguments through the walls. The sounds of crying and pleas that I always thought were down to my father. I never believed for one second that it was my mother who was the cause. Then again, surely my father must have known. Did he turn the other way and pretend it wasn't happening?

There are so many answers I need from him, but the most important one is why he abandoned us? He should have been better than that, and yet he wasn't.

The anger tightens like a ball of bad memories inside me, and I prepare to fling it at my father if I ever get the chance.

But not now. Not today because today is the beginning of the rest of my life with Domenico Ortega.

I never thought I'd be *that* woman. The one who accepted this life and craved it, even. That was always my sister and yet are we so different. I fucking hope we are because if I turn out anything like her, I may as well end it now before someone does it for me.

The fact she is walking around with a target on her back doesn't concern me in the slightest. If anything, I hope they get a direct hit because that woman deserves it. In fact, the more painful the better when I think back on what she put me through the past few years.

With a sigh, I push everything away as I head into the kitchen to find the housekeeper, Gretchen. Apart from her curious glances when she serves us, I have yet to make her acquaintance.

She stares up as I enter the room and smiles curiously.

"Hi, um, Gretchen. I'm sorry, but Mr. Ortega told me to ask you if there is anything I can grab to eat."

I smile because I'm more nervous about meeting her than I would have believed, and yet she just smiles kindly and nods to the stool set against the marble countertop.

"Of course, I'll fix you a sandwich, or would you prefer something hot? Neither is too much trouble."

"A sandwich will be lovely, thank you."

As I perch on the edge of the stool, she regards me with a fascinated curiosity, which makes me squirm a little before she laughs. "I'm sorry, my dear. I've made you uncomfortable. It's just that you're the first woman I've ever met here."

"Seriously?" I stare at her in astonishment, and she shrugs. "Mr. Ortega doesn't like guests."

"But the Gala?"

I'm confused and she shrugs. "Once a year, he opens his door to keep the men that run this town happy. He raises money for charity but never stays longer than an hour, leaving Pasquale to deal with the guests on his behalf."

"So, he's a recluse then." I chuckle, causing her to smile.

"I suppose you could call him that." She begins preparing the sandwich and I say with curiosity, "Have you worked for him long?"

"Two years. He's a good employer. He pays well and keeps out of my way, so I have no complaints."

"I'm glad to hear it." I smile and then picture the dungeon that's not far away and wonder if she knows about that and his dark preferences.

"I guess he works from here, too." I know I'm prying and regret it when her face falls. "I don't know anything about his work, Miss…"

She arches her brow and I mumble, "Flora, please."

"Well, Flora, if I can give you one word of advice concerning Mr. Ortega, it's to ask no questions. If he wants you to know, he'll tell you. It's best that way."

Now I know Gretchen is discreet I relax a little. Any secrets inside these walls will not spill from her lips and that includes my own. It settles my nerves and makes me comfortable and, for the first time since I arrived, I relax. I'm home.

CHAPTER 34

DOM

As always, we travel in convoy and head to my casino in the center of Vegas. Business is good and for the most part trouble free, but there has been talk of my manager not playing by the rules that has irritated me.

Sylvester Brennan has run my casino for ten years, which makes me wonder if something has happened to change his loyalty. Thousands of dollars aren't making it into my bank account and after a spy operation, we discovered he was pocketing the cash.

"Any news on his family?" I ask Pasquale, who sits beside me and frowns at his phone.

"His wife left him last year and took the kids with her. They live in Miami and word is she's got a new boyfriend."

"Anybody we know?"

"Hardly, he's a doctor. I'm guessing she's had enough and wants a respectable life for once."

"It happens." I shrug, wondering how I'd feel if Flora decided this wasn't for her and took up with an accountant or something like that. I hate the mere thought of that and snap, "His bank account. What's the story there?"

"Overdrawn."

I raise my eyes.

"He's been in the red since she left."

"She cleaned him out?" I'm mildly interested, but Pasquale just laughs. "He has an expensive habit."

Now I sit up because if he's pissing my money on drugs and women, there is no hope for his future, meaning he hasn't got one when I get my hands on him.

Pasquale shrugs. "He's a victim of circumstance. Addicted to gambling and streetwalkers."

"You're kidding." I stare at him in astonishment because Sylvester could fuck any of the staff if he wanted to. He's a man of power in this town and the women that flock to the casinos would be turned on by that.

"Why is he paying for something he could get for free? It doesn't make sense."

Pasquale laughs out loud and says with a wicked grin, "Apparently, he thrives on the danger. He fucks them in dark alleys where anyone could see them. The dirtier the whore, the harder he comes."

I'm not sure what to think about that and sigh heavily. "The gambling. Where?"

"Private games in rival casinos. House parties and clubs. He's in deep."

I lean back against the leather upholstery and exhale sharply. "How much?"

"Two hundred thousand dollars."

"Fuck."

Now there is no way back for Sylvester Brennan. Unless he has an extremely good card up his sleeve, his death is about to be a long and painful one.

* * *

WE HEAD into my casino like avenging demons and as the customers part to let us through, I set my mood to bastard. My soldiers surround me as we move through a gambler's paradise in search of the one man who is about to learn that gambling is extremely bad for your health.

The stench of greed and desperation fill my lungs and gives me the energy I need to deal with a man who should have known better. *Don't piss in your own back yard.* It's the golden rule, one that he's broken and is about to pay dearly for.

We head to the manager's office on the top floor and the casino security turn the other way as we pass through them. They know who really calls the shots around here and work for me. My loyal soldiers follow me and, as we reach the office, take up their positions guarding every exit and without a cursory knock, I slam the door open, much to the surprise of my manager who is currently balls deep in a woman who is barely legal.

She screams as I growl, "Get the fuck out of here!"

Sylvester stutters, "Mr. Ortega, I'm…"

"Fucked, Sylvester. You're fucked, which is ironically what we interrupted."

The girl grabs her cheap clothes, telling me she's something that blew in off the street and without a glance back, she heads out of the office to the walk of shame outside.

"Please…" Sylvester stutters as he zips his now flaccid cock back into his pants. "I can explain."

I kick out the chair opposite his desk and sit astride it as my men move behind him and force him back in his chair.

"Explain what Sylvester?"

"The money." His eyes scan the room as if he's possessed and he whispers, "My wife cleaned me out. She's demanding more and the only way I can keep her off my back is to pay up. You see…" He licks his lips nervously. "She knows all the dirt on your empire and is blackmailing me. Said she'd go to the cops and bring us all down. I did what I could to protect you. I didn't involve the casino. I used other establishments to try to keep her happy."

He is flailing around for excuses, which is all they are, and I exhale sharply. "So, the fact she's now replaced you with a doctor isn't enough."

Sylvester turns ashen.

"The new life she has in Miami in a modest home with her kids at the local school isn't good enough?"

I lean forward and glare at him fiercely. "You're treating me as a fool, Sylvester, and we both know how much I hate that."

He turns another interesting shade and clutches his chest.

"Please, help me, I'm…"

"Having a heart attack. Go ahead, I'll watch."

I lean back and fold my arms, and the wild glint in his eyes is not new to me. They all wear that look when their time's up and to add more drama to the occasion, I take out my gun and spin the barrel in my hands.

"Two hundred thousand dollars, Sylvester. That is the cost of your life."

"Please, no."

He looks as if he's about to faint and I drive the knife in deeper. "No? Perhaps you'd rather I waste your wife instead of you. Your kids perhaps?" I lean forward and snarl. "Or the whole fucking family."

"No, please, not my family. I'm begging you."

I glance up and catch Pasquale's eye and he grins, obviously enjoying the show, as he always does.

I turn my attention back to the manager and growl, "On your knees."

He hesitates, and that's all it takes for my men to reach out and force him down on the floor before me and I take the gun and hold it to his temple. "Any last words, Sylvester? An apology perhaps?"

He begins to shake. "I have information."

"I'm listening." I press the barrel in deeper and he shouts, "Word on the street is you're being framed for murder."

"You think I don't know that?" I yawn loudly. "Keep going."

"It's true. I've got evidence on the cameras."

I pull the gun away and snap, "Show me."

He rushes to his feet and heads to his computer, frantically pressing the keyboard until he says with relief, "Here. It was last week."

He spins the monitor around and I stare with interest at the picture of the detective playing a game of poker. That's not unusual. He often gambles here but never to extremes. Most of Vegas plays the tables, but it's who else is at the table that interests me more.

I nod to Pasquale, who peers closer, and I know he has noticed it too as I growl, "This is your evidence?"

Sylvester nods vigorously. "Keep watching."

He forwards the recording and I stare as the detective stands and throws in his hand, gathering his chips before draining his glass and without another look, heads for the exit. The other person at the table does the same and follows him out.

Sylvester says with excitement. "Now look."

He taps on his computer and the next image of the two men is at the staff exit out the back of the club. Their faces are turned away from the camera, but it's obviously them. As Sylvester turns up the volume, there is no doubting whose voice it is, even though the words are too low to comprehend. Mario Bachini.

I share a look with Pasquale, who stares back with a grim determination. A silent message passes between us because that man is walking with the biggest fucking target on his back right now. The fact he was even in one of my establishments is like acid pouring into my heart, and the fact I wasn't even notified has sealed Sylvester's fate.

"When was this?" I snarl and Sylvester says confidently, certain he's done enough to get him off the hook.

"Three days ago."

"And you're telling me this now?"

I bite back and the fear increases in his eyes as he senses he's only made things worse.

"I... I..." he stutters, but I push his excuses aside and growl, "Sit down and write these words on your desk blotter."

He starts to shake as he lifts a pen and I say slowly, "I'm sorry."

He lifts his eyes in confusion. Probably wondering if that's all it will take and as he pens the words, I hiss, "Sign your name."

As he does so with a flourish, I nod to Pasquale, who wastes no time at all in pressing his gun in Sylvester's hand, raising it quickly and using his own finger to blow his fucking brains out before he even knew it was happening.

As the shot finds its mark, I stare at the wasted life before me, his blood dripping down onto the polished wooden floor.

Then I stand and without looking back, we all exit the room as if we'd never been there.

* * *

WE MAKE the short journey down in the elevator to the basement and as the door opens, it appears I have a welcoming committee because standing waiting with a team of officers is Detective Woznowski. Before I can ask what he wants, he steps forward and says loudly, "Domenico Ortega. I am arresting you for the murders of Senator Billings and Desdemona Gray. You do not…"

As he rattles off the caution, I whisper to Pasquale, "Protect Flora. Take her to the retreat."

He nods and as the cops slip the cuffs on my wrists, I know exactly what I must do next.

CHAPTER 35

FLORA

It's good to chat about normal things with Gretchen. I help her clean up and ask her about her family. Normal stuff that calms the fear building inside me that won't go away after Diana's visit.

The fact I am in love with Dom is the sweetest antidote. Through all this madness grew something pure, and it has been totally unexpected.

It must only be less than an hour after Dom left that one of the soldiers heads into the kitchen with the detective we met after the Gala.

Gretchen appears as surprised as I am, and the soldier is obviously on edge about the invasion.

"What can I do for you, detective?"

I inject some steel into my voice because there is something about this man I don't trust and he smiles kindly, making a mockery of my suspicions and glances at the two staff listening intently nearby.

"I'm sorry, ma'am, but I'm afraid I have bad news."

"What is it?" My world stops spinning as I imagine something terrible has happened to Dom and he shakes his head sadly. "I'm afraid I must take you to a safe house right away."

The soldier steps between us and says darkly, "She stays here. This is the safest house for her."

The detective appears irritated and beckons to the soldier to follow him and, as they huddle in the corner of the room, I don't miss the confusion on the soldier's face.

Gretchen slides beside me and whispers, "I don't like this. I'm going to call Mr. Ortega."

"You have his number?" I am so grateful as Gretchen winks. "Of course. Believe it or not, I know what to do when unwelcome visitors come calling. Leave it with me. I won't be long."

As she heads outside, the two men return, and the detective says pleasantly, "I've agreed that Max can accompany you. You will be perfectly safe, but we need to leave now."

"Now!" I look around me wildly, desperate to know what's happening.

"Tell me why?" I say roughly and he says in a whisper, "I'm afraid your, um, boyfriend has been arrested for double homicide."

"DOM!" I cry out and the tears pour from my eyes in disbelief. "Who?"

"Senator Billings and Desdemona Gray."

"Desdemona, but..." The sob catches me unaware, and I blurt out, "But how? Why? I don't understand."

"Neither do we yet, but an eyewitness saw it all. Both murders have been caught on camera and the person responsible appears to be Mr. Ortega."

"You're lying!" I yell, knowing this isn't true, and the detective shakes his head and says with a sigh, "Listen, we don't have time for this. Apparently, his stepmother has been informed and is on her way to deal with the problem. Mr. Ortega pleaded with me to remove you and take you to a safe house before she gets here."

"Diana. She's coming here." I am almost drowning in fear as I contemplate what that will mean for me and the detective nods, saying urgently, "Please, Miss. Corlietti. I promised to relocate you in return for his cooperation."

Gretchen returns and shakes her head. "There's no answer."

The detective glances between us and says tightly, "We are wasting time. Come."

He turns to Gretchen. "Mrs. Ortega will be here within the hour. When she arrives, tell her nothing. We weren't here. OK?"

Gretchen nods miserably. "Yes sir."

Knowing I have no choice makes me keen to get this over with, so I impulsively hug the housekeeper and whisper, "It will be OK. Dom will be released and then I'll return. Just don't tell Diana anything."

"Take care miss."

"Flora." I smile through my tears. "Call me Flora, Gretchen. We're friends now."

The troubled look on her face doesn't make me feel any better but facing my sister with no back up is not a pleasant thought, so I follow the detective out to the waiting car in nothing but the clothes I'm wearing and pray it won't be long before Dom sorts this mess out.

* * *

THE DRIVE to the safe house is a strange one. The detective appears on edge as he glances in his rear-view mirror at every opportunity he gets.

"Is something worrying you, detective?"

I say after ten minutes and he says a little too quickly, "It's fine. Standard practice when escorting a guest to the safe house. It won't take long, and we need to make sure we're not followed."

"Who would follow us?" I'm quick to ask because as far as I know, Dom is in a cell downtown and Diana is on a flight right now.

He merely laughs softly and injects a lightness into his voice that I can tell is as false as he appears to be.

"Sorry, old habits and all. Anyway, when we get to the safe house, you must trust me. Nobody will find you there. It's not on any maps or satellite navigation systems. If you like, it's a ghost house. Not literally, though."

He laughs, but it sounds forced. "It's a place we use when we need maximum security away from prying eyes. You'll be safe with Max."

If anything, I'm grateful that the silent soldier is sitting behind us, watching over me like an avenging angel. He doesn't say much, but I'm happy he's here because there's something about him I trust. His expression alone regarding the detective tells me he's even more unhappy about this than I am.

It takes another thirty minutes before we turn off the highway and a further ten minutes before he turns sharply through some old iron gates that are held up by two stone pillars.

As we drive through them, it strikes me there is no light at all and I wonder if there is anything hiding behind the thick tree line.

However, as we turn the corner, I see a majestic house looming up before us, and it makes me shiver.

"Is this really a safe house?" I question because something about it doesn't feel safe at all and he nods, saying lightly. "It's a little spooky; I'll give you that, but the fact it's so hidden is the reason we're here at all."

He screeches to a halt outside the main door, and I say nervously, "Is anybody inside?"

Shaking his head, he unlocks the door and steps outside, peering back in and saying firmly, "No. It's just us. Actually, it will just be the two of you, because I must return and question Mr. Ortega."

A painful emotion grips my heart knowing Dom is locked up and I say quickly, "He didn't do it, detective. I was with him the entire time."

The detective sighs and says almost as an aside, "You would say that Flora, you see, you are from the same world. You close ranks and back up horror stories. Please forgive me if I don't believe a word that spills from your pretty little lips."

The low growl from the silent soldier warns him from saying anything else and as we head through the door, I shiver at the gloomy residence I must call home until Dom is released.

The detective follows and says to Max, "You check one half, I'll check the other."

He nods toward me. "The kitchen is through that door. Wait there until we give you the all clear."

Resigned to my fate, I nod and head into the large kitchen and am surprised when the door locks behind me.

"Hey!" I protest, and the detective's muffled voice reassures me.

"It's for your own protection until we've checked this place is secure."

As he walks away, I stare around the kitchen and shiver inside. There is something freaky about this house. I know it's a ghost house and unlived in but it's as if there are ghosts all around me warning me to run like hell.

There are shutters covering the windows and when I try them, I realize they are locked tightly and with a sigh, I head to the cupboard to check if there's anything to make a hot drink because I need something to do before I go crazy.

I'm not sure how long I wait, but the door opens, and the detective enters and smiles. "It's all clear. I'll show you to your room. Follow me."

"Where's Max?" I'm reluctant to move until I have my

guardian angel beside me and the detective smiles. "He's checking the grounds. He won't be long."

I follow him unhappily, wishing I wasn't here at all, and as I step out into the gloomy hallway, I pray this is over soon.

* * *

As places to stay go, this one is creepy, and I would have rather taken my chances anywhere but here.

As we walk, it occurs to me I haven't asked about my employer and say with concern. "You said Desdemona is dead. What happened to her?"

"Her body was found inside her car, not far from where Senator Billings died. The cameras revealed she left the Ortega Mansion and was heading back down the hill."

"But you said the cameras revealed it was Dom. I swear he was with me at the time."

"Can anyone else confirm that, Miss. Corlietti?"

The detective's voice is hard and disbelieving and with a sinking feeling, I shake my head.

"No, we were alone, but his staff will tell you he never left the house."

"Really, Miss. Corlietti. Is that the best you've got? Those men would lay down their life for that monster. Their word means nothing."

I'm taken aback at the vitriol in his tone and as we reach a door, he opens it with a flourish and as I step inside, I see a bedroom that consists of one narrow bed and no other furniture.

"This is…" I half turn, but that's all I manage before I experience a sharp pain in my arm and my world turns dark.

CHAPTER 36

DOM

I have never been so angry. In fact, I can't even speak my mind is racing so fast. I know this is a setup. Diana lied to me and said I had twenty-four hours, so why the fuck am I facing these charges now?

I just pray Pasquale gets Flora to safety before Diana finds her, because there is no doubt in my mind she wants Flora back along with the money and I'm guessing she hates that her sister is free and finally happy. If there is anyone I hate more than Diana, it's that fucker Mario and as soon as I get the hell out of here, neither one of them will be safe from me.

After the usual shit, I am thrown into a cell to burn with anger, and it takes a further hour before I'm granted my single call.

My brother Leonardo answers immediately.

"Who is this?"

"Leo, it's Dom."

"What the fuck's going on? What is this number?"

"Fucking jail, man. They've arrested me for the murder of Senator Billings and Desdemona Gray."

"Fucking bastards." His hiss of anger matches my own, and

he growls, "I've got you, brother. I'll call Declan Cole; he'll get you out in no time."

Declan Cole is the most feared attorney around and my heart sags with relief. He knows all the official's weaknesses and will be putting in a call to the chief of police within seconds of Leo's call.

"Just get me the fuck out of here. Flora's vulnerable."

Leo lowers his voice. "Where is she?"

"Back at the house. Pasquale should be there by now, and I instructed him to take her to the retreat."

Leo takes a minute and then says with concern, "There are no cars at the retreat. I've got the image on my monitor."

We all have access to our family's bolt hole that is heavily monitored by surveillance. His words are unwelcome, and I shout, "Fuck!"

Leo says calmly, "Settle down. I'll deal with it. You concentrate on getting out of there and leave the rest to me."

The cop nudges me and I say angrily, "I've got to go. Just make sure Flora's safe, that's all I ask."

He cuts the call leaving me feeling so helpless I want to smash something and yet the only thing to hand is the cop by my side, so with a groan, I allow him to escort me back to my cell where I hope to God, Declan Cole will visit soon.

* * *

As I WAIT, I try to piece together the events that led me here, and the only reason I can think of is the money we stole. Why is Flora so important to Diana? It doesn't make sense that she'd do all of this just to get her sister home. I know how her mind works and there must be something bigger that I'm not seeing.

I totally get that she wants me and my brothers removed from the family. Without us to challenge them, Diana and Mario can take over the Ortega empire and finally have a family of their own. Just contemplating Diana's fascination with that low life pimp shocks me because he's a weasley little fucker who belongs on the streets selling whores and crack, not as the don of a well-established crime family.

So many things rattle through my mind as I wait for someone to move this on and when the door flies open, I breathe a sigh of relief because standing there is the man who is going to get me the hell out of here.

"Domenico."

Declan shakes his head in disgust and sits beside me on the narrow bunk and lowers his voice. "The detective's timing was impeccable."

"What do you mean?"

I'm confused and he whispers, "The chief of police is on vacation. He's currently in mid-air and won't land for another eight hours. There's nobody else who can authorize your release."

"You had better be fucking kidding me." I hiss darkly and he shrugs, not at all intimidated by me. Then again, this man is probably the only man alive who intimidates me and so I back down and say tightly, "I didn't kill them. I've been set up."

"You're an easy target." Declan taps his finger on his briefcase and growls, "The detective knows how it works. One call from his superior and you would be driven home with an apology. The charges would be dropped due to lack of evidence, and he would be back to checking tickets in the car lot."

"So, he chose his moment for his own agenda. Is that what you're saying?"

Now I'm even more alarmed because Declan's right, he has approximately ten hours to carry out his own reason for banging me up and Declan replies in a low voice, "Whatever the detective is planning must be something concerning you. To remove you from the picture, knowing your hands are tied. Can you think of anything I need to know about?"

"My stepmother." I lower my voice to a whisper.

"We liberated our father's money from her bank account. If I was guessing, I'd say she's on her way to my home to retrieve it. Flora has knowledge of it and will be her best chance at getting it back. I've asked my consigliere to take her to the retreat, but Leo told me they haven't arrived."

"Sounds likely." He huffs, "Leave it with me, Dom. I'll pay the mansion a visit on the pretext of getting some files. Is the money safe?"

"Unregistered and untraceable accounts. Flora doesn't have a clue where they are. Only me."

"Good." Declan nods. "I'll see what I can do. I may be able to pull some strings higher up the food chain. The detective may think he's got this, but he hasn't met me yet."

As Declan stands and moves to the door, he grins. "They will regret this, Dom. You have my word on that. I love nothing more than eating the authorities for breakfast and it's been a while. I'm going to enjoy this."

As he leaves, I pray he's right because the more I think about it, the more danger Flora is in and if anything happens to her, hell won't be painful enough for its new inhabitants.

CHAPTER 37

FLORA

That's a strange noise. I must be dreaming and wait for the dream to switch and reveal itself. However, there is nothing but a weird humming and as I struggle to open my eyes, all that lies before them is darkness.

As the shadows part, I stare up at a ceiling that I definitely don't recognize. In fact, it's so high it can't be anywhere I'm familiar with. If anything, it appears I'm in a church.

I make to sit up but am held down by my wrists, my ankles are also bound and my heart fills with terror. I've been here before—in this position and the cold fingers of dread curl around my heart and tell me I'm right back where I started.

I turn my head to the side and make out a shadowy figure standing a short distance away, covered from head to toe in a black robe. At least I think it's a person. I can't be certain of that and then I realize it must be because the gentle hums around me are definitely human.

There is more than one figure standing around me and I frantically spin my head and witness what must be ten people all holding candles and wearing the same cloak.

"What's happening?" My voice bounces off the chilling

walls and my head thumps with a blinding pain, causing me to wince. I get no answer at all and if anything, the humming increases.

Whatever I'm lying on is cold against my back and for the first time, I realize I'm naked.

This is not good.

"Please, who are you?"

My voice shakes but I get no acknowledgment that I even spoke, and the humming is beginning to seriously freak me out. Then the figure moves and heads toward me, the hood effectively disguising their identity as they lift the candle, blinding me from seeing anything but the flickering flame.

The noise continues and I gasp as candle wax drips onto my vulnerable body and as the molten liquid sears my skin, I cry out in alarm.

"What the fuck, you demented bastard, let me go!"

It's as if I'm in the weirdest nightmare as instead the figure turns and walks silently around me, a second figure taking its place and doing the exact same thing.

As more wax drips across my body, I feel the burn of wax on skin and one by one they all take a turn, causing me to scream in agony as I struggle to avoid it. It's almost as if they can't hear me because nobody reacts and just patrol around me, dragging their candles the length of my body, depositing the wax on any exposed of part of it they can. I'm not even sure how long it lasts and it's as if they will only stop when the contents of their candles are relocated to my skin.

The tears fall unchecked as I struggle to make sense of this. The only thing I can remember is being shown to the stark bedroom by the detective. I must be dreaming. Surely this can't be happening, and I try my hardest to wake from this sadistic nightmare.

Suddenly, they figures stop humming and retreat back to the shadows and if anything, that scares me even more because a bright light suddenly blinds me to anything, hurting my eyes, causing me to snap them closed. A weird chanting replaces the humming and yet I can't see a thing, which gets fainter as if the shadows are fading away. I still can't see anything because of the infernal light, and I feel a sharp pain in my arm before sliding into oblivion.

* * *

THE NEXT TIME I WAKE, I'm in a different position. This time I'm face down on what appears to be a slab of concrete. My wrists and ankles are cuffed in metal and this time my eyes are obscured by a blindfold that is tight around my head.

I can tell I'm not alone and once again the humming alerts me to the freak show all around me and I struggle to move but am held down so firmly all I can manage is a twitch.

Suddenly, I note the crack of a whip and my heart almost stops beating as the sting in its tail hits me hard against my back. It hurts so badly, causing me to scream with the pain, my fear echoing back at me as it fills the dark space.

I'm not sure how many blows hit my body, each one more painful than the last, and like the candle wax, it causes my body to burn, setting it alight in the most painful way.

As I steel myself for the next blow, it's eerily quiet and then something soft brushes against my ear, causing me to freeze as I anticipate even more torture.

I was right because this is the worst yet when the voice that slides into my subconscious is one I hoped I'd never hear again.

He whispers huskily, "You thought you could run from me. Bad luck, honey, you're home."

As the terror overwhelms me, another painful sensation travels down my arm, which plunges me deep inside a living nightmare with my biggest fear coming along for the ride.

***

I must have been dreaming. That's my first thought as I drift back into consciousness and wake in the narrow bed, telling me it must have been a nightmare.

As I stretch my limbs, I'm relieved to find I'm free at least, however, when I sit up, I groan as the ache from my body confirms my worst fear. I wasn't dreaming.

It's as if my body is on fire and I glance down in the gloomy light and see dried wax littered across my body. The raw pain on my back tells me my skin has been torn and damaged, and I gasp as a burst of pain shoots through my body.

It hurts so badly and then I see a tray on the floor by the door, and my heart drops. Somebody else is here. Is it Max? Did he betray me and Dom and take part in this?

With a huge effort, I slide off the bed and stagger to the tray, noting the bottle of water standing beside a couple of pills. There's a note attached, and I grab it and read, "Welcome to hell. You may want to take these for the pain."

I note the Advil and wonder if they are what they seem, but I'm in so much pain I have no choice and chuck them back, loving how the cool water slides down my throat. Then I register a chunk of bread that is apparently all the food I'm getting, and I laugh hysterically. Bread and water. How fucking original.

However, I need to eat something if I'm to stand any chance of surviving whatever this is and so I retreat to the bed and stuff small pieces of bread into my mouth and try to figure a way out of this.

CHAPTER 38

DOM

The detective sits across from me, looking as if he has won the fucking lottery and merely shrugs as Declan growls, "Release my client. There is no evidence to charge him with anything, not even a traffic violation."

"I have…" he peers at his wristwatch. "Ninety more hours if I wish, because murder is a serious charge."

"You know I'm fucking innocent, you bastard." I growl and Declan places his hand on my arm in a warning as the detective's eyes narrow.

"I know I have two bodies. Two victims minus their hearts and two crime scenes a short distance from your home. There is also the video evidence from your own security cameras that shows them both leaving your home minutes before they died. I'd say there is enough evidence to keep you locked up for a very long time."

"Circumstantial evidence, detective." Declan growls, "That wouldn't stand up in court. We need DNA, fingerprints at the scene, and probable cause. You must do better than that if you hope to build a case against my client who, as he said, is innocent and has several eyewitnesses along with that same security evidence proving he never left his home. So, I will repeat my request, release him."

The detective leans back and appears to be enjoying every minute of this as he shrugs, almost with amusement.

"I don't make the laws, or the rules, Mr. Cole. I'm sworn to carry them out, so you must abide by the law and let me do my job."

I am so frustrated. I can't bear the thought of Flora out there on her own with her vicious sister heading her way, and yet there is absolutely nothing I can do about it.

The detective says with interest, "Why the heart, Mr. Ortega? That's particularly gruesome, even for you."

"Why don't you ask the twisted fucker who did this instead of wasting time with me."

I growl and whisper to Declan, "Shut this fucker down."

Declan nods and says icily, "There will be no comment until you present the charges. My client is innocent, and it's up to you to prove otherwise."

The detective merely smiles and then I'm happy to see it wiped off his smug face when Declan peers at his phone and his expression changes in an instant.

"May I have a word, detective? In private."

The detective narrows his eyes as he watches my own expression change when I read the text on Declan's phone.

Without saying a word, the detective scrapes back his chair and waits for Declan to exit the room before him, not even glancing back in my direction as they leave me with a silent detective who appears to wish he was anywhere else.

As I lean back in my chair, I would give anything to see the detective's expression now because that text was from the governor himself, demanding my immediate release. I don't know how Declan does it, but it appears every official is indebted to him and all it would take is one word from him and I'd be serving life with no hope of parole. He is that powerful.

It makes me wonder why the detective has even bothered and I'm guessing it's to buy him some time and remove me from life, even for a few hours. I think hard about the reasons why and can only think of one. Diana. She must have something on the detective and is using him to remove me from the situation so she can go in and take back what she believes is hers. Not just the money either, it's Flora too and my heart thumps so hard when I consider I could be too late.

* * *

WHEN DECLAN STRIKES, its fast and within the hour I step inside my car after assuring the bent attorney of my eternal loyalty. All charges were dropped, and the detective was forced to issue a groveling apology, which I would relish if I wasn't so impatient to leave.

Pasquale looks at me as if his cat just died and my chest tightens as I prepare myself for something I'm not going to like.

"Flora." I growl as soon as the door slams behind me and he visibly turns a whiter shade of pale.

"Gone."

"How?"

I don't bother with emotion, that is not required now, and he says in a worried voice, "Before I made it back after your arrest. Gretchen told me the detective had taken her to a safe house."

"And my fucking soldiers allowed it?"

I'm incensed and Pasquale shakes his head. "Max demanded that she stay, and Gretchen told me the detective agreed he could accompany her."

"Well, that's something I suppose."

"Not really. Max's body was discovered at the same place as the others, just outside the mansion with his heart cut out."

"You are fucking kidding me." I roar and Pasquale nods miserably. "We dragged him in before he was discovered. Tony was heading back from a visit home and found him."

"What the fuck is going on?" I lean back and he says with a deep sigh. "I'm guessing the answer lies wherever they took Flora."

"You mean you don't know?" Now I'm a desperate man and Pasquale shakes his head. "The only lead we've got is that the good detective wasn't so good after all. We shook a few informants, and it turns out he's involved in serious shit that nobody wanted any part of."

"Do we have eyes on him now?"

"Of course. Our best shadow is following him. If he takes a piss, we'll know about it before he even shakes."

I don't have time to sit and wait for information and reach for my phone. There is only one man who can help me now and I fucking hope he's up to the job because I have a strong feeling the next heart that will be cut out will be mine when Flora's body arrives outside my mansion, if I don't find her and fast.

"Dom. Declan worked his magic, I see."

"Now I need you to work yours."

I don't mess around and Matteo's tone changes in a flash as he says darkly, *"How can I help?"*

"Detective Woznowski. He's keeping dark secrets and has Flora. I'm guessing she doesn't have long."

"I'm on it."

As he hangs up, I'm confident my brother will discover everything known about the detective after a few well-placed calls and words in the right ears by the time I return home.

Matteo isn't our consigliere for nothing. He has always loved planning, plotting, and discovering a person's weakness, which is why he is so good at his job. My father never appreciated him and when Diana seduced Matteo along with the rest of us, he was sent to run the Ortega business in New York and if I know my brother, he hasn't been idle. He hates Diana and Mario just as much as I do and probably has a file on them as thick as War and Peace, waiting for the opportune moment to use the information.

In fact, the car has barely made it through my security gates when he returns my call.

He doesn't waste time with pleasantries and says in a voice etched in steel,

"There's an abandoned house one hour from you. Hadleigh Hall. You won't find it on any Sat Nav, or any google search though, so I'm sending you the GPS. Follow that and it will take you there."

I don't even know how he discovers this shit, but I trust him with my life, despite the fact we turned on one another after Diana seduced every one of us.

"It turns out your detective was the errand boy of a secret society that uses the place for weird rituals and depraved shit."

The conversation I had with Desdemona comes back to bite me and I curse my stupidity in not paying closer attention to that.

"Do you know who's involved?"

"No. I'm working on it but I'm guessing whoever it is, has ties with our enemies. I'm guessing that's why they have Flora now."

"What about security? Do I need to go in mob handed?"

My mind is already preparing my battle plan and Matteo snarls, *"What do you think? We're not dealing with amateurs. They already have three bodies all pointing their fingers at your door, and I'm guessing that number is far greater. You must protect yourself and your family because these men are dangerous, Dom."*

"Thanks bro." There's a small pause before he says in a softer tone.

"I'm always here for you, you know that, right?"

"Same." I cut the call because my heart is doing some weird shit right now and I'm conscious of Pasquale regarding me curiously, waiting for the plan.

Without even glancing at him, I say icily, "Prepare for war, Pasquale. You have ten minutes."

He nods and as he calls the guard house, I hear him issuing orders like bullets and as we sweep around the driveway of the mansion and head back the way we came, I watch my soldiers pouring from my home into the heavily armored SUVs we use, tooled up with machine guns and God only knows what else.

In one hour's time, Hadleigh Hall will be a smoldering pile of ash and if she's there, Flora will be once again by my side.

CHAPTER 39

FLORA

I am so cold. There are no sheets or even any drapes I can pull down to cover my naked body. There is nothing and I curl up in a ball on the bare mattress in the vain hope there is any heat left inside me to take the chill away.

He's here.

That thought alone causes me to shiver uncontrollably because Mario's voice burns in my brain and drives intense fear through my soul. They found me and there will be no escaping this time and death is looking like a mighty fine proposition, yet all I can think about is Dom. If anything, I'm glad he's locked up because at least he will be protected. I've known Mario and Diana too long and know they fight dirty, and I'm guessing his arrest had a lot to do with them.

I jump when the lock is turned in my prison cell and I'm afraid to look at who is on the other end.

Then her voice washes through me like a poisoned river. "Flora."

I jump from the bed as a defense and face my sister, regarding me with interest from the door she closed behind her.

"This is just like old times, huh?"

Her giggle grates on my frayed nerves and I hiss, "Let me go you fucking mad bitch." She shakes her head and says with disappointment. "Is that any way to greet your loving sister who has only ever had your best interests at heart?"

"Best interests." I bark out a harsh laugh. "The only interests you've ever had are your own. You're not my sister, and I doubt you even care about that. I'm merely someone else to manipulate in your desperate need to keep Mario interested."

"Is that what you think?" She laughs as if she's watching a fucking comedy show.

"Oh, Flora, you have never understood the deep love Mario and I share."

"Deep love." This time, I laugh out loud. "Don't make me laugh. You may love him, but he definitely doesn't love you."

For the first time, I detect a hint of uncertainty in Diana's eyes, and she hisses, "You know nothing about our relationship."

"I know you're his whore. I know he uses you to make money, and I know you're the pathetic fool who can't see that."

In a couple of steps, she crosses the room and slaps me hard across the face and, to my surprise, I hit her hard back. I'm not sure who is more astonished as she stands staring at me in shock and I take courage from that and bark, "Have I surprised you? The meek fool has retaliated for once."

She steps back and snarls, "Then you *are* a fool, because unless you listen to me, the only place you're going is to hell."

She shakes her head and regains a little of her self-assurance.

"Do you really think you can walk out of here? You obviously haven't grasped how serious this is for you."

I maintain a brave expression, but inside I'm shaking as she says almost conversationally. "You see, Mario has decided we need to teach the Ortega's a lesson. To remove them from the picture and take over their empire. I'm guessing it's only a formality because Giovanni left everything to me in his will and as his consigliere, Mario will step up as don when Giovanni's sons are in no position to do so."

"But they are, you thick bitch, and they're coming for you."

I take great satisfaction in watching her fear peer out from behind her eyes before it is quickly replaced by anger.

"They are amateurs. We have planned their downfall and there is nothing they can do about that. Forget them, they are ghosts already. However, you, Flora, you owe us money and it's in your very best interests to return the money that you stole from us or die."

She studies her fingernails. "You see, Mario is not a patient man, and you have me to thank that you're still breathing."

"Don't make me laugh, Diana." I snap. "Mario wants the money and I'm the only person who can help with that, so I'm a valuable commodity to him right now. If he wants it, he needs to keep me alive, and this is his way of intimidating me so I surrender it to him. I'm not a fool. I understand as soon as the money hits his account he will have no further use for me, so jog on out of here and report back that I would rather die than tell him where his precious money is."

I'm breathless on adrenalin. For the first time in my life, I'm standing tall and not backing down. I am facing my fear head on and challenging it to bite me.

Diana obviously doesn't know how to deal with the warrior in me and snaps, "You think Dom wants you?"

She's really trying everything, and I sigh. "Does it matter?"

"To you it does."

She leans against the door and laughs softly. "I saw you together. The puppy dog wagging its tail for its master. As always, dear sister, you are happy to follow rather than lead. You believe he loves you? He's *using you*. It's me he loves. Me, he craves like an antidote to death and me he sees when he's fucking you. What's it like knowing I've been there first? His cock inside me pledging his love—for me. The anguish in his expression when I chose his father over him and the fact both his brothers enjoyed fucking me too. I broke them all and only I can control them. The Ortega brothers fell in love with me and one glance in their direction, one shy smile and one regretful tear from my eye, would have them sprinting back to my side. You..."

She points her finger at me and laughs. "You are second best and you always have been."

"And you would know a lot about being second best, wouldn't you, Diana?"

"What are you talking about?"

"Abigail Kensington."

As I mention her name, Diana's eyes narrow and I laugh softly. "The only woman Mario loves and would ditch you in a heartbeat if she showed any interest at all. The one woman he can't have because she can't fucking stand him. She is the reason you're by his side at all, because you are desperate to be relevant in his life. You're not. In fact, you're not relevant in anyone's life except your own. You say the Ortega brothers love you. Well, love turns to hate pretty damn quickly when you crush a soul. It forms into retribution and yours is heading your way at a frightening speed, so if you think you're calling the shots, you are so far off the mark it's laughable."

I straighten up and throw her a pitying look. "At least I have a man who loves me for who I am. Not what I can give him. Someone whose soft touches and whispered words of love are something you long to hear spill from Mario's lips. How does it feel knowing he fucks other women while you watch? That he pimps you out to his friends because you're the fool who lets him. It must hurt knowing you're only a commodity to him. Someone he can manipulate to his own agenda and that if

Abigail Kensington walked into the room declaring her love for him, you would be history."

Diana's eyes flash, revealing the truth hurts, but she forces a laugh and says, "Keep telling yourself that, Flora. The only one disposable around here is you, and you always have been. Ask yourself why we had to leave the Matasso mansion that night and why our father was never seen again."

My blood freezes as she strikes back with a devastating blow. "It was you, Flora. You he couldn't bear to be around because you're the bastard child that caused the death of our mother."

"You're lying."

I am trying so hard to be strong but the quiver in my voice tells her she's scored a direct hit, and she smiles sweetly, "Maybe I'll tell you about that some time, but time is something you don't have a lot of. You see…"

She grins and the madness in her terrifies me as she giggles, "What you experienced on the altar was foreplay. Mario is keen to move things on and unless you agree to return the money, you will be tortured until you agree. First, they drug you so you can't move. Then they chain you to the stone altar that is drenched in the blood of the sacrifices that went before you."

I'm so afraid but try not to show it as she giggles, "Then they fuck you, brutally and interminably. They cut you, whip you, and dismember you. Your heart will still be beating though and your eyes witnessing every minute of it as they systematically make your passing the most painful one possible. All the time you can make it stop by giving Mario what he wants. They will leave you to bleed, but not enough to kill you and even if it takes weeks, they will keep you alive."

She laughs as if it's hilarious and grins. " You see, Flora, Mario will always win in the end because nothing can touch him. He is always one step ahead and Desdemona paid the price for not doing as she was told. In fact, she lay on that altar and pleaded with the lords to grant her mercy and they rewarded her by cutting out her heart while she watched. Senator Billings was equally pitiful when they removed his own heart with the aim of making life extremely uncomfortable for the man who you foolishly believe loves you but would trade you in a heartbeat for me."

She fixes me with a withering look. "Let's be clear, Flora, your boyfriend is nothing compared to Mario, and you are nothing compared to me, so do us all a favor and give back the money you stole from us and spare yourself the cruelest of passings. Then you can work off your debt on your back like you always did so well and nothing more will be said of this whole unfortunate episode."

A knock on the door interrupts her speech, and she leaves at once, locking the door behind her.

As the silence wraps around my shivering body, the demons circling tell me they're coming for my soul because it's doubtful I'm going to survive this latest attack, even though I will die trying.

CHAPTER 40

DOM

One hour is one hell of a countdown when the life of the person you love hangs in the balance.

I'm not sure how I get through the journey at all, and to keep myself sane, I spend the entire time planning what happens when we get there.

Pasquale is also on edge because as my consigliere, he is in charge of making sure this shit doesn't come back to bite us and spends a great deal of time on his phone double checking our plan.

"Run me through it again."

I regard him through malevolent eyes, and he nods. "Apparently, Senator Billings was into dubious shit that barely made it out of the press. Someone high up kept his name hidden, but he was becoming a problem, getting careless and threatening this organization."

"Tell me again about that." I still can't believe this shit was going on under our noses the entire time, and I'm looking hard for answers to that.

Pasquale says grimly, "One of the whores working the streets told her pimp about her roommate going missing.

Apparently, she'd been picked up off the street by the good senator."

"Sloppy." I shake my head and Pasquale nods.

"Sonny didn't want to lose one of his best girls and started asking the wrong people and was found hanging in his apartment by his latest fuck."

"Any idea who was involved?"

"Luckily, the block manager thought on his feet and before he called the cops, he copied the security footage."

"Why?"

"Because shit had gone down in his apartment block before, and he set it up as protection and a way of making a few extra bucks."

He grins, "He made it known that the tape was for sale to the highest bidder, so congratulations, you win."

He pulls up an image on his phone and I watch as a car parks at the rear of the building and four shadowy figures exit. They are dressed completely in black, their heads obscured by balaclavas.

They head into the building where the camera picks them up in the hallway outside the pimp's apartment and I observe as they break in, leaving ten minutes later.

"This tells us nothing. I hope you didn't pay the creep actual dollars."

I shake my head in disgust and Pasquale smiles secretively. "Watch."

As the four men leave, a man steps out of nowhere and shouts. His voice is muted, but I can tell he's angry, probably a tenant who thinks the place is being robbed. A have a go hero if you like and as he tackles one of the four men, he pushes him to the ground and starts raining blows to his head, pulling off the mask and subsequently revealing his face.

Two of the others come to help their accomplice but whoever this guy is, he's a pro, because he defends himself like an assassin and as he tears into the four men, he rips their balaclavas off to get easier access, while he smashes their faces in.

"Who is this guy?"

I'm impressed and Pasquale laughs. "Jonny Freeman. An ex special forces soldier who was discharged a few months back."

"Does he need a job?" I fucking hope he does and Pasquale shakes his head. "He has one."

"Shame."

"For us."

I stare at him in surprise, and he waves to the car in front. "Started today and couldn't wait by all accounts."

Pasquale obviously notes my expression because he says hastily, "You were locked up. I thought you wouldn't want him knocking on any other families' doors, so as soon as I saw this footage, I sent Salvatore around to recruit him. On a trial basis, of course."

"Of course." I laugh softly. "Good job. Anyway, back to these fuckers. Who are they?"

"Nobody knows. We circulated their head shots around and only one person had a guess."

"Who?"

"It was one of your dancers at the strip club. Lily belle Blake. She told me one of them had been in last week and paid for her attention, in private."

"And?"

"She said he gave her the creeps. He was unusually rough and slapped her around a lot."

"Why the fuck wasn't she protected? She was in the fucking club, for Christ's sake."

I pride myself on my security and Pasquale obviously shares my concern.

"I asked the same question to the guys on duty that night. They told me it wasn't worth their pay grade to interrupt a Dark Lord."

"Dark what…?"

I can't believe what I'm hearing, and Pasquale's expression tells me he's not that impressed either.

"They told me of a secret society nobody knows much about. It's an organization on the dark web ironically called The Dark Lords, and they recruit their staff there."

"Their staff?"

"Security, cleaners, the usual shit and word is, it's like a haunted house of sin. There are reports of ritual sacrifices and sadistic orgies that all happen in the place we are heading for now."

I feel like smashing something, and Pasquale is obviously concerned that he's the closest thing to me right now and shifts away a little.

"I've done some more digging on your stepmother."

My ears prick up.

"What did you discover?"

That she landed in Vegas the night Flora came to the gala with the senator. She rented a suite at the Four Seasons."

"Was she alone?"

"No." Pasquale spits, "Accompanied by Mario Bachini."

The pounding in my head is almost drowning out his words as he says tightly, "As soon as I heard, I instructed Vito to head up surveillance. They left the hotel this morning and headed to the airport. Apparently, their trip is over, and they watched the private plane take off."

"Did they see them enter the plane?" I growl, hoping like hell they didn't, and Pasquale sighs.

"They can't be certain."

"Why not?"

This is not what I want to hear, and Pasquale looks worried. "Another plane taxiing in obscured their view and when it passed, the door was closed, and the engines started."

"And the car?"

"Gone."

"So, they could still be here."

"Unlikely. Why go to the airport if they weren't leaving?"

"Possibly because they knew they were being watched. To make it appear they left, enabling them to commit a crime and give them an alibi."

I sometimes wonder if I'm the only one with a brain in my organization and Pasquale falls silent as he realizes his mistake.

"This dark lord shit is right up Mario and Diana's alley. I'm guessing her visit to my home was a smokescreen, too. The fact she gave me twenty-four hours that she had no intention of honoring tells me it was to gather information."

I contemplate where we're heading and despite having a small army surrounding us, I know that Mario and Diana have probably planned for this, in fact, I wouldn't put it past them to have engineered the whole set up as a trap, so I say roughly, "Change of plan."

"What?" Pasquale stares at me in shock and I snarl, "We stay in the shadows and go in covertly. Maybe your recruit can help us with that."

Pasquale nods, his eyes shining with excited adrenalin and as he calls each car in turn to change his instructions, an excitement builds that I recognize.

I smell blood. I sniff fear and I relish the pain I will unleash on the people who dare mess with my family and I'm going in hard to get my woman back because until she is safe by my side, no one is safe from me.

CHAPTER 41

FLORA

It must be only thirty minutes after Diana left that the door opens, and two hooded figures enter my room wearing devil masks. It's creepy as fuck and I say fearfully, "Let me go, you fucking weirdoes."

I attempt to keep the bed between us, but they move fast and before I can put up a fight, my hands are held behind my back by one of them and the other strikes me hard across the face. I taste the blood trickling into my mouth as they force me face down on the bed and snap metal cuffs on my wrists. Then one of them hauls me over his shoulder like a sack and moves silently outside, back into the dimmed hallway.

I try so hard to wriggle and fight, but every time I move the other person flicks a whip against my ass, causing me to scream in pain as I feel the bite.

They say nothing at all as they proceed to a door at the end of the hallway, and something is telling me I'm not going to like what's inside.

The door opens as if by magic as we approach and my heart almost fails when I see the huge church like chamber I was in before. This time I see the whole room and note the burning candles set around the large stone altar set in the middle.

My breath falters when I see the hooded figures watching from their positions in a circle around the altar, holding candles before them, the same devil mask on their faces obscuring their identities and as I am slammed down hard on the altar, my arms are raised and hooked to a restraint above my head. My feet are unshackled and as I kick out, the two figures grab an ankle each and attach them to a pulley and my legs are raised into the air, exposing me to the entire fucking room.

"Let me go!" I scream and get silence back in return before that infernal humming begins again as the figures start circling the altar like sadistic demons from hell.

I yell, "I know you're here, Mario, you sick fuck. You won't get away with this!"

They carry on and I shout, "Dom is coming for you, and I'll watch him send you all to hell."

Still nothing, so I call out, "Oh, and Diana, I'm glad we're only half related because that weakens the levels of toxic blood running in my veins. Oh, and just in case you didn't know this already but you are a deluded idiot if you believe that creep Mario will ever fall in love with you the more you obey him."

The tears flow unchecked as I realize none of my words are finding their mark and as I continue to scream and cuss their souls to burn in the eternal fires of hell, my heart almost stops beating when one of the devils stands before me and punches me hard around the head. I almost black out but a voice dripping in sinister intent whispers, "Give us back our money, you bitch, and save yourself."

I don't recognize the voice, but it's muffled, and my ears are ringing from the punch, so I spit on the mask and hiss, "Not fucking likely."

Once again, the whip scorches my breast and I scream out

in pain and the voice hisses again, "Wrong answer. I'll ask you again. Where's our money?"

"I don't have your fucking money, you deranged shit. Dom has it, so go and ask him if you dare."

Once again, I scream as something hot burns my thigh and my skin sizzles as a hot poker dances close to my face.

"I can arrange this to be shoved up your ass if you prefer, Flora."

I am openly crying because what the hell is happening to me? I suppose this is the moment my life flashes before my eyes, telling me it's now or never. Agree to their demands or die an increasingly slow and painful death.

I'm conscious of the figure's excitement that sparks a twisted energy in the room. Their heavy panting reveals their sick pleasure as they anticipate the kill, and my heart goes into free fall as one of them stands at the foot of the altar and brandishes a huge dagger that rests against my heart.

The figure by my ear whispers, "One by one, we will fuck you until you lose consciousness. Then, unless you agree to return the money, we will cut out your heart as a souvenir and toss your body back to your boyfriend as a warning he's next."

I scream as the hooded figure shifts between my legs and the robe parts, revealing he's naked underneath. His hard angry cock firmly positioned to thrust inside me and as the man beside me laughs like a demon, he whispers, "Then let the party begin."

I tense as the man thrusts forward at the same time as a shot rings out, the sound of it bouncing off the stone walls and magnifying several times over. I stare in horror as the man between my legs staggers back, a gaping hole in the side of his head causing what was inside to explode all around us. Further shots ring out as chaos enters the room and I am helpless as I lie chained like a human sacrifice in the middle of an obvious massacre.

The figures scream and run for cover as the sound of death fills the already chilling space.

It all happens so fast I can't think straight and only when a body lands on me do I scream before a familiar voice whispers huskily, "I've got you, baby girl. Stay still until I tell you to move."

The tears flow down my face unchecked as the man I love shields my body from harm and just feeling his protective body over mine causes my shock to desert me, leaving me a sobbing mess.

* * *

THE STENCH of death surrounds me, the acrid smoke of burning flesh and the footsteps of heavy boots and urgent voices. Most of all, though, I smell salvation as the musky scent of the man who has become everything to me in an alarmingly short space of time, covers my burning body with his. As the noise subsides, he pulls back and rips off his jacket, covering my modesty as he sets about releasing me from my prison and ignoring the chaos surrounding us, pulls me into his strong arms.

He nuzzles my hair and whispers, "I thought I was going to lose you."

As I cling onto him, nothing else matters. What happened no longer matters because he came for me. He was there when I needed him most and is the first person in my miserable life who has ever done that.

He holds his hand flat on the back of my head in a protective move that I appreciate and, as I cling on tight, he growls over the top of my head, "Are they here?"

"No boss."

I recognize the husky voice of his consigliere and Dom

growls, "Search every fucking corner of this house of horrors. They must be here. Search for any evidence."

I hear a low groan and Dom snaps, "Bring that fucker over here."

I tense as the sound of a man moaning in agony approaches and Dom straightens up and pulls me safely into his arms and whispers, "We will find them, baby. This man is going to help us, and I need to deal with that. Stay brave for a little longer and then I'm taking you home."

I gulp away my tears because I know he's right. This isn't over all the time Mario and Diana still breathe, so I pull his jacket tighter around my aching shivering body and nod, stepping to the side, trying to ignore the pain in my leg as my skin deals with the burn they inflicted on me.

As Dom moves, I peer past him and notice a couple of soldiers holding one of the hooded figures down, replacing me on the altar, and set about restraining him in the cuffs they used on me. They rip off his robe, making sure he's naked and his hands are bound at the wrists before being hooked on the same device mine were. His legs soon follow, and I get a moment's satisfaction knowing that Karma is a bitch.

I am curious and move to Dom's side to stare at the man who is now cowering under Dom's ferocious gaze, and I stare in shock as a familiar face peers back at me.

Detective Woznowski doesn't appear so confident now as his eyes stare back at us with fear and resignation.

"So, detective, this is an interesting situation we now find ourselves in." Dom shakes his head and appears almost amused.

"You don't understand who you're dealing with. Release me." The detective growls and yet it's hard to be scared of a man who looks pathetic as the roles reverse.

"I know exactly who I'm dealing with, and they won't be safe. They will *never* be safe from me." Dom snarls and yet the detective merely smiles.

"Keep telling yourself that. You see, this goes way further than two wanna-bee crime lords fighting for relevance. This is about power, absolute power, to control this damaged world we live in."

Dom leans forward and says lightly, "Power is the drug of fools. However much you have, it's never enough. There is always someone with more than you and it can drive a once sane man mad."

"Is that what you think—we're mad?"

Dom waves his hand around the room. "What do you think? This is like some weird fucking frat initiation shit. Guys who never grew up taking part in something any ordinary person left behind at puberty. Preying on defenseless women to make themselves feel powerful and dressing murder up in excuses to join a fucking sick club."

"Maybe but ask yourself what rewards membership brings. Protection, riches, and power. A solidarity of brothers who have each other's backs. Knowing you are part of a family who will protect you and make certain your future is walking down a path paved with gold.

"And yet, where are they now?"

Dom sneers and glances around at the room that is filled with the mafia. Soldiers who are staring at the detective with a grim animosity that makes me shiver as threats and intimidation dances with death around the room.

"Safe." The detective barks out a laugh.

"The most important thing to do when under attack is to save the organization. You won't find them; you'll *never* find them, and you'll probably never understand the reason behind any of this. That is if you survive long enough to figure it out. Mr. Ortega, your future is written in blood and always has been. The arrest was only the beginning. There will be more bodies, more accusations and it will become relentless. You may as well have saved yourself the trouble, because nothing you can do will ever come close to hurting the Dark Lords."

"The Dark Lords. What a fucking joke."

Dom turns and grins at his men.

"Have any of you ever come across shit like this before?"

"I have."

The detective snaps his head to the side as a man steps forward who could probably wrestle a bear and his disgusted gaze falls on the detective as he growls. "I heard about them when I was in special ops."

For the first time, I note the detective appears less confident as the man carries on.

"One of the guys spoke about it on a stakeout one night. We had shit else to do, and he told me they had been briefed about an organization of powerful figures in local communities forming some kind of ancient club. They work together to protect their interests and operate above the law, mainly because most of the people responsible for that are in the fucking club themselves."

"So it goes further than Vegas, then."

Dom addresses the man as if they're having a conversation over a couple of beers and he nods.

"The soldier told me they were under orders to storm one of their meetings. To shoot on sight and take the ringleader out. They were in position, somewhere in Texas, and at the last minute they were told to stand down."

"Interesting."

The detective openly laughs.

"Even then, the Lords found out about it and protected themselves. What makes you think a fucking low life mafia soldier can win against the power that the Dark Lords enjoy? You're a fool, Domenico and that will be the death of you and..." His gaze flicks over to me and he says with derision. "And all because of a hot, wet pussy. You're pathetic."

As he speaks, I notice the expression on Dom's face change in a heartbeat. From easy going interest to murderous intent and I catch my breath as he reaches for the dagger that is lying beside the altar and holds it flush against the detective's heart, causing him to break out into an immediate sweat. As he presses the blade in deep enough to cause the detective to cry out in pain, he growls, "Then let's find out how pathetic I can be."

CHAPTER 42

DOM

The most important thing right now is to drag answers out of a dying man. It's interesting to test a man's limits, and the detective is stronger than most. Despite inflicting the same method he tried on Flora, he remains tight-lipped and, as I stare down at his body, bearing several marks from the same hot poker he used on Flora, I'm impressed by his resilience. He now bears scars courtesy of the same blade he rested against her heart and the resignation in his pain-filled eyes is impressive as I hold the knife against his own twisted heart. The air is thick with anticipation as I hold it close to his skin and whisper, "Last chance, detective. If you only tell me one thing, tell me Mario Bachini's involvement in your organization."

He glares up at me and with a small smile twisted with pain, whispers with a ragged breath. "Go to hell."

I step back and throw the blade to the ground and sneer.

"Say hi to the Devil because you're heading there first."

Turning, I see Flora watching with a fascination that makes me smile and I reach for her hand and whisper, "I'm taking you home."

As her soft hand closes around mine, I say to Pasquale, "Have you checked the building?"

"Clear."

I sigh with exasperation.

"Our work here is done. Torch the place, making sure nothing can be identified and all that's left is the smoldering tomb of a man who burned alive for his sins."

As I make to leave, the detective cries out, "Wait, you can't leave me here. At least finish the job, you fucking coward."

I keep on walking.

"You're a fucking joke. I heard you were a killer. A man who took no prisoners, but you're a coward. You can't even bring yourself to kill the man who hurt your whore."

Flora shivers beside me and I fight the red mist away that's threatening to blow my cool and then I hear, "Stop. I'll give you names."

I stop.

I turn.

Then I say roughly, "Go on."

"Untie me first. Guarantee my safety and then I'll talk."

I turn away and continue walking.

"Abel Jackson."

His pitiful wail reaches out and causes me to sneer. Abel Jackson is the most powerful Judge in town, and I'm not surprised that bent fucker is involved.

I carry on walking.

"Clayton Hass."

"Fucking banker." I whisper to Flora, "He heads up City Bank. Now we know where Diana got her information from. Interesting."

We don't turn around.

"Carlos Matasso."

We stop walking.

Flora gasps beside me and almost stumbles and says fearfully, "My father."

This time I stare at her in shock and growl, "What the fuck, since when?"

"Diana told me when she visited me in the room they kept me in."

"She was here today?"

I'm incensed and Flora nods miserably. "Earlier. She told me Carlos Matasso was my father after we traded insults. She could have been lying, but what if it's true?"

Her beautiful eyes gaze at me with so much pain it's like a physical blow to my heart and I turn and say roughly, "I'm listening."

The detective shouts, "Untie me and I'll explain, but you must guarantee my safety."

"Must I?" I head back to his side, with Flora close behind me.

As I stare into his maddened eyes, I hiss, "Tell me what I need to know, and I'll untie you."

He visibly relaxes and says with a deep sigh. "Carlos Matasso is one of the elite five."

"Elite what?" I can't believe the shit I'm hearing, and the detective says irritably, "Listen and I'll tell you. More so you can see how pathetic you are in believing you will ever defeat the Dark Lords."

He takes a huge gulp of stale air.

"The elite are the men at the pinnacle of the organization. The five pinnacles of the crown. I only know of Carlos because he is the Great Lord of our region."

I glance at Flora, who is frozen in disbelief, and the detective barks out a laugh. "Mario Bachini thinks he will take that position on the crown one day. All of this..." He points to Flora, "Is to show Carlos he is worthy of a place on the council."

His eyes flash. "His mission is to take over your business

and pledge allegiance to the Matassos. To form a bigger empire that Carlos will ultimately control. Apparently, Diana was the Trojan horse they used to seduce you all and by all accounts, it was easy."

He laughs at his own fucking joke and then immediately stops when I drive my fist through his fucking stomach. His cries of pain are the sweetest sound and as he coughs and splutters, he hisses, "So you see, this is bigger than all of us and when you stole their money, you wrote your own death warrant."

I turn to Flora and note the pain and fear casting a shadow across her face and I snarl, "Anything else?"

The detective whispers, "You can't win. They are too powerful, have too many people in their pockets and the backing of the elite. If I were you, I'd give their money back and prepare for a painful ending because they have no mercy."

"Thanks for the advice."

I reach for the restraints holding him in place and release them before saying to Flora, "Wait for me by the door."

She steps back, and the detective says in fear, "You promised to release me. Everybody heard it. You have to let me go."

"I did release you." I pull him effortlessly off the stone altar and hold my gun to his head, pressing the barrel in hard, causing him to shake, the sound of him pissing echoing around the dark and gloomy space.

I snarl. "Consider this a favor; an easy entrance into hell where they've prepared your room."

Before he can register my words, I pull the trigger and as his head explodes the contents rain down on me, drenching me in satisfaction. I throw his body down in disgust and growl, "Now torch this fucking place. Let's go home."

CHAPTER 43

FLORA

I don't utter one word until we reach Dom's mansion and as we enter the place, I now think of as home, Gretchen races out and stares at me in horror.

"Oh my God, Miss Corlietti, let me help you."

Dom places his protective arm around me and says shortly, "There's no need for that, Gretchen. Just some brandy and a hot tea will be fine."

She scurries off with a pained look in my direction, and as the soldiers drift once more into the shadows, Dom says softly, "Let's get you cleaned up."

I follow him to the bedroom, and he leads me straight into the bathroom where he proceeds to fill the gigantic tub and, as I sit shivering on the bench, he says gruffly, "I let you down."

"Never!" I glare at him fiercely, and he sighs heavily. "My lack of planning and security meant the detective took you from what should have been the safest of places into a nightmare. I will never forgive myself."

"You weren't to know; none of us were."

I stand and my legs shake as I head toward him and wrap

my arms around his bloodied body, pressing my cheek to his beating heart.

"I love you, Domenico Ortega."

He stiffens as I whisper, "I want to be strong for you. To be the woman you deserve and everything my sister wasn't."

He pulls back and tilts my face to his and the emotion in his face makes my breath hitch.

"You already are, baby girl."

As his lips claim mine in a soft and loving kiss, I swear my toes curl. I don't even register that another man's blood smears across my chest as I kiss the man I love with all my heart, in a frenzied passion, needing to demonstrate just how much he means to me.

I love him.

I've known for a while now. It didn't take long either. When I was locked in that room, I was more afraid for him than me, telling me that he has fast become the most important person in my life and with him beside me, I can conquer any demons that fly at me.

He whispers against my lips, "Let me care for you, Flora. Stay here with me."

"You thought I was leaving?" I laugh softly. "You don't get rid of me that easily, Domenico."

I reach up and run my fingers through his hair and as the steam from the tub fills the room, I say breathlessly, "Fuck me now, Dom. Fuck me with another man's blood on me and the words of our enemies ringing in our ears. Fuck me knowing they can't touch us; will never touch us. We are stronger than all of them and fuck me because I love you and can't wait another minute until you are inside me."

With a deep growl, he lifts me hard against the tiled walls and wastes no time in pushing in deep. Slow, gently, and luxuriously perfect. He stares into my eyes the entire time as he takes it lingering and deep, my back sliding against the cool tiles, counteracting the wet heat that flows through my body. Soft, seductive, and memorable. This moment is ours and we are grabbing it with greedy hands.

I gasp as his thick cock grazes my throbbing walls and love the sense of ownership that he commands of me. We are one unit now, so deep inside one another's souls there is no room for anyone else. Any fears, jealousies and doubts were left smoldering in the ash back in the horror house and what rose from the ashes is magical, beautiful and breath-taking.

His seed shoots deep inside me as my orgasm dances with his and my screams echo around the steam filled room, meeting his loud roar that reminds me who I am dealing with. A conqueror, an assassin and a man who loves hard and deep, and I'm the lucky lady on the receiving end of that.

We don't have long because Dom's business needs him and after we clean up, I slip into leggings and a sweater, my mouth watering as I watch him dress in his customary black suit that reflects his dark and dangerous personality.

As we head downstairs together, he raises my hand to his lips and whispers regretfully, "I must go to work. You will be safe. The mansion is on lockdown, and I am leaving my newest recruit to be your personal bodyguard."

I'm not sure I understand when he laughs with a wicked glint in his eye. My mouth dries when he nods toward the huge bear of a man heading our way and says abruptly, "Jonny, you have the most important job in my organization. Guarding my woman. Don't let me down."

The man nods and just fixes a blank expression on his face, but when Dom turns away, he throws me a wink, making me instantly relax. I can tell Jonny is one of the good guys, ironic when you consider where I'm standing right now and who with.

Dom leans down and kisses me slow, lingering and so sexily, almost as if he's savoring every delicious moment and it makes my heart pant. Then he pulls back and whispers, "Go and spend time with Gretchen. The poor woman is out of her mind with worry."

I nod and watch him leave, Pasquale appearing from the shadows and taking up his position by his side and my heart does a strange somersault as he leaves through the main door.

My man.

How did I get so lucky?

I glance at the soldier, who says respectfully. "If you need me, yell. I won't be far away, but I'm guessing you could use some personal space."

"Thanks."

I smile shyly. "Thanks for what you did back there."

"Just doing my job, ma'am."

He winks and heads off, leaving me smiling. Something tells me Jonny is the perfect man for the job and for the first time since I came here that fateful night, I finally feel at home.

CHAPTER 44

DOM

We head to every business I own, banging a few heads for information and checking my investments haven't been tampered with. I don't trust Mario, Diana and certainly not Matasso and it's now of the ultimate importance that I secure my business.

The final stop is my strip club and as I sit in a booth with my men around me, I have half an eye on the show as I caress a tumbler of whiskey as my reward for a very hard day at the office.

My phone vibrates and I note my brother Matteo on the other end, and I growl, "Brother."

He says quickly, *"I've been doing some digging on Matasso as you asked."*

Earlier, I texted him my request, filling him in on what I know and I still, the glass cold in my hand.

"He's into shady shit that is buried under fear."

"Stop talking in riddles, you fucking bastard."

His low laugh makes me smile, and he says gruffly. *"He has most people with any authority in his pocket. There is no dirt on him, despite the fact we know otherwise. One source spoke of his infidelity. Apparently, he likes to fuck the hired help and takes whores to his home for his own pleasure, despite the fact his wife is there. He's a wicked bastard with no morals and word on the street is if anyone challenges him, they end up on the missing person's list."*

"Business as usual then." I growl because none of us are the tooth fairy here.

"I'm guessing you should pay Flora's father a visit. If anyone can enlighten you, it's him. You have the perfect reason to get it from the horse's mouth and search for a weakness in his organization to bring him down."

"And Bachini, how is he connected?"

My blood boils when I think of Mario at the heart of all this and Matteo snarls, *"He's a wannabee and it's obvious Matasso is using him. Don't be surprised if he winds up a ghost when his use by date runs out."*

At least that's something I suppose, and I say with interest. "Any news on his weakness?"

I'm surprised when Matteo laughs softly. *"An interesting project. I'll fill you in when it's over."*

The fact he knows how much is at stake tells me my brother won't leave anything to chance and if this woman is the weapon that will cause Bachini to crumble, I can only imagine the pleasure that will bring to us all.

He cuts the call, and my attention is distracted by the stripper moving across to our table, gyrating seductively before us, running her hands over her glitter dressed body. Her long red hair gleams as the light catches it and her flashing green eyes gaze at me seductively as she palms her breasts and pouts in my direction. I'm interested to note that it has no effect on me at all, which surprises me because usually I would be taking full advantage of her services to end a hard day at the office in the most pleasurable way. Not now I have my own woman who could do a much better job of that and so I chuck some dollars on the table and stand, noting the disappointment cloud her eyes.

"Time to go." I move toward the exit surrounded by my men, ignoring the curious gazes of the customers enjoying the hospitality. Sometimes it's good to be me because I can have anything I want and right now there is only one thing I want more than oxygen. Flora.

* * *

I FIND her in my cinema room, deep in the basement of my mansion. I'm not surprised she's here. It's the one place that feels removed from the shit that surrounds us daily. A cocoon, a place to shut the door and indulge in escapism, courtesy of the huge screen and deep luxurious chairs. A small bar sits in the corner of the room making the inhabitant self-sufficient as they help themselves to drinks both alcoholic and otherwise. There is a well-stocked fridge with everything required, and a coffee machine that is permanently loaded. In the cupboard are bags of potato chips and pretzels of every flavor sitting alongside popcorn and most varieties of nuts. This space has always been a favorite of mine and now it's even more enjoyable because she's here.

I lock the door.

She turns and in the dark light, smiles as she sees me approaching, shrugging out of my jacket and crossing the deep luxurious ivory carpet that curls into my toes. I rip off my shirt, revealing my flexing muscles as I reach for my belt and slide it quickly from my pants.

Her eyes glitter with excitement as I reach her and, without a word, I curl the belt around her neck, using it to pull her toward me with one hand, reaching for the remote with the other. As I increase the volume, the sound of classical music fills the room, and her soft gasp tells me this is just what she wants.

Chucking the remote to the floor, I pull her clothes from her body with a violent haste, loving the anticipation building in her beautiful blue eyes.

Kissing Flora raises a multitude of emotions and the one engulfing me now is dominance. Sweet loving comes later, but after the day I've had, I have a certain need of her right now.

"Have you missed me, baby girl?"

I growl as her breath rains down hot on my lips and she licks those luscious lips and whispers, "Yes."

I lean down and bite hard on the cherry and her small scream drives lust in my heart as she licks the blood pooling in her mouth.

Then I push her down onto the soft seat and hook her legs around my neck before burrowing my face into her glistening pussy, inhaling deeply as I bathe in her scent.

Her small moan reveals what her body is desperate for, and I take a long leisurely swipe up her pussy, her desire resting on my lips. She tastes so good, so sweet, the perfect honey and as I suck her throbbing clit into my greedy mouth, her sharp intake of breath tells me she's balancing on the edge of ecstasy already.

I am relentless in giving this woman pleasure and as she convulses under me, I dip two fingers inside her and reach for the spot that has her screaming my name.

"Dom! Oh fuck…"

Her pleasure flies away on the breeze from the air conditioning and then I spin her around, so she is face planted against the plush fabric of the seat. Grabbing her hair in one hand, I graze my tongue the length of her body settling in the crease of her ass, causing her to squeal, "What the…"

I slap her hard on the ass causing her to groan, "Fuck me."

causing me to laugh as I lower my pants and palm my throbbing cock.

"If you insist."

As I press the crown against her ass, she pants, "Do it."

"Do what, baby girl?"

I laugh softly as she hisses, "Fuck my ass."

I press in slowly, her desire coating my balls, causing me to groan out loud. "Fuck me, Flora, you're incredible."

As I slide in, she pushes down hard and this time my roar fills the dusky space as I unleash my inner beast. I tighten my hold on her hair and ride her like a cowboy, in and out, hard and fast, her body grazing the fabric beneath her as if she's on rails.

This is primitive fucking, the best kind there is and as I dominate my woman, I come so hard I swear I black out for a second.

It's as if my release has no ending and spills through the crack between us, dripping down her body and onto the seat. Her wild screams tell me she's more than a match for me and as she climaxes, I slap her ass hard.

"I fucking love you, woman."

I cry out as she gifts her soul to me and as the classical music plays all around us, filling our minds and promising a lifetime of intense pleasure, I know Flora will be my wife before the month is done.

CHAPTER 45

FLORA

We pull up outside a small house on a suburban street that looks as if normal lives here. The white picket fence and the trailing ivy covering the porch is add odds with everything I know in life. I don't belong in a place like this, surrounded by God-fearing folk who play by the rules and struggle to make ends meet.

There is no wealth here. Not material wealth, anyway. However, this place is my dream. What I pictured when I closed my eyes as the current bastard thrust inside me. When I was beaten, stripped, and humiliated on repeat. When the cruel words reminding me how worthless I was rained down on me, I came to this place in my head. Obscurity, safety and my desperate dream.

"Are you ready, baby girl?"

Dom's husky voice dives into my heart and I take a deep breath, only courageous because he is with me.

"I guess."

He nods his approval. "That's my girl."

The door to the car flies opens, and I am comforted by Jonny standing outside, promising back up for the one who guards me the closest. The two men in my life who have vowed to protect me and I'm about to meet the one who should have made the same vow.

However, the man I called daddy may not deserve that title, so, as we step outside the car, my focus is on what waits inside.

We walk as if in slow motion up the wooden steps to the front door and my heart is beating so fast, I may not make it out alive.

Jonny thumps on the door. Twice. Hard.

A few seconds pass while my life flashes before me and then the door opens and a pleasant, smiling woman peers at us with curiosity.

"May I help you?"

My mouth dries and I lick my lips in the vain attempt to lubricate my words and say with a tremor to my voice, "We are here to see my, um, Benjamin Corlietti."

She nods as if there is nothing unusual about the freak show at her door and opens it a little wider.

"He's expecting you."

Every step I take into the pleasant house is a painful one as the reality bites that I know nothing about my father at all. Who is this woman? Is this his house and why has he never tried to get in touch with me?

We enter a sunny room filled with roses in vases and soft comfortable furniture and sitting in a chair watching us keenly is the man I always thought of as my father.

For a moment, as our eyes connect, I think I register a little emotion in his that is quickly replaced with indifference.

"Flora."

At least he remembers my name. That's a start at least and he nods respectfully to Dom.

"Mr. Ortega, it's an honor."

Dom tenses beside me as he offers him a warmer greeting than me and then waves toward the couch before him.

"You must have questions. I'll do my best to answer them."

He nods toward the woman and it's as if a knife twists in my heart as his expression softens and he says pleasantly, "Sadie, fetch our guests some refreshments will you, beautiful."

Beautiful. He used that term a lot when I was growing up. For my mother, for my sister and for me. We were beautiful, and it made me feel loved, even when he struggled to demonstrate that. My father was always cold and distant, and I always thought that was due to his job. Second in command to a monster. Carlos Matasso, head of the Matasso family, and feared by all who knew, or had even heard of him.

When 'beautiful' leaves, he sighs heavily.

"Sadie's my wife, just in case you were wondering."

I nod because that doesn't surprise me. His old one died and it was inevitable he would replace her. However, what confuses me more is this place. We lived in the Matasso mansion. We never had a house of our own and I wonder what's changed.

His words reach out to me like cruel flying bullets as he says with no emotion. "The day your mother died was inevitable."

Dom tenses beside me as he says with a slight shrug. "She was Carlos's whore. I knew that, in fact, the whole family knew that and on that fateful night Diana knew that."

I tense at the mention of my sister and his twisted expression tells me there is no love lost there.

"She overheard them arguing. Apparently, your mother was tired of being used and demanded Carlos divorce Giselle and marry her. She received the back of his hand across her face for her trouble and by all accounts Diana heard her threaten him. She told him everyone would know that you were his child. She would tell Giselle's family and they would make life very difficult for him. He just laughed in her face and told her she was a cheap whore that no longer held any interest for him."

He sighs heavily. "Diana heard her mother scream and ran into the room, rushing Carlos before he could react. She grabbed a statue off the table and attacked him and he rewarded her by punching her hard in the stomach. Your mother screamed, and he did the same to her as she rushed at him, and he knocked her out."

I feel emotionless as I hear his story, almost as if I'm a stranger listening in.

"Giselle, by all accounts, heard the screams and went to investigate. She found Carlos deep inside Diana and it sent her over the edge. A huge fight broke out and Diana ran from the room and when I arrived, Giselle was holding your mother's heart in her bloodied hands."

Dom reaches for my hand and whispers, "Are you ok, baby?"

I must be in shock because I just blink twice and whisper, with a ragged breath, "Then what happened?"

"I took out my gun, intending to kill the bastards, but Carlos taunted me and told me you were his child. He was going to keep you as a reward and Diana would become his whore in the place of her mother. That I had a choice. Stay quiet and keep my job knowing that my wife betrayed me and deserved her untimely death, or carry on and end up dead for my efforts."

He doesn't appear as if he gives two fucks about how I'm feeling now as he shrugs. "I told him I would agree under the condition you were both allowed to leave. I couldn't live in the same house as either of you anymore, knowing you were his bastard child."

Dom growls beside me and I say fiercely, "Don't hold back daddy dearest. Tell us how you really feel."

His eyes narrow and he spits, "I did it for you, Flora. You were innocent. You never asked for any of it, but your sister, well, she was a different story entirely."

"In what way?" I'm confused, and he shakes his head in disgust.

"I left the room, and she was standing there. She told me she heard every word, and she was going nowhere. That she wanted to take her mother's place and to trust her. That she would make him pay and get our revenge."

That doesn't surprise me, and he says darkly, "Your sister begged to be that man's whore, which told me I had to send her away to try to salvage any remaining sanity she had. That night, I packed you both into a car and sent you to your grandmothers. I knew that was the best place for you both and hoped that Diana would benefit from living in a loving home. Be normal, not end up as an old man's whore and for my own sanity, I turned my back on the whole experience and tried to put it behind me."

"And your daughters. You didn't think to check on them when your mother died?" Dom snaps angrily and my father's eyes narrow as he spits, "Daughters, Mr. Ortega. I had one daughter, remember? They both looked so alike I couldn't be sure Diana wasn't Carlos's daughter as well. The fact he fucked her brought with it a different level of depravity I couldn't live with. I removed myself from their lives for their own good and I hoped never to see them again because if I did, it meant they hadn't made it past the shadows we live among."

He shakes his head sadly. "And it appears I was right just from the fact you are holding her hand."

He turns to me and says with some disappointment. "It appears you are more like your mother than I hoped."

Dom stands and I say quickly, "Enough."

I join him and we stare down at the pitiful man who I called daddy once.

"Thanks for your honesty, and thanks for the ride out of hell. Just so you know, we never made it out and I have you to thank for that. Diana did become a cruel man's whore and forced me into a life I didn't deserve. In abandoning us, you are no better than the rest of them, so enjoy your 'normal' life with your apple pie 'beautiful' wife because one day it will all come back to bite you.

As I turn to leave, his low laugh rings in my ears as he hisses, "It's good to see you, Flora. Tell your sister not to bother looking me up. You're both dead to me."

I don't react and just walk away and then I hear a single gunshot and as I turn in shock, Dom pushes me to the door as Sadie's screams echo through the entire house. We completely ignore her and leave through the front door with her tears serenading our departure.

Pasquale shifts off the porch beam and stares at Dom with curiosity and he snaps, "Send in the clean-up crew. Pay the woman off and threaten her to keep her mouth shut. We're heading home."

Jonny holds the car door open and as I slide in bedside Dom, I am numb inside. As we pull away from a house that will be forever etched in my memory, I whisper, "Tell the driver to drive fast because from this moment on, I have no past. Only a future and I promise you now, it will be *nothing* like that."

As I snuggle in beside him, his strong arm wraps around my shoulder and he kisses my head lightly.

"I couldn't have put it better myself, baby girl. Now it's time to hand the baton to my brothers. We have a future to enjoy, and I will make it my life's work to make it a happy one."

As the car speeds away from my past, I settle my head on my future, who is holding me so tenderly, knowing that whatever happens next, I made it through and found a man who loves me for *who* I am, not what I am. This mafia princess is about to marry her king and God help anyone who stands in our way.

EPILOGUE

MATTEO

The door opens, and Cesare, my consigliere, enters the room with a wry smile.

"Boss." He nods with respect, and I wave to the chair set before my desk.

"How did it go?"

I reach for my lighter and flick the flame against the finest Cuban cigar, taking a deep drag and then clipping the end, before replacing it in the box.

Cesare barks out a laugh.

"I thought you gave up."

"I have." I grin as he settles back in his seat and shakes his head.

"It never ceases to amaze me how gullible rich kids are."

"So, he took the bait."

Cesare nods, his eyes glittering with devilish mirth.

"A private booth and champagne on the house to celebrate his birthday. Invites for ten of his friends and a complimentary lap dance."

"He would be a fool to refuse."

I glance at the photo on my phone and consider the beauty staring back at me.

"And his girlfriend? Will she be joining him?"

"What do you think?"

Abigail Kensington. Billionaire's daughter and, by all accounts, the love of Mario Bachini's life. The one woman he never had and desired more for it. Currently hooked up with Jefferson Stevenson, the son of a powerful Judge and friend of her parents. They are obviously orchestrating a union between their families and Abigail is the pawn in their game, which is a coincidence because she's also the pawn in mine.

We move onto other business, but I keep the phone with her picture by my side, glancing at it occasionally and familiarizing myself with an important piece of the puzzle. I will use her, probably abuse her and ruin her and it will all be because I am thirsty for revenge.

Later that evening, I watch from my office as Jefferson arrives with nine of his friends. There is not one girl among them which tells me everything I need to know.

The booth is positioned at the correct angle for my security cameras to film every detail, and I wait for the inevitable with a cut glass of whiskey in my hand and the unlit cigar in the other.

Show time.

At first the group is rowdy but not out of line and enjoys the endless champagne I ply them with. Rich kids never question a gift. They believe it's their right and probably think my establishment is sucking up to them for their business.

My manager is under instructions to make this a night to remember, but it won't be for their benefit. No, it's purely for mine to drive my kill into my sights.

Sherrie, one of my most skilled lap dancers, sways across to the booth and proceeds to do what she does best. She gyrates, titillates, and provokes and only when she asks who the birthday boy is, does she strike.

I watch her straddle Jefferson, who appears to be loving every minute of it, and he soon has his hands over her as she sucks on his neck.

His friends encourage him on and as she drops to her knees and unzips his pants, their cheers can be heard over the loud music.

The camera zooms in on Jefferson's face and from the look of it he's enjoying every minute and when Sherrie pulls back and shifts onto his lap, there's no mistaking what's happening now.

He thrusts up inside her and my camera catches every sordid minute of it and when they finish, it's to cheers and requests for the same. I make a fist when he takes out a roll of dollars and slips it into her mouth, slapping her on the ass as she leaves. Fucking creep, at this moment I want to waste the prick myself, but that wouldn't help my plan.

As they congratulate their friend, another waitress stops by with a silver tray lined with ten rows of cocaine and they need no further encouragement to inhale their lines like the good little rich kids they are.

More lap dances involve their friends and it's not far off a fucking orgy and then Sherrie returns and fastens a leather collar to Jefferson's neck before leading him away to a private room.

I switch cameras and record the entire sordid freak show as she humiliates him by whipping his ass, caning his legs and making him crawl around the room before eating her pussy.

Job done, humiliation complete and as I press send, I wait for the recipient to beat down my door.

* * *

ONE HOUR LATER, the fun really begins.

I study her arrival with interest. The car draws up outside and my uniformed guard on the door opens it and a long shapely leg exits first, followed by a woman who could grace any Paris runway.

Her silver dress moves independently of her, dusting her knees as she towers on the highest heels that give me an instant hard on.

She straightens up and tosses her auburn hair across her shoulder and glances up at the name above my club, her lips set in a grim line and her vivid green eyes flashing as she nods her thanks to the guard who holds the rope aside to let her pass.

Cesare is waiting just inside the door and approaches her with a respectful smile and as he guides her past the door leading into the club, I prepare myself for battle.

Mere seconds later the door opens, and she enters my office, trying to appear unconcerned, but I already sense her emotion.

"Mr. Ortega, I presume."

She glances past me, and I notice her skin pale as she witnesses her current boyfriend fucking one of my staff doggy style.

For a moment she falters, and her dark stormy eyes sparkle with unshed tears.

"Please take a seat, Miss. Kensington."

She drops into the seat opposite me, and I hand her a glass of champagne, causing her to flinch.

"Are we celebrating, Mr. Ortega?"

She glances back to the screen and her lips tighten as she witnesses what her boyfriend does in his spare time.

"Of course."

I sit behind my desk and smile, nodding to the screen and saying huskily, "Have you seen enough?"

"No." She fixes her eyes on the screen and raises the glass to her lips and for once I'm surprised by a reaction. I thought she'd be inconsolable, tearful, and hysterical. Not this cold fury and desire to watch every sordid second of her boyfriend's infidelity.

She doesn't tear her eyes from the screen as she says conversationally, "So, what's this about? Why send this to me with an invitation to meet you?"

"Because I have a business proposition for you."

"I'm not in business."

She cringes as Jefferson slaps Sherrie's ass hard.

"I beg to differ, Miss. Kensington."

"You know nothing about me."

I'm impressed with the fire inside her and I say slowly, "Let me refresh your memory, then. You are in the business of being set up as a trophy wife. Your husband to be is currently starring in his own porn movie that could end up in the public domain if you choose to walk away."

Her eyes flick away from the screen, and I almost flinch under her derisive gaze.

"What do I care? Publish it. It's his shit to deal with, not mine."

She raises her glass to the screen and then to me and for some reason that impresses me more than anything so far. She has a fiery spark in her and I kind of love my women like that and so I bark out a laugh and then fix her with my deadliest look that definitely gets her attention.

"Miss. Kensington. I don't believe you have understood how serious this situation is. Jefferson's father is Judge Stevenson. The most powerful judge in the state who is currently on your father's radar as your future father-in-law. You have entered into an agreement that your engagement will be announced at the beginning of summer, allowing for endless parties and social gatherings to celebrate that fact."

I lean forward and stare at her hard. "In doing so, your

father makes the perfect marriage for his daughter, to the man who is tipped to follow in his father's footsteps. Your future is guaranteed and yet one leak on the internet would have Jefferson up on drugs and prostitution charges, not to mention the scandal that would destroy his family."

I lean back and smirk. "By association, your family would be affected. The scandal would create a wide berth around them. Social invitations would dry up, business deals withdrawn and socially you would be humiliated and ridiculed. Need I go on."

She sighs and studies her fingernails as if I'm a mild irritant that she needs to deal with before pulling her boyfriend back in line and then straightening the gilded mirror they live their life staring into.

So, I go in for the kill.

"I need you to ditch Jefferson and agree to be my girlfriend."

"You are kidding me."

Her eyes widen and I nod, feeling extremely smug about this.

"You see, every kid goes off the rails at least one time in their life and this will be brushed under the Persian rug as yours. Your parents will make excuses that you are overseas for the summer, educating yourself and helping build an orphanage, or something along those charitable lines. Jefferson will receive a copy of this recording with instruction to play along or face his future blowing up in his face. You help me with a problem I have and we're all happy when you return home and take up where you left off. It's a small price to pay for a few weeks of rebellion, wouldn't you agree, Miss. Kensington?"

She stares at me as if I'm the Grim Reaper and then her gaze flicks back to the screen as her boyfriend pulls on his trousers and then beckons Sherrie to sit on his lap, proceeding to suck her tits as she fists his hair.

To my surprise, Abigail sighs heavily.

ORTEGA MAFIA – THE ENFORCER

"What do I have to do?"

"I told you. Play the part of my girlfriend and come home and meet the family. That's all I ask."

"But why?"

"I have my reasons."

The last thing I'm revealing is who will be there. I am looking forward to that more than anything.

The fact this woman is eye candy of the sexiest kind has already re-written the contract from the one I first had in mind.

Yes, Abigail Kensington is a challenge. Mario failed, but I never do. As my girlfriend, I expect her to fulfill the job description in every way and when Mario Bachini realizes I'm fucking the love of his life, it will push him to the edge and I'm the man who will be waiting to push him off.

Abigail sets the glass on the desk and stands, flicking one hard look toward the screen.

"You have a deal, Mr. Ortega. Text me the details. I've seen enough. I'll be your girlfriend, but in name only. I'm not my boyfriend, I don't cheat, and I don't sleep around. Whatever your reason for staging this…" she waves her hand at the screen. "event, is not my concern. What does concern me is my future and if that is with or without Jefferson, I have yet to decide."

She tosses her hair behind her like every rich princess I have ever met, and the way she looks down on me tells me exactly what she thinks of me. If anything, I'm glad about that because it will make my job a much easier one. Dominate the princess and bring her in line, wiping that regal smirk from her face and crushing her soul.

Once again, I light the cigar and prepare to ruin Jefferson Stevenson's life along with his girlfriend's and the people I detest most in the world.

Mario Bachini and Diana Ortega, my wicked stepmother. It

will be cruel, vindictive, and glorious and at the end of it, I will walk victoriously over their broken souls.

* * *

Thank you for reading The Enforcer. If you want to continue reading Matteo's story, click on the link.

Ortega Mafia – The Consigliere

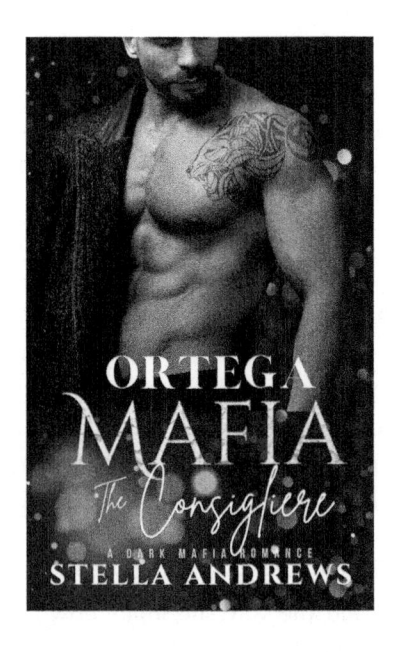

Thank you for reading this story.
If you have enjoyed the fantasy world of this novel, please would you be so kind as to leave a review on Amazon?

Join my closed Facebook Group

Stella's Sexy Readers

Follow me on Instagram

Carry on reading for more Reaper Romances, Mafia Romance & more.
Remember to grab your free book by visiting stellaandrews.com.

ALSO BY STELLA ANDREWS

Twisted Reapers

Sealed With a Broken Kiss
Dirty Hero (Snake & Bonnie)
Daddy's Girls (Ryder & Ashton)
Twisted (Sam & Kitty)
The Billion Dollar baby (Tyler & Sydney)
Bodyguard (Jet & Lucy)
Flash (Flash & Jennifer)
Country Girl (Tyson & Sunny)

The Romanos
The Throne of Pain (Lucian & Riley)
The Throne of Hate (Dante & Isabella)
The Throne of Fear (Romeo & Ivy)
Lorenzo's story is in Broken Beauty

Beauty Series
Breaking Beauty (Sebastian & Angel) *
Owning Beauty (Tobias & Anastasia)
Broken Beauty (Maverick & Sophia) *
Completing Beauty – The series

Five Kings
Catch a King (Sawyer & Millie) *
<u>Slade</u>

Steal a King

Break a King

Destroy a King

Marry a King

Baron

Club Mafia

Club Mafia – The Contract

Club Mafia – The Boss

Club Mafia – The Angel

Club Mafia – The Savage

Club Mafia - The Beast

Club Mafia – The Demon

Standalone

The Highest Bidder (Logan & Samantha)

Rocked (Jax & Emily)

Brutally British

Deck the Boss

Reasons to sign up to my mailing list.

•A reminder that you can read my books FREE with Kindle Unlimited.

•Receive a monthly newsletter so you don't miss out on any special offers or new releases.

•Links to follow me on Amazon or social media to be kept up to date with new releases.

•Free books and bonus content.

•Opportunities to read my books before they are even released by joining my team.

•Sneak peeks at new material before anyone else.

stellaandrews.com

Follow me on Amazon

Printed in Great Britain
by Amazon